'I make no apologies for who I am,' Nate said. *'Not even to you.'*

Cyn didn't know what to say. How could she ever explain to him that she had been having dreams about him for twenty years, that she had thought her dream lover was a gentle man, comforting and caring? How could she accept the fact that her green-eyed protector was actually a warrior?

He saw doubt and confusion in her eyes, and wished that she had never stepped out of his dreams into reality. When she had come to him in his dreams, she hadn't judged him, hadn't cringed at the sight of the battle scars on his body.

'I won't bother you again," he said, turning away from her.

She wanted to reach out, to call him back, but she couldn't. She was afraid…

Available in June 2003 from Silhouette Sensation

This Side of Heaven

BEVERLY BARTON

SILHOUETTE®
SENSATION™

*Silhouette, Silhouette Sensation and Colophon are
registered trademarks of Harlequin Books S.A., used under licence.*

*First published in Great Britain 2003
Silhouette Books, Eton House, 18-24 Paradise Road,
Richmond, Surrey TW9 1SR*

© Beverly Beaver 1992

ISBN 0 373 07453 0

18-0603

*Printed and bound in Spain
by Litografia Rosés S.A., Barcelona*

BEVERLY BARTON

has been in love with romance since her grandfather gave her an illustrated book of *Beauty and the Beast*. An avid reader since childhood, she began writing at the age of nine and wrote short stories, poetry, plays and novels throughout school and college. After marriage to her own 'hero' and the births of her daughter and son, Beverly chose to be a full-time homemaker—wife, mother, friend and volunteer.

Some years ago, she began substitute teaching and returned to writing as a hobby. In 1987, she joined the Romance Writers of America and soon afterwards helped found the Heart of Dixie chapter in Alabama. Her hobby became an obsession as she devoted more and more time to improving her skills as a writer. Now, her lifelong dream of being published has come true.

To Linda Howard
Okay, so you were right—again!

Prologue

They walked together along the isolated beach, the small Timucuan maiden and her big Spanish conquistador. Each knew the other's thoughts and could feel the other's pain, but they could not touch in a physical way, for their mortal bodies had long since returned to the earth's soil.

They knew the time was near. The fulfillment of the ancient legend's prophecy was at hand. Soon a troubled warrior and the woman who could give him sanctuary within her heart and body would come to their beach, would abide within the walls of the old mission, and discover a passion known only by a precious few.

The maiden and her conquistador had known such passion, but had lost their lives in the hatred and destruction wrought by mankind's greed for wealth and power. For centuries the two lovers had roamed this Florida beach waiting for the heirs of their love to arrive and set them free.

"Soon," she whispered. "Soon, they will come."

"Yes," he said. "They will share the same eternal love that we do."

"And when their lives are united as ours could never be, we will be allowed to go."

"Yes, *querida*."

And they continued their nightly stroll along the surf-kissed sand, waiting here, this side of heaven—waiting for the day they could enter paradise.

Chapter 1

He heard the blood-curdling scream. Tremors racked his body. He knew he couldn't save her. With a moan of anguished pain and animalistic rage, he cursed the powers of heaven and earth.

Nate Hodges opened his eyes. His harsh, erratic breathing gradually slowed as he lay on his sweat-dampened bed. He looked around the dark bedroom, seeking reassurances in the familiar, reassurance that the agony he had just endured had, indeed, been a dream. No, not a dream—a nightmare. The same gut-wrenching nightmare that had tormented his sleep for the past few weeks.

Even though he knew why the dreams had begun again after all these years, he didn't understand why this dream was so different from the old nightmares, those cursed souvenirs of the war. Until two months ago when he had moved into the ancient coquina house by the ocean, he'd never experienced this particular dream. Unlike the ones that had plagued him after Vietnam, this one didn't involve the war.

He had not been overcome by the sickening smell of rotting

flesh. He hadn't felt the splattering of a friend's blood on his face, or heard the moans of a teenager dying in his arms. He hadn't seen piles of pulverized bodies lying on the deck of an incoming boat. Those had been the old dreams, the substance of long-ago nightmares.

Only two things had been the same. Ryker had been there, his one icy blue eye staring triumphantly at Nate, his thin lips curved into a smile of psychotic pleasure. And *she* had been there. In the past, the woman had been his salvation—the calm voice, the soothing hand, his sanctuary from the madness from which he could not escape.

But in these recent dreams, she had cried out for him, and he had not been able to save her. His only hope for peace— destroyed by an old enemy.

Nate eased out of bed, the feel of the cold stone against his feet chilling his feverish body. He rubbed the back of his neck, stretching as he took several deep breaths. Reaching down to the cane-seated chair beside the bed, he picked up his jeans and pulled them on over his naked body. He retrieved the K-Bar knife that lay beneath his pillow, slid it into its sheath and attached it to his belt that hung loosely through the loopholes in his jeans. It had been almost five years since he'd worn a knife—since he'd felt the need for constant protection.

But for the last five years he'd thought Ryker was dead.

Nate slipped into a pair of leather sandals, then, as an after-thought, he grabbed his shirt and threw it over his shoulder.

Opening the heavy wooden door, he walked out into the long narrow hallway and, moving slowly, made his way to his den. The room lay in darkness, except for the shadowy glow of moonlight.

Looking through the wide, open-shuttered windows, Nate noticed the nearly full moon, its silvery yellow light illuminating the patio, the unkept gardens, the rock walkway leading from the back of the house to the gravel road. He opened the huge, arched wooden door and stepped outside. The salty, airy smell of the ocean filled his nostrils, mingling with the thick, heavy aroma of verdant Florida vegetation.

The cool night breeze caressed his bare chest, shoulders and arms. He slipped into his shirt, leaving it unbuttoned. Slowly, cautiously, he walked along the patio, through the high arched openings that ran the length of the L-shaped porch that extended from the back to the side of the house.

He'd done little to improve the shabby conditions of his new home since he'd moved in the last of January. But he hadn't purchased this place for its beauty or with any desire to redecorate or restore. This sturdy, solid fortress of a house had been purchased because of its isolated location. Except for the lone cottage across the road right on the beach, the nearest neighbors were a mile away at the state park. The realtor had assured him that the owners of the cottage seldom used the place except in summer. And that was good. Nate didn't want anyone else around when he had to confront Ryker. That was why he'd left St. Augustine, left his business—to protect his friend and partner John Mason, and John's family. Even with his departure, Nate wasn't sure the Masons were safe from a man as diabolically bent on revenge as Ryker, who would use anyone and anything to settle an old score.

Nate knew the final battle would be over long before summer. Ryker had been spotted in South America three months ago. It was only a matter of time until that mad dog would make his way to the States, find out where Nate was, and come after him.

Nate walked across the road, leaned against a massive cypress tree dripping with thick Spanish moss, and looked out at the ocean. So peaceful. So serene. Comforting—like the woman in his dreams. If there was one thing on earth Nate wanted, it was peace, blessed sanctuary from the scars of a war long ended, the savage memories of a lifetime spent as a navy SEAL, the bitter regrets of a childhood he could never change.

He had given up any hope of love or happiness so many years ago he could barely remember thinking such emotions existed. In childhood, he'd learned that he could count on no one except himself. As a protective mechanism, he'd closed his heart to love, and over the years, he'd found no woman capable of teaching him to entrust his life to another.

His years in the special services had only reinforced his negative attitudes. He had seen the ugly side of life more times than he cared to remember. He'd thought he could find the peace his soul craved when he left the navy nearly five years ago. But that had been when he'd thought Ryker was dead.

Nate rested his head against the tree, closed his eyes and remembered tonight's dream. He hadn't known where he was. He'd been lost in a dark, gloomy room filled with dirt and cobwebs, the smell of rotting wood and damp mustiness everywhere. He had realized he was in terrible danger. Ryker was there. Close. Yet out of reach. And *she* was there. What the hell was she doing with Ryker?

Nate opened his eyes suddenly, not wanting to see. But with his eyes wide open, he saw her lifeless body in Ryker's arms. The pain ripped through him hotter and more deadly than any blade could have. No. No. She couldn't be dead. She was his lifeline. She was his sanctuary. And Ryker had killed her for revenge. To get even with him.

Restless with a need he could not explain, Nate started walking toward the beach. He felt like a fool. The woman in his dreams had no name, no face. All he ever remembered afterward were her eyes—rich, warm brown—and her body. When she'd given herself to him in his dreams, he'd found a sanctuary for his heart and his soul in her arms.

The first time he'd dreamed of her, he'd been eighteen and a newly trained SEAL in Nam. He hadn't dreamed about her in at least a dozen years, not until—until he'd moved to Sweet Haven, to the secluded house where he waited for a man who was as ruthless and dangerous as he was himself.

Suddenly, Nate stopped dead still. His trained instincts told him he wasn't alone. Then he saw her. In a long, flowing dress—white and shimmering in the moonlight—she walked along the beach, at the very edge of the ocean. For one split second he felt as if his heart had stopped beating. Was it *her,* the woman from his dreams? He shook his head, then looked again. She was still there. She was real. No dream. No fantasy.

He knew she wasn't aware of him, of a stranger so close. She seemed to be lost in her private thoughts, and somehow, Nate could feel her loneliness. It was as if her frustration and pain and anger had invaded his mind.

"Damn idiot," he mumbled under his breath. "You've been by yourself for too long." That's what's wrong, he thought. Whoever she is, she isn't *her*. The woman in his dreams didn't exist.

Nate made his way back to the tree, stopping briefly before starting across the road. He slowed his steps, cursing himself for the need to see her again. He turned around and watched while she walked farther up the beach, then stopped, slumping down, cuddling her body up against her knees.

Who was she? he wondered. What was she doing here? And what was wrong with her? He resisted the temptation to go to her.

For what seemed like hours, Nate stood in the shadows of the ancient tree and watched her. Once, he thought he heard her crying and had to fight his desire to comfort her. He wasn't the kind of man who comforted women, and yet...

She stood up, her long blond hair blowing in the mild spring breeze, her dress billowing around her small body. He watched, fascinated by the way she moved, the way her waist-length hair created a shawl around her shoulders. When she came nearer, he saw that her dress wasn't white. It was pale yellow—a pale yellow lace robe that hung open all the way down the front, with a matching nightgown beneath.

Nate's body hardened with arousal. He groaned inwardly. So what? he told himself as she headed toward the two-story stucco-and-wood cottage. *She's a beautiful woman and you haven't had sex in a long time.*

He didn't turn and go back to his house until she disappeared inside the cottage. He had no idea who she was, but obviously she was now his nearest neighbor. She was too close. He'd have to see what he could do to get rid of her.

* * *

Cynthia Porter poured herself a cup of hot coffee, laced it with low-calorie creamer and a sugar substitute, then walked outside onto the patio. The morning was crisp and clear, the sky baby-blue and filled with thin, wispy clouds. The early morning sun warred with the sharp April wind for dominance, one issuing Florida warmth, the other a reminder that winter had just ended in the Sunshine State.

She set down her cup on the glass-and-concrete table before pulling her royal blue sweater together, closing the top button. Seating herself in an enormous wooden rocker, Cyn picked up her coffee, sipping it leisurely as she tilted her head backward and closed her eyes.

It was her first night back here at her family's beachfront cottage in nearly six months, and she hadn't been able to get more than a few hours' sleep. Late in the night, she'd been so restless that she'd gotten up and taken a long walk on the beach, then she'd slept for a while. But she'd had that dream again—the familiar vision that she'd first had at fifteen, a week after her mother's tragic death in a plane crash.

But the familiar dream had been different this time—different from when she'd been fifteen; different from when she'd been twenty-one and the dream had come to her after her father's stroke; and different from when, four years ago, Evan had been brutally murdered. Always, at times of grief and great stress, the dreams would come, and somehow they comforted her. They gave her strength. *He* gave her strength.

The man in her dreams had no name, no face, no real identity, and yet she knew him as she had never known another man. Her heart knew him. Her soul recognized him as its mate. When she awoke, the only things she could remember were his eyes—the most incredible, moss-green eyes she'd ever seen— and his body, big and strong and protecting. This phantom of her dreams came to her to give her strength and protection and…love.

Cyn opened her eyes quickly and ran trembling fingers down the side of her face. Dear God, she had to stop this! She had to stop fantasizing about a man who didn't exist. Taking another sip of her sweet, creamy coffee, she began to rock.

The shrill ring of the portable phone brought her back to reality. She knew before she answered that the caller was Mimi. Dear, good-hearted Mimi. Her title could best be described as chief cook and bottle washer, but what would Tomorrow House do without Mimi Burnside's grandmotherly wisdom and love? How many runaways had been saved because of her generous nature?

"Hello," Cyn said.

"So, was I right?" Mimi asked. "Wasn't getting away to Sweet Haven just what you needed?"

"You were right, as usual. All I need is a few days to recover from the trial—"

"I'd say a few weeks." Mimi's tone was gentle, yet commanding. "Everybody, including me, expected you to be able to handle Darren's death." When Cyn made no reply, Mimi grunted. "If only we could have gotten through to that boy when Evan first brought him to Tomorrow House."

"It was already too late…even then." Cyn's hand quivered. The warm liquid sloshed in the cup. Standing abruptly, she threw the last drops of her coffee into the yard, then set the cup down. Clutching the phone tightly with both hands, Cyn choked back the tears, trying not to remember her husband's death, trying to forget the sight of his bloody body.

"Evan didn't think so," Mimi said.

Cyn remembered how Evan, in his gentle and caring way, had been so sure they could help Darren. Evan had been wrong. "Darren's drug addiction had taken over his life and turned him into a monster capable of killing."

"You'll come to terms with this the same way you did with Evan's death," Mimi assured her. "You have to continue Evan's work at Tomorrow House. There are so many hopeless kids out there who need our shelter, and need someone like you who really cares."

"I thought that I had put the past behind me when I went to see Darren in jail and accepted his pleas for forgiveness."

"None of us expected another inmate to kill Darren. It was a shock to all of us."

"I shouldn't have gone to pieces the way I did. People are counting on me, depending on—"

"Well, honey child, we all know you're a tower of strength. You've held your family together more than once, and you kept Tomorrow House running when the entire staff fell apart after Evan was murdered. But you're human. You're a woman who takes care of everyone around you. What you need is someone to take care of you for a change."

"Oh, Mimi, you're always trying to take care of me." No one understood, least of all Cyn, why she'd fallen apart, why the murder of her husband's young killer had affected her so strongly.

"Well, somebody's got to," Mimi said. "What you need is time away from us here in Jacksonville. You need to forget the problems at Tomorrow House and stay away from the real world for a while."

"I can do that here at Sweet Haven."

"Stay for as long as you need to. I'll try to keep the natives from getting too restless."

"Thanks." Cyn knew she could count on Mimi. They were kindred souls, both dependable and nurturing women.

"I'll call you in a few days. Take care, honey child."

"Bye, Mimi." She laid the phone on the table, then focused her attention on the beach, the sound of the lapping water soothing to her nerves.

Cyn knew that Mimi was right. What she needed now was to escape from the real world. And she'd done just that for a few hours last night, but the dream world she had entered hadn't given her any comfort. *He* had been there. Big and strong. But he had been in danger. She had felt his fear, and knew that it was an alien emotion, one he'd long ago forgotten. He had not been afraid for himself, but for her.

Suddenly, without warning, Cyn saw him running along the beach. Her breath caught in her throat, her chest aching, her heart beating loudly. He was big and powerfully built, yet his tall, muscular body was trim. He ran with the speed and ease of a wild stallion, his shoulder-length black hair flying around his face like a silky mane.

Cyn blinked her eyes several times, uncertain whether or not the man was real. She looked again. He was still there. His powerful body, clad only in cutoff jeans, raced into the wind, moving farther and farther up the beach.

She realized how foolish she'd been, even for one moment, to have thought that the runner on the beach was *him,* the phantom protector from her dreams.

No matter how hard she tried, Cyn couldn't turn around and walk away. She watched, fascinated by the stranger, by his incredible physical condition, the absolute perfection of his darkly tanned body and by the length of his inky black hair. Even at this distance she could tell he wasn't some long-haired youth. He was obviously a man in his prime. The shoulder-length hair gave him a roguish quality, as if he were a buccaneer. No, she thought, as if he were an ancient warrior.

The conquistador? Cyn couldn't stop the image from flashing through her mind. Since childhood, when she'd first heard the legend, she had visualized the ancient warrior and his maiden. And now this man, this stranger on her beach, brought to life the haunting story of tragic love and a prophecy that the present would one day heal the wounds of the past.

Cyn gazed out across the horizon, noting that the morning sun was just beginning to ascend into the sky. She glanced back and saw the stranger run into the ocean, the surging tide covering his bronzed body in an aqueous caress as his powerful arms and legs glided through the water.

Who was this man, she wondered? And what was he doing on her beach? The nearest neighbor was over a mile away. All the land past her family's cottage and the old building across the road were part of a state park. Perhaps that was it. Maybe this man had run along the beach for miles and somehow ended up taking a morning swim near her home.

Time seemed to stand still for Cyn as she watched the stranger swimming, coming out of the ocean, walking along the beach. Then time began again when he suddenly turned and looked at her. He stood yards away, the sun bright behind him, but she could tell that he was staring at her. She had the oddest feeling that he wanted her to come to him. She stared at him for endless moments, until he turned and ran back up the beach. It took every ounce of her willpower not to follow him, not to run after him, not to call out.

Her whole body trembled, inside and out. When she went back into the cottage, she began to wonder if she'd imagined the stranger, if all the mental stress she had endured recently was causing her to have delusions.

Well, whoever he was, real or imaginary, it didn't matter. She'd never see him again. The last thing on earth she needed at this particular time in her life was a man.

Nate sat on the huge tan leather sofa in his den, the only room in his new residence he'd bothered to fix up. Once things were settled with Ryker, he'd get rid of this musty old house and return to his place in St. Augustine. With his feet propped up on an old trunk and a beer in his hand, Nate felt relaxed for the first time that day. A second run on the beach after lunch and another rigorous swim in the ocean had helped ease the constant tension with which he lived these days.

She hadn't been outside on her patio or on the beach when he'd gone out the second time. He'd noticed that a white minivan was parked around on the north side of the cottage and assumed it was hers. That meant she was still here, still too close for comfort, still in danger if Ryker showed up sooner than expected.

Whoever she was, she was beautiful, Nate thought. He couldn't erase the memory of her standing on the patio, the early morning breeze whipping her blond hair around her face, molding her thin cotton slacks to her rounded hips and legs. Although he'd sensed her presence when he'd been running, he hadn't allowed himself to acknowledge her until he'd come out of the ocean and faced her. He had stood there staring at her like some lovesick teenager, as if he'd been struck deaf and dumb by the very sight of her. Hell, he'd seen gorgeous women before, he'd even had his share of lovely ladies, but there was something about this particular woman. Something that sent a surge of both fear and longing through him. The longing he understood. The fear puzzled him.

He had wanted to speak to her, to ask who she was and how long she'd be staying at the cottage. But he'd just stood there staring at her while she stared back at him. After what had seemed like an eternity, he'd turned and run away. If he'd stayed another minute, he'd have been on her patio, taking her in his arms. His body had been hard with need.

Nate laughed, a mirthless grunt. If he'd gone toward her, she probably would have run into the house screaming her head off. If he'd gotten near her, he would have frightened her to death. After all, he was a stranger, a big, Hispanic-looking man with hair nearly to his shoulders. Hell, he was surprised she hadn't already called the police.

The insistent ring of the telephone jarred Nate from his thoughts. Before answering, he knew the caller had to be one of two people. John Mason or Nick Romero. They were the only two people on earth who knew where Nathan Rafael Hodges was.

"Yeah?" Nate asked when he set his beer down and picked up the phone sitting on the enormous Jacobean table behind the sofa.

"I need to see you," Nick Romero said.

"Maybe you should come here. See if anyone follows you. Let Ryker know where I am and get this thing over with."

"Meet me in Jacksonville. Tonight," Romero said. "We know where Ryker is, where he's been and who he's working for."

"You boys have been busy."

"The CIA kept track of him before he entered the country. Our man Ryker has made some powerful friends in Colombia."

"You could give me the information over the phone," Nate said as he ran one big hand up and down the moist beer can he'd placed beside the phone.

"Probably, but I think we should talk, face to face."

"When and where?"

"Let's make it an early night," Romero said. "How about nine o'clock at a bar called the Brazen Hussy?"

"I know the place." Nate recalled the sleazy bar where scantily clad ladies of the night and streetwise punk drug pushers mixed and mingled with the clientele. "Wise choice. Nobody's going to notice two more shady characters in a place like that."

Romero laughed. "Yeah, that's us, a couple of shady characters."

"Hey, Romero."

"Huh?"

"Have you done something about protection for John and his family?" Nate knew that Nick Romero would have to call in a few favors to get any type of protection for John and Laurel Mason and their son, Johnny. But there was no way to be sure that once Ryker found out about Nate's business association and friendship with the Masons that they would be safe. Nate had distanced himself from the Masons, hoping to protect them, but there was always the chance that Ryker would harm Nate's friends regardless of the circumstances. Ryker would do anything to see Nate sweat, to prolong the torture.

"I'm working on it. It's just a matter of time."

Nate could hear the hesitation in his old friend's voice, and instinctively knew that there was more. Something Romero didn't want to talk about. "What is it?"

"I've got to ask you something," Romero said. "But I don't want an answer right now. Think about it and tell me tonight."

"What?"

"Do you know a man named Ramon Carranza?"

"Carranza?"

"Think about it, Nate. This Carranza has been showing a definite interest in you."

"Who is he?" Nate asked, certain he'd heard the name before. Where or when, he wasn't sure.

"We'll discuss it tonight. The Brazen Hussy. Nine," Romero said and hung up.

Nate replaced the receiver, picked up his beer and walked across the room. The whole den was filled with knives. Elaborate display cases covered the walls, the desk and the tables. Nate reached down on the wide pine table by the windows, picked up a small wood-and-glass case and opened it. He lifted a sinew-sewn hide sheath into his big hand, then removed the Apache scalping knife with its sinew-wrapped handle.

What does this guy Carranza have to do with Ryker? Nate asked himself. *What ungodly secret has Nick Romero unearthed?*

Cyn pushed the bits of lettuce and tomato around in the salad bowl. She had tried to convince herself that she didn't really want any of the chocolate-marshmallow ice cream she'd picked up at the store less than an hour ago. After all, she'd made it through the entire trial without reverting back to her old habit of using food as a crutch. But, with each bite she took, the nutritious veggies with which she'd concocted her enormous salad tasted more and more like cardboard.

Shoving the bowl aside, Cyn stood up and turned toward the refrigerator. *Don't do it,* she told herself. *Stay away from that ice cream and your hips will thank you for it.*

With her hand on the freezer, Cyn closed her eyes, cursing under her breath. *It's that man,* she thought. *He's got me acting irrationally.*

She had survived Evan's death, four years of loneliness, the year-long trial to convict her husband's killer. She had sought refuge here at the beach so she could come to terms with Darren Kilbrew's senseless murder. Somehow she could make sense of it all. She had to. But what she didn't need was the intrusion of some stranger, a man she identified, foolishly, with her phantom dream lover.

She wished she hadn't been sitting at the desk beside the back windows when he'd taken his swim in the ocean this afternoon. If only she hadn't seen him again, she never would

have made that hasty trip into town. There was something
about the stranger that unnerved her. Somehow she knew he
was no ordinary man. Her instincts told her that he was dangerous.

Cyn let her hand drop from the freezer door. Maybe what
she needed was a swim, a vigorous swim in the cool springtime
ocean. Anything was better than this nervous hunger inside her,
a hunger she had hoped chocolate-marshmallow ice cream
could appease.

Leaving the kitchen, she headed for her bedroom to put on
a bathing suit. Just as she walked down the hallway, the telephone rang. Who on earth? she wondered. Even though her
father and her brother David knew she was here, she doubted
either of them would have reason to call her. And Mimi certainly wouldn't be calling again. That left only one person.

Cyn opened the door and walked across the bedroom to
where the portable phone lay at the foot of the twin bed by the
window.

"Hello?"

"Cyn, how are you?" the man asked. "Everyone here at
Tomorrow House is very concerned about you."

"I'm all right, Bruce," Cyn lied. She wasn't all right. She
probably would have been if some savage-looking stranger
hadn't appeared on her beach and stirred her imagination into
overdrive. But, of course, she couldn't tell Reverend Bruce
Tomlinson such a thing. "Is there something wrong? I know
you wouldn't have disturbed my vacation otherwise."

"Well…I hated to call, and Mimi practically threatened me,
but—"

Cyn thought Bruce sounded whiny. Scratch that. She thought
he sounded more whiny than usual. The current director of
Tomorrow House had little in common with Reverend Evan
Porter, who, although he'd been the gentlest of gentlemen, had
been quite capable. "What's the problem?"

"It's that Casey kid who came here about a week ago. I told
you he would be a problem."

Cyn wanted to scream. For the past four years, Bruce had

come to her with every situation too nasty, too dirty, or too much trouble for him to handle. "What has he done?"

"It's not what he's done," Bruce said. "It's what he's going to do tonight. Mary Alice overheard Casey on the pay phone. I thought maybe I should call the police, but Mimi is totally opposed."

"Bruce, you're not making any sense." For the eleven millionth time in four years, Cyn wanted to shake dear Reverend Bruce Tomlinson until his teeth rattled.

"Casey is meeting some guy tonight to buy drugs, and he's…he's taking Bobby with him."

"Bobby!" Cyn had suspected that Casey was a user, but Tomorrow House had made many a runaway addict welcome for brief periods of time, had even helped a few kick the habit. Evan's death had been the only tragic result of giving safe haven to a junkie.

"I thought I should just confront the boys, but Mimi said confronting them would do no good, that Casey will leave in a few days and Bobby might go with him if I push him too far. She suggested that I speak to Bobby alone."

"Did you?" Cyn asked, praying silently. Bobby was a good kid, only thirteen. He'd been at Tomorrow House for nearly a month, longer than most, and there was a chance he would eventually agree to try another foster home.

"I couldn't. He's gone."

"What?" Cyn cried, gripping the phone tightly.

"And Casey's gone, too. I imagine they left early for their night on the town."

"Did Mary Alice overhear where they were going to meet this dealer?" Cyn asked.

"Some place called the Brazen Hussy at around nine-thirty, tonight. I've never heard of it, but I can guess by its name what sort of establishment it is. What on earth am I to do?" Bruce's voice sounded as distraught as Cyn felt.

"Don't do anything Bruce. It isn't our place to play policemen with the kids who come to Tomorrow House." Cyn recited the words she'd been told over and over again. "If we start calling in the police, the word will get out and none of these boys and girls will come to us when they need help so desperately.''

"But Bobby—"

"I'll take care of this."

"What are you going to do?" Bruce asked.

"I'm not sure, but I'll think of something." Cyn knew she should take her own advice, but she also knew that she wouldn't.

"I'm sorry I bothered you at a time like this. I realize how badly you needed to get away from all the problems here, but I didn't know who else to call. You're our tower of strength around here, Cyn. We just don't know how to deal with you being...well, out of commission, so to speak."

"Don't tell Mimi that you called me," Cyn advised the minister. "She'd never bake you another pineapple upsidedown cake as long as you live."

Bruce chuckled in his good-natured way. "Thanks, Cyn. You take care, and hurry on back to us. We miss you."

"Goodbye, Bruce. And don't worry about Bobby. Just leave him to me."

Cyn punched the off button and lowered the antenna, then tossed the telephone back onto the twin bed. She moved her overnight bag off the wicker settee, put it on the floor and sat down. Dear God, what was she going to do?

Bobby, abandoned at the age of five by his parents, had moved from one foster home to another. His last foster father had physically abused him and he'd run away. He'd been eleven at the time and had been on the streets ever since. Cyn could only imagine the nightmares the boy had lived through, but she knew one thing for certain. Bobby had never used drugs.

What would Evan have done in this situation? she asked herself, and immediately knew the answer. Evan would have gone after Bobby and Casey. He would have talked to the boys and, in his own loving yet professional way, would have talked Bobby into returning to the shelter. Cyn had become just enough of a realist in the past four years to know that Casey might be a lost cause.

Did she have the nerve to go to a place like the Brazen Hussy? She'd be a fool to go alone at night to one of the most notorious bars in town. But what choice did she have, other than calling the police?

She would just put her can of Mace and her whistle in her purse, dress appropriately and pray that her guardian angel would protect her.

Chapter 2

"**R**yker is in Miami," Nick Romero said, then took a leisurely sip of his Scotch and soda, eyeing Nate Hodges over the rim of his glass.

Instead of replying immediately, Nate let the information soak in as he glanced around the smoky bar. Tonight the Brazen Hussy was as loud and smelly and crowded as it had been the last time he had stopped by, over a year ago.

Noticing the small group of teens crowded around a table at the far side of the room, Nate took a deep breath before turning his attention back to Romero. "Some of them aren't dry behind the ears, but the scum that owns this place doesn't give a damn. He's been busted twice for allowing minors in this place, but somehow he manages to stay in business." Nate grunted with disgust. "Just look at them. They're smoking pot and waiting around for their dealer to show up."

"When did you start worrying about kids you don't even know?" Romero asked. "I'll bet if you bothered to check every boy would have an ID to prove he's of age."

"Yeah, fake ID."

"They really think they're tough, don't they? I was just like them once. I thought that growing up in a tough neighborhood had prepared me for anything. Until I went to Nam."

"They'd all flip out if they knew a big, badass DEA agent was sitting across the room from them."

"I'm not here tonight as an agent." Romero gave his old SEAL comrade a hard, intent look. "I'm here as your friend."

"Yeah, I know, and I'm grateful even if I don't act like I am."

"I've arranged for some protection for John's family. Un-officially, of course. By the way, how is he now that he's a happily married man?" Romero grinned, then took another sip of his drink.

"Happy," Nate said, not looking directly at Romero, but at some point over his shoulder where a tall, buxom brunette was giving him the eye. "He says he's in love, and damn if I don't believe him."

"Who would have thought it, huh? The three of us shared some good times together, didn't we?"

"Yeah." Nate gave his head a negative shake when he noticed that the brunette was coming straight toward him. He wanted her to know he wasn't interested. He'd lost his taste for her type years ago. "But you and I shared some bad times, too."

"Mm-mm, starting with when we first got to Nam and our entire platoon got the runs from drinking the Vietnamese water."

Nate chuckled, the memory distant and harmless enough to laugh about. "So, Ryker's made it to Miami. No big news. We knew it was just a matter of time." Nate lifted the glass of straight bourbon to his lips, savoring the taste when it hit his tongue.

"He's working for the Marquez family as a bodyguard."

"Big-time drug dealers." Nate wasn't surprised. Ian Ryker had been a mercenary, a soldier of fortune and a drug smuggler. He was the type who understood the system and used it to his advantage. No matter what, he always found a loophole, a back door out of trouble. "What else does Ryker do for them?"

"He's an enforcer," Romero said. "He's been with the family for over a year, first in South America, now here."

"Were they the ones who got him out of the prison where we thought he'd died?" Nate asked.

"Our information is sketchy, but it's possible. All we know is that Ryker was reported killed five years ago when he was serving a sentence for smuggling, then miraculously, he reappeared a few months ago, alive and well and back to business as usual."

"Who spotted him?" Nate knew that Ryker would have taken no chances of being seen, of making himself visible, and, with his looks—a patch over one eye and his left hand missing—it would have been difficult for him to move around Miami incognito.

"Not one of our guys." Romero looked squarely at Nate. "Remember the man I asked you about earlier today?"

"Ramon Carranza?"

"It seems Señor Carranza's right-hand man made a discreet phone call to someone at the agency. He knew the connection between you and Ryker. He used your name. The man knew too much about you, Nate."

"Just what was the message, and why didn't Señor Carranza make the call himself?"

"Carranza never gets his own hands dirty. You know the type. But I'd say, for some reason, he wants you to know that he's involved," Romero said, shrugging. "As for the message, well, I'd call it a warning."

Nate grunted as he rubbed the side of his jaw. "A warning from Carranza?"

"Oh, yeah. From the big man himself. You've been advised to go into hiding if you're smart."

"Just who is this Ramon Carranza?" Nate asked.

"He's a retired businessman. A former Miami resident. He moved to St. Augustine a few years ago, about the same time you came back home.'' Romero picked up his glass, downing the last drops of his Scotch and soda.

"Are you saying there's a connection?" Nate narrowed his eyes, wrinkling his forehead.

"I was hoping you could tell me. Carranza is associated with all the right people and all the wrong people. The man knows everybody, and I mean everybody. He ran a ritzy casino in Havana back in the forties and fifties. When he moved to Miami before Castro took over in Cuba, he already had connections.'' Romero opened his dark eyes in a wide if-you-know-what-I-mean stare. "He's an old man, late seventies, but he's still powerful."

"Did you get the name of the guy who called the agency for Carranza?"

"Emilio Rivera. They've been together for years."

Nate shook his head. "Never heard of him."

"We've been doing some checking—"

"We?" Nate didn't like the sound of this. Something was damned queer about the whole thing.

"When a man like Ramon Carranza starts giving us information, it's only natural that we'd wonder why."

"What did you find out?"

Romero glanced around the room, motioned for the barmaid, then ran one dark, lean hand across his face. "This isn't the first time Carranza has shown an interest in you. It seems that, through both legal and illegal sources, he's been keeping track of your activities for years."

Nate felt a hard tightening in the pit of his stomach. Some man, some former godfather figure, had been keeping tabs on him. "How long?"

"Best we can figure out, ever since Nam."

"Ever since I first met Ryker. Is that what you're saying?" Nate asked.

"Carranza and Ryker have friends and associates in common. Presently the Marquez family. Who's to say that Ryker wasn't working for Carranza back in the seventies? The black market, drugs. Could be Carranza's been keeping tabs on you as a favor for an old buddy.''

"Then why would Carranza have his man send me a warning?''

"To add a little extra pressure, maybe?''

"Ryker wants to see me sweat,'' Nate said.

The barmaid appeared, took the men's order, and left.

"The DEA is very interested in Ryker, and even more interested in his connection with the Marquez family, so we're in on this with you Nate, whether you want us or not.''

"I don't have much choice, do I?'' Nate finished off his bourbon just as the barmaid set his second drink down in front of him. "And what interest does the DEA have in Carranza?''

"None, other than his possible connection to Ryker.''

Nate gripped the glass in his big hand, sloshing the contents around and around as he stared down sightlessly at the liquid. He had enough problems in his life right now without having a puzzle to solve. Was Carranza friend or foe? Was he really trying to warn Nate or was he trying to help Ryker?

"Well, well, take a look at that, would you?'' Romero said, emitting a low, sensual growl as he stared across the room. "What is something like that doing in a place like this?''

Slowly, with total disinterest, Nate glanced across the room, looking at the woman who'd gained his friend's attention. He felt as if he'd been hit in the stomach with a sledgehammer. It was her. The woman from the beach. The woman who was staying at the cottage across the road from his house. And she looked sorely out of place walking into the Brazen Hussy, although she had obviously tried to dress for the occasion. Wearing a red silk jumpsuit, a pair of four-inch red heels and teacup-size gold hoops dangling from her ears, she should have looked like any of the other "working girls'' casing the bar for an easy mark, but she didn't. Even with the added touch of red lipstick and red nail polish, she still emitted an aura of innocence. Her beautiful face was too fresh, her eyes too warm and bright, her movements too hesitant for her to be a pro.

"Maybe her car broke down," Nate said. "Or maybe she's slumming."

"I don't think so," Romero said, smiling as he watched the woman cross the room. "She looks too classy for a one-night stand. But, if I thought she was interested—"

"You always did have a weakness for blondes." Nate had seen his friend succumb to the charms of more than one blond beauty over the years. But this woman wasn't for Nick Romero.

Laughing, Romero slapped Nate on the back. "And you, my friend, never had a weakness for anything."

Until now, Nate almost said. Hell, what was the matter with him? The woman didn't mean a damn thing to him. He didn't even know her. So what if just looking at her aroused him? Half the guys in the bar were probably readjusting their pants right now.

"Weaknesses can get you killed," Nate said.

"Oh, but what a way to die!" Romero reared back in his chair, bringing the front legs up off the floor. "She's bound to get into trouble, alone in a place like this. Maybe I should offer my assistance."

When Romero lowered his chair back on the floor and started to get up, Nate threw out a restraining hand. "Don't."

Romero sat back down, glaring at Nate. "Hey, old pal, I saw her first. Remember the rules."

"The rules don't apply here." Nate looked past Romero, his gaze riveted to the woman who had approached the table of noisy, swaggering teens. "But if they did, then she'd be mine. *I* saw her first."

"You what?"

"Last night. On the beach." Nate watched as she placed her hand on a boy's shoulder. What the hell was she doing in a place like the Brazen Hussy? he wondered.

"Tell me more," Romero said.

The group of teenage boys stared up at her when she approached their table, Casey easing back his chair as if he intended to stand. When she put her hand on Bobby's shoulder, he slumped down in the chair and hung his head so low his chin rested on his chest.

Casey smiled at her, a cocky look on his youthful face. "What are you doing here, Ms. Porter, checking out the action?"

"Shut up," Bobby said in a whispered hiss.

"Hey, you two know this sexy freak?" A husky young blonde asked, turning in his chair, sticking out his muscular chest.

"Yeah, we know her," Casey said, standing up to face Cyn.

The blonde stood up and walked behind Bobby's chair to stand beside Cyn. "Introduce us."

"Lazarus my man, meet Cyn Porter." Casey's laughter chilled Cyn. Obviously, the boy was already high.

The husky youth reached out and ran the tips of his fingers across Cyn's cheek, watching her, obviously waiting for a reaction. "Cyn, huh?" He laughed, the sound menacingly unnerving. "I like it. Lazarus Jones, at your service, baby doll."

Cyn's earlier uncertainty when she'd made the decision to come to the Brazen Hussy turned into outright apprehension. Jutting out her chin, she tried to appear undisturbed by the boy's crude come-on.

When she slowly pulled back away from his sweaty touch, he snickered and flashed Cyn a lascivious smile that turned her stomach. "Tell me, is Cyn ready to sin tonight?"

She looked down at his hand, noticing the thick coiled snake tattoo that began at his knuckles and ran up past his wrist. "Are you the *man* Casey and Bobby came here to meet tonight?" Cyn asked, trying to keep the tone of her voice calm and steady.

"Ms. Porter, please…" Bobby knocked Cyn's hand from his shoulder in an effort to stand, but Casey shoved him back down into his chair. "How did you know where to find us?" Bobby began to tremble.

"You don't really want to be here, do you, Bobby?" Cyn asked. "Why don't you and I leave, go get a hamburger and talk?"

"Hey, baby doll, you can't leave yet," Lazarus Jones said, placing his arm around Cyn's waist. "Besides, you can't have any fun with a kid like him. Hell, he's probably still a virgin."

Bobby jumped up, his big blue eyes glaring at Lazarus. "Leave her alone! Come on, Ms. Porter, I'll go with you."

"Sit down, kid. You came here for a little blow, didn't you? The party hasn't even started yet." Lazarus pulled Cyn up against him. "I got enough for you, too, baby doll. Enough of everything."

When Lazarus rubbed himself against Cyn, fissions of panic exploded in her stomach. Her whistle and Mace were inside her purse, which was inconveniently trapped between her and the muscle-bound delinquent.

"I'm not interested in anything you have, Mr. Jones," Cyn said, staring him directly in the eye, hoping her false bravado would pay off.

Lazarus released her momentarily, long enough to shove another teen out of his chair and onto the floor. "Get up and give the lady your seat."

When Lazarus grabbed Cyn by the arm, she tried to pull away. He held fast. She began raising her leg, slowly, intending to knee her overly zealous admirer in the groin. Bobby knotted his hands into fists, thrusting one out in front of him.

Suddenly, Lazarus Jones released Cyn, then dropped to his knees. A very big man stood behind Lazarus, his hands on the boy's shoulders, the pressure from his hold keeping him subdued. Letting out a stream of colorful obscenities, Lazarus squirmed, trying to free himself, but to no avail.

Cyn looked up at her rescuer. Her head began to spin. Her knees bolted. She grabbed the back of a chair to steady herself. It was him. The man on the beach. He was even bigger, darker and more deadly close up.

He looked different fully clothed and with his long hair pulled back into a short, neat ponytail. Wearing faded jeans, a dark cotton shirt, tan sport coat and snakeskin boots, he looked a little bit like a cowboy, Cyn thought. No, not a cowboy—an Indian dressed in white man's garb.

While Lazarus, still on his knees, continued his tirade, the other boys at the table began to get up, one at a time, and move backward. No one else in the Brazen Hussy paid much attention, except another big, dark man a few tables over who was watching the situation with amusement. Cyn couldn't help but notice him when he nodded at her and smiled.

"What would you like for me to do with him?" Nate asked Cyn, tightening his hold on the boy.

"Hey, man, what's she to you?" Casey asked. "Lazarus didn't mean no harm. He just considers himself a ladies' man."

"Is that right…Lazarus? Are you a ladies' man?" Nate didn't smile, but the tone of his voice was teasing.

"Let me go," Lazarus said, snarling his features into a threatening look. "If you know what's good for you, you'll let me go and get the hell out of here before I kill you."

Nate did smile then. Cyn thought it was the coldest, most dangerous expression she'd ever seen on a man's face. Nate released his hold on the boy.

Lazarus jumped up, pulled a switchblade from his pocket and thrust it toward Nate in a show of manly triumph. Cyn sucked in her breath and stepped backward. Dear God, what was she doing here? Why had she been stupid enough to think that dressing like a hooker and carrying a can of Mace and a whistle in her purse would protect her? Hadn't Evan's senseless murder taught her anything? The very sight of the knife in Lazarus's hand intensified the terror that had been building inside her for the last few minutes. Since Evan's death, the sight of a knife in another person's hands created irrational fear in Cyn.

The other boys at the table backed up further, even the swaggering Casey. Bobby stood beside Cyn, grabbing her hand, trying to pull her away.

"I don't know what kind of hold you had on me, man," Lazarus said, swaying from side to side in a macho strut. "But you came up on me from behind. Things are even now. We're face-to-face, and I'm going to stick you, big man, and watch you fall to your knees."

Nate knew that he could take care of this cocky young hood quickly and efficiently in the way only a trained warrior could. After all, he knew more ways to kill a man than most people even knew existed. But he had no intention of physically harming this streetwise punk. Scaring a little sense into him, however, was a different matter.

"Please, don't do this." Cyn heard a pleading female voice say, then realized she had spoken the words. Dear God, this couldn't be happening. It just couldn't! One of these men was going to get hurt, maybe both of them, and it would be her fault. She had thought she could handle the situation, been so confident in her ability to do what Evan would have done. But Evan died like this, a tiny inner voice reminded her, stabbed to death when he'd tried to help a wayward teenager.

While Cyn and the group of boys watched, while the dark man several tables over simply glanced their way, while a couple of barmaids stopped to view the scene, Lazarus Jones lunged toward the older man. The switchblade in his hand gleamed like shiny sterling silver in the smoky, muted light of the barroom. Cyn cried out. Bobby held her hand so tightly she winced from the pain.

From out of nowhere it seemed to Cyn, her rescuer pulled a knife—longer, wider, larger than his opponent's. Within seconds he had knocked Lazarus's knife to the floor and turned him around to face Cyn, twisting his arm behind his back and holding the deadly blade to the boy's throat.

Cyn could see the fear plainly in Lazarus Jones's eyes. Obviously, he thought he was going to die. Cyn prayed he was wrong.

"I think you owe the lady an apology," Nate said, letting the sharp blade of his knife rest against the boy's flesh.

"I...I'm sorry. I—"

"Please, let him go," Cyn said.

"Should I let you go, Lazarus?" Nate asked, leaning down slightly so he was practically whispering in the boy's ear. "Should I set you free so you can keep on selling drugs to other kids? So you can rob again, maybe even kill?"

"Hey, man, how the hell did you know—" Lazarus trembled with the certain fear of a man facing death.

Cyn felt hot, salty bile rise in her throat when she realized what kind of human beings she was dealing with. The boy was so brutal and uncaring, and her rescuer was twice as deadly as the boy. Dear Lord in heaven, this wasn't the kind of world she wanted to live in. She had spent the last ten years of her life trying to help change things, trying to make a difference. She hated violence, and yet she seemed unable to escape it.

Nate shoved Lazarus toward his companions. "Get out of here, and pray to whatever God you believe in that our paths never cross again."

Lazarus and his entourage left in a big hurry, Casey following quickly. Bobby released Cyn's hand, but continued staring at the big man coming toward them.

"Bobby—" Cyn had no more than said his name when he ran. "No, Bobby. Wait," she cried out, but didn't try to follow him, knowing she would never catch him. Bobby was too adept at running and hiding.

Nate hadn't felt such rage in a long time. It had been years since he'd wanted to kill another man, but the moment that cocky boy had touched her, Nate had wanted to rip him apart. He hated to admit it, but the brutality within him, the way he so often used violence as a means to settle problems, made him, in a strange way, no better than the smart-mouthed young hood he'd just subdued. Violence breeds violence. It was a fact he couldn't deny.

"Are you all right?" he asked, as he folded his lock-blade knife, reached beneath his jacket and slipped it into a leather sheath attached to his belt.

"Yes." She stared up at him, her heart pounding so loud and wild she thought surely he could hear it.

"What the devil are you doing in a place like this? Don't you know you could have gotten yourself raped or killed?" He wanted to grab her and shake the living daylights out of her. Then he wanted to pick her up and carry her out of here to some isolated place where he could make love to her.

"Look, no one asked you to interfere," Cyn said, tilting her chin upward in a defiant manner. "What made you think I couldn't handle the situation?"

"What made me...?" Nate glared at her flushed face, noting the anger in her dark brown eyes. Rich, warm brown eyes. "That young stud had plans for the two of you."

"Do you realize that your interference could well have ruined a boy's life?" Even though she knew she should be thanking this man for coming to her rescue, she was lashing out at him, some deep-seated instinct warning her to protect herself from the emotions he had stirred to life within her.

Nate moved closer, but didn't touch her. "What are you talking about? Which boy?"

"Bobby, the boy that was clutching my hand." Cyn took several deep, calming breaths. "Bobby's a runaway who has been staying at Tomorrow House, and we had just about talked him into trying a new foster home."

"Tomorrow House?" Nate's stomach tightened. Hell and damnation, what was she, some sort of social worker? Might know, the first woman he'd truly wanted in years would turn out to be some bright-eyed, sanctimonious do-gooder. "Don't tell me, you're some sort of undercover nun, out to save the world."

Cyn stiffened her spine, gritted her teeth and glared up at Rambo-to-the-Rescue. "I'm Cynthia Porter, and I'm assistant director at Tomorrow House, a church home for runaway children. Two of our boys, Bobby and Casey, came here tonight to buy drugs. I came here to try to persuade them not to. To try to get Bobby to return to a place where he feels safe."

Nate could see the zealous determination in her eyes. Rich, warm brown eyes. "The kid will probably come back on his own."

"After what happened here tonight, I'm not so certain. You scared him half to death." Cyn noticed that the man who'd been watching from several tables over had just gotten up and was walking toward them. "Your friend?" she asked.

Nate felt Nick Romero's approach, slanted his eyes just

enough to pick up the other man's shadow in his peripheral vision, and nodded affirmatively. He wondered if this woman realized that they'd met before. She'd made no reference to having seen him on the beach. "Romero, meet Cynthia Porter, assistant director at some shelter for runaways."

Romero reached out and took Cyn's hand, brought it to his lips and brushed a feather-light kiss across her knuckles. "I'm delighted, Ms. Porter. I was afraid Nate might forget to introduce us. I'm Nicholas Romero, and the man who just saved you from a rather unpleasant evening is Nathan Hodges. But you can call him Nate."

Nathan? Nathan Hodges. Nate. His name was Nate. Cyn noticed the stormy darkness in his eyes as he glared at his friend. Up until this very moment she'd thought his eyes were deep, dark brown because they appeared almost black. But they weren't brown. They were green—an incredibly dark green. Powerful eyes. Stunningly green, set in a hard, bronzed face with sharp cheekbones, a strong nose and a wide, full mouth. Recognition shot through her like a surge of electricity. Those were *his* eyes. Her phantom protector. Her dream lover.

She stared at him, unable to stop herself. Her breathing quickened, her pulse accelerated, her flesh tingled with some unknown excitement.

It isn't *him,* she told herself. It can't be.

Nate studied her closely as she stared at him. He didn't think he'd ever seen such a beautiful woman—every feature perfect, combining to create an unforgettable face. Large brown eyes framed by thick dark lashes. Small, tip-tilted nose, luscious, full-lipped mouth. And golden blond hair hanging in long silken waves down to her tiny waist.

He looked at her, lost in the warmth of her rich brown eyes. He knew those eyes. They had haunted his dreams for twenty-five years.

The blood in his veins ran hot and wild, some primitive longing surging through him. He couldn't, wouldn't, give a name to what he was feeling.

It isn't *her,* he told himself. It couldn't be.

"Could we give you a ride home, Ms. Porter?" Nick Romero smiled as he looked back and forth from Nate to Cyn.

"What?" she asked, aware of nothing and no one except the big, dark man whose green eyes held her under their spell.

"I asked if you came here in a cab and need a ride home. I'd be glad to take you." Romero grasped Cyn's hand.

"I'll take her." Placing his arm around Cyn's shoulder, Nate gave his old friend a warning glare.

Romero released her and stepped backward, grinning.

"That…that won't be necessary, thank you," she said. "I drove here. I'm parked out front."

"Then let us escort you," Romero said.

"I will." Nate pulled Cyn close to his side, completely ignoring Romero.

Before Cyn knew what had happened, Nate had escorted her outside. She felt overwhelmed. Nate Hodges was quite a commanding person.

"Where's your car?" he asked.

"It's the white van over there." She pointed down the street. "I'll be all right now. Thanks."

Nate didn't release her. Cyn sighed, and allowed him to walk her to her van. Opening her purse, she fumbled with the keys, almost dropping them. Nate took the gold initial key ring from her trembling fingers.

"Don't ever do something this stupid again," he said as he inserted the key and unlocked the van.

"What did you say?" How dare he issue her orders.

"Coming into this part of town alone was a stupid thing to do. You were asking for trouble. You were damned lucky that I was here tonight."

"I've lived thirty-five years without your help, and I think I'll make it another thirty-five. Just who do you think you are, my guardian angel?"

He took her chin in his big hand, tilting it upward so that she was forced to look into his eyes. "Tonight, that's exactly what I was."

His words sent a tremor racing through her. This man was

a dominant, protective male, and for some reason she felt as if he'd staked his claim on her. "Then thank you, Mr. Hodges and…and goodbye."

Cyn stepped up into the van, inserted the key into the ignition and started the motor.

"Don't come back to this part of town even if Bobby and Casey don't show up at the shelter." Nate leaned down into the van, his face so close to hers she could feel his breath. "Has anyone ever told you that you're—"

"I'm used to giving orders and having them obeyed," he said.

"That's obvious."

"Go straight home."

"Yes, sir!" Cyn slammed the door, then maneuvered the minivan out of the parking space.

Nate watched until the van's taillights disappeared into the traffic. He turned, walking in the opposite direction where his Jeep Cherokee was parked. When he passed the front entrance of the Brazen Hussy, he noticed Nick Romero coming out the door.

"She's quite a woman, isn't she?" Romero slapped his old friend on the back.

"Stay away from her," Nate warned.

"Well, well. I've never seen you so proprietary when it came to a woman. What is it with you and her?"

"Nothing, absolutely nothing." Nate began walking away, moving toward his car.

Nate neither wanted nor needed Cynthia Porter in his life, especially not now when just being his friend was potentially dangerous. All he wanted was peace. Blessed peace. He had longed to put the past behind him. He wanted to forget the memories of a war that still haunted him, and to come to terms with the man he had been, the man who had served his country for twenty years.

Romero followed. "You said you'd met her before?"

Nate slowed his quick strides and turned to face his old SEAL comrade. "There's a cottage across the road from the house I bought. It's the only other house within a mile. She's staying there. She was there last night and again this morning, and I've got to find a way to make her leave. She's in danger.''

''Hey, pal, Ryker's coming after you, not after Cynthia Porter.''

Nate tried to erase the scene forming in his mind, the vision of *his* woman's lifeless body in Ryker's arms. ''Anyone near me when Ryker shows up will be in danger.''

''Whatever your feelings are for Ms. Porter, they're mutual. I saw the way she looked at you.'' Romero put his hand on Nate's shoulder.

''I have no feelings for her, and if you think she has any for me, then you're mistaken.'' Nate unlocked his car. ''She isn't going to be in my life long enough for Ryker to know of her existence.''

Cynthia Porter wasn't the woman in his dreams. She couldn't be. Ryker was going to kill that woman—and destroy Nate's soul.

Chapter 3

The drive from Jacksonville to Sweet Haven seemed endless to Cyn. Her mind was racked with utter confusion, and her heart rioted with a mixture of far too many emotions. She had never experienced a night quite like this one, and she'd certainly never met a man like Nate Hodges.

Gripping the steering wheel tightly, Cyn turned east off Interstate 1. She glanced in her rearview mirror to see if he was still following her. He was. Damn him. She tried to tell herself that if he was staying somewhere in the state park he was on his way home, too, and not actually following her. But her feminine instincts told her that his Jeep would still be behind her van when she left the highway in Sweet Haven and drove down the narrow road to the beach.

While keeping her eyes glued to the road, she rummaged around in the cassette holder between the bucket seats, counted the tapes until she reached the fourth one, then pulled it out and slipped it into the player. Within seconds, fifties sound filled the inside of the very nineties van.

Cyn loved the music from the period just before and after

her birth, the romantic, sentimental songs that promised love and happiness no matter how many times your heart had been broken. The song playing on the tape was "True Love," and Cyn found herself humming, then mouthing the lyrics along with the singer.

No one seeing her now would believe that the trim, attractive, mature Cynthia Porter had once been a plump, naive teenager who had lived in a world of romantic fantasies, listening to dreamy songs like the ones Johnny Mathis sang and watching movies like *Love Story* and *Dr. Zhivago*.

The songs on the tape changed again and again as Cyn raced through the dark night, her speed ten miles over the limit, as if she thought she could outrun the feelings that the man driving so close behind her had created. Nate Hodges's eyes might remind her of the man in her dreams, but he wasn't *him*. Nate was too big, too mysterious…too dangerous to be the gentle, protective guardian who had always come to her to offer her comfort and hope in times of greatest loss and deepest sorrow. But why, then, did she sense that she knew Nate, that it was inevitable that their lives would be joined, that sometime, somewhere, she had belonged to him?

The bright headlights of an oncoming car nearly blinded Cyn. She slowed the van to several miles below the speed limit just in time to see the turnoff to the beach. Taking a right, she glanced in her rearview mirror and saw that Nate had turned directly behind her.

She was tempted to pull off on the side of the road, wait until he stopped, then get out and demand that he quit following her. She wanted to tell him that he didn't have to see her safely home, that there was no danger for her in Sweet Haven. But she didn't stop until she pulled into the driveway at her cottage.

Jerking the keys from the ignition, she opened the door and hopped down onto the stone walkway. Expecting Nate to drive his Jeep in beside her van, Cyn turned around to greet him, the words "thank you and goodbye" on the tip of her tongue. Her eyes widened in surprise when she watched him pass her cottage. Where is he going? she wondered. Didn't he realize she lived on a dead-end road, and even though he probably lived nearby, there was no way out except the way he'd come in?

He turned into the overgrown drive across the road. She sighed with relief, assuming he was going to turn around. When his Jeep disappeared behind the old shell-rock and wooden house that had stood deserted since its last owner had died nearly two years ago, Cyn planted her hands on her hips, shaking her head in bewilderment. What did he think he was doing?

She waited for a few minutes, thinking his Jeep would reappear. It didn't. Well, whatever kind of game he was playing, she wasn't going to cooperate. With an exasperated groan, Cyn went into her cottage.

Stumbling over a footstool in the living room, she cursed herself for not leaving on a light when she'd left. She kicked off her heels, then reached out to turn on a nearby table lamp. Hopping around on one foot, she massaged the throbbing toes that had collided with the footstool. She headed toward the kitchen, flipping on light switches as she went. She opened the freezer, pulled out a half-gallon container of chocolate-marshmallow ice cream and set it on the table.

"Where is he?" she said aloud. Was it possible that he planned to stay the night in the abandoned house across the road so he could watch over her? "You're fantasizing again, Cynthia Ellen. Nate Hodges is not your protector. He's a ruthless, deadly man. Tonight, you saw what he's capable of doing."

Cyn retrieved a long-handled spoon from a nearby drawer, sat down at the table and opened the ice cream carton. Sticking the spoon into the frozen dessert, she lifted a huge bite to her mouth.

Think about something besides him, she told herself. *You've got enough problems without borrowing trouble. You took a dangerous chance tonight hoping to help Bobby, and maybe even Casey, and where did it get you? Into trouble—trouble spelled N-A-T-E. Stop that now! Concentrate on finding a way to help Bobby.* There was no telling where the boy was right now. She only prayed that he wasn't with Casey.

Cyn slipped the smooth, creamy chocolate concoction into her mouth, savoring the rich, sweet taste. She dipped the spoon in again and again as she devoured her edible nerve-soother. That's what Mimi called Cyn's addiction to sweets, especially ice cream.

Mimi. That's it. She needed to talk to Mimi. Checking her watch, she saw that it was after midnight. She couldn't call the elderly woman at this hour, no matter how badly she needed a motherly shoulder to cry on. The heart-to-heart talk she so badly needed would have to wait.

While Cyn finished almost a third of a carton of ice cream, she tried to figure out just what she would do if Nate should appear at her door tonight. She'd tell him to get lost. No. She'd thank him again for coming to her rescue, then she'd say a polite goodbye. Or maybe she would invite him in for coffee.

Without even thinking about what she was doing, Cyn got up and prepared her coffeemaker. Just as she flipped on the switch, she realized what she'd done. What was wrong with her? Did she actually want Nate Hodges to come by for coffee? A man like that? A man who carried a deadly knife. A man who had subdued a muscular young man half his age with the ease of a wolf overpowering a rabbit.

She took a deep breath, groaning at the pungent odors her own body and clothes emitted. God, she smelled like a sweaty, smoky, whiskey-perfumed streetwalker. Running her fingers over her face, she realized she probably didn't look much better. She'd overdone the makeup just a bit tonight in the hopes of fitting in at the Brazen Hussy.

Forget about Nate Hodges, about phoning Mimi, about where Bobby and Casey are, she told herself. What she needed was a long soak in the bathtub and a good night's sleep.

Maybe she wouldn't dream about a man with incredible green eyes.

Nate prowled around the den, feeling like a caged animal. If he let himself, his feelings for Cynthia Porter could close in, corner and trap him. He didn't know why, now of all times, she had come into his life. He'd been alone most of his forty-two years. He didn't want or need the complications of a permanent relationship—now or ever. He'd never been in love, had never believed the crap about that undying, forever-after emotion.

Love was only a word. His mother had loved his father, but that love had given her nothing but grief. The man for whom she'd borne a child hadn't cared enough about her to marry her. For all Nate knew, his mother had been one of countless women his father had *loved* and left behind.

And when his mother had died, he'd been handed over to his uncle, a man who'd taught Nate, early on, that love was for weaklings and only the strong survived. Nate was strong. He'd lived through years of physical and verbal abuse from the man who'd taught him to trust and depend on nothing and no one except himself. Hate was a powerful teacher. And Nate hated Collum Hodges—almost as much as his uncle had hated him.

He didn't want or need a woman in his life, depending on him, caring for him, demanding more of him than he could give. Oh, he'd had his share of women over the years, but he'd never allowed one to mean more to him than a temporary pleasure. No woman had ever pierced through the painful scars that protected his heart—except *her*. The woman from his dreams, the woman with the warm, rich brown eyes, the woman who gave his heart and soul sanctuary within her loving arms.

And for some stupid reason he had allowed himself to think, for a few crazy minutes, that Cynthia Porter might be that dream woman come to life. What had given him such delusions? Even if his beautiful neighbor did have the same hypnotic brown eyes, it didn't mean that she was— *Stop it!* He cursed himself for being a fool. He had more important things to worry about than a woman—any woman.

Ryker was in Miami working for one of the most notorious drug families in the country. Nate knew his days were numbered. Soon, maybe sooner than he'd planned, Ian Ryker would go hunting, searching for a man he blamed for the death of his lover and the loss of his eye and hand.

Nate had relived that day a hundred, no, a thousand times, and he knew there was nothing that he or any of the other SEAL team could or would have done differently. They had all regretted that the woman had been killed, accidentally, in the crossfire when she'd tried to protect Ryker. Momentarily paralyzed by the sight of his Vietnamese lover's lifeless body, Ryker's reaction to Nate's attack had been a second off, costing him his eye, his hand and perhaps, over a period of time, his sanity.

Nate longed for a drink, a stiff belt of strong whiskey, not the watered-down bourbon he'd been served at the Brazen Hussy earlier tonight. He didn't want to remember Nam or any of the death-defying assignments he'd taken part in during the years he'd been a SEAL. He wanted no more violence in his life. All he wanted was peace.

Running his fingers through his hair, he loosed the band that held the thick black mass into a subdued ponytail, releasing it to fall freely down his neck and against his face. He walked over to the three-legged pine cabinet sitting in the corner of the den, opened a drawer and pulled out an almost-full bottle of Jack Daniel's. Undoing the cap, he tipped the bottle to his mouth and took a short, quick swig. The straight whiskey burned like fire as it coated his mouth, anesthetizing his tongue, burning a trail down his gut when he swallowed.

Hell, he shouldn't need this. He'd never been a man to use liquor to solve his problems. He recapped the bottle and shoved it into the drawer.

Cyn. He'd heard the boy named Casey call her Cyn. What a name for a church shelter worker. She looked like sin—pure, damn-a-man's-immortal-soul type of sin. All soft, female flesh, with round hips, tiny waist and full breasts. And golden-blond hair. God, a man could go crazy thinking about that mane of sunshine covering his naked body.

But the one thing he couldn't forget about her, no matter

how hard he tried, were her eyes. Those rich, warm brown eyes.

Nate took in a hefty gulp of air, then released it slowly. The heady aroma of sweat and smoke and liquor clung to his body, hair and clothes. Damn, he needed a shower—a cold shower—and about eight hours of dreamless sleep.

Within minutes, Nate had stripped and stood beneath the cleansing chill of the antiquated shower in the house's one bathroom, located just off the kitchen. For a while he simply stood and let the water pour over his hot, sticky body. A body heavy with desire.

He had to focus on something besides Cyn Porter, or he'd be up half the night if he didn't settle for a less-than-satisfactory, temporary solution. Think of something pleasant, he told himself. He tried to recall the carefree shore leaves he'd shared with Nick and occasionally with John, days they'd sowed their wild oats in countries all over the world.

But his most pleasant memories were hidden deep in his heart, tucked away in a private section he had marked with No Trespassing signs. The happiest moments of his life had been spent with his mother when he'd been a small boy. Although she'd died when he was six, he could still remember what she looked like, what she smelled like, how she'd felt when she'd held him close.

Grace Hodges had been a beautiful woman. Tall, slender, elegant. She had been the only person who'd ever loved him, and in the years since her death, he'd often wondered why she hadn't hated him. After all, he'd been a child born to her from a brief affair with a man who had deserted her, and soon afterward had gotten himself killed. Nate's father had been no good. And he was just like his father. His uncle had told him that—often.

"Your old man was some mixed-breed sonofabitch who ruined my sister's life," Collum Hodges had delighted in telling Nate. "If I'd had my way, she would've had an abortion. Our family had the money—we could have found a doctor. But no, she had to have you, and keep you, a constant reminder of her dead lover. She disgraced herself and the whole family. And now, I'm stuck with you, you dirty little bastard.''

Nate told himself that his uncle's taunts no longer hurt him, that he was immune to the racial slurs his dark, Hispanic looks had garnered him over the years, especially as a boy growing up in an affluent north Florida Anglo neighborhood. The only anguish he endured now was knowing how badly his mother had suffered because she had refused to give away her lover's child.

And what about that lover? Nate had wondered about his father. Who had he been? Had he known, before his death, that Nate existed? And if he had, had he cared?

What difference did any of that make now? Nate asked himself as he stepped out of the shower and reached for a huge white towel. He had enough immediate problems without dredging up any from his childhood.

Drying off quickly, he walked down the hall, his body still damp and totally naked. His bare feet made a slight slapping noise as he moved over the slick stone floor. As soon as he entered his bedroom, he reached down, checking under his pillow for his K-Bar knife, then fell into bed. The night air felt chilly, but he didn't pull up a blanket or even a sheet. He lay there in the dark room, listening to the quiet, blessing the solitude. He closed his eyes. Restless and frustrated, Nate tossed and turned, longing for peace, for the pure dark moments of sleep when all his problems vanished.

If only he could sleep without dreaming—without seeing *her* lifeless body and Ryker's one gloating blue eye staring at him.

Cyn slipped the cassette into the tape deck sitting on the first shelf of the bookcase near the back door. The living room in the cottage ran from front to back, the entire length of the house, so that both front and back doors exited from the same room.

Listening to songs from the fifties always reminded Cyn of her mother. Her father had often said she had inherited her romantic nature from Marjorie Wellington, who had lived an ideal life with a loving husband and two children—until it all ended tragically when the small airplane on which she'd been traveling crashed. Denton Wellington had been devastated, and had blamed himself because Marjorie had been touring the state on behalf of his congressional election.

Cyn would never forget how amazed family and friends had been that the plump, shy, fifteen-year-old Cynthia had shown a strength and courage that quite literally held both her father and younger brother together in the weeks and months following Marjorie's death. Cyn suspected that it was then that her fate had been sealed. Soon, everyone who knew her grew to depend upon her strength—in any crisis and under any circumstances.

Perhaps it was because others quickly forgot that Cyn, too, needed occasional support and comfort that the dreams started. For months after Marjorie's death, she dreamed of the strong, protective man with the incredible green eyes.

Cyn heard the small antique clock in her bedroom strike twice. Two o'clock. Pre-dawn hours when the world slept, when most people were lost in comforting renewal. But she couldn't rest.

After taking a long, soothing bubble bath, she'd slipped on her aqua silk gown and crawled into bed. After over an hour of endless tossing, she'd gotten up, put on her robe and rambled around the cottage, finally making her way into the kitchen to pour herself a cup of the coffee she'd prepared earlier. She knew sleep would be impossible. She couldn't stop thinking about what had happened tonight.

She had met the stranger, the handsome and magnetic man she'd seen on the beach. The man with the green eyes that so reminded her of her dream lover. She found it difficult to imagine Nate Hodges as a comforting protector, someone capable of unselfish care and ultimate gentleness. Cyn felt certain that he was as hard and cold and dangerous as the knife he had put to Lazarus Jones's throat tonight. And yet…she couldn't dismiss the feeling that she knew this man, that she'd known him all her life. Perhaps in another life?

Cyn shook her head, crossing her arms over her chest and gripping her elbows in a fierce hug. What made her think something so outrageous? She was tired. Exhausted. The stress that had been building in her life for the last year had taken its toll on her emotions. The always-strong, always-reliable and in-control Cynthia Ellen Wellington Porter had finally reached the limits of her control. She had begun imagining things, things like seeing a resemblance between that brute Nate Hodges and the man from her dreams.

Opening the door leading to the patio, Cyn watched the sky, dark and mysterious, filled with countless stars and one big, bright moon. She breathed in the sharp, poignant smell of the ocean, felt the crisp, cool wind coming off the Atlantic. Leaning backward, she rested her head against the door-frame.

Sooner or later, she'd have to sleep. But not tonight. What if *he* came to her to comfort her? What if, after all these years, she would awaken to remember more than his eyes? What if, as he held her within the strength of his arms, she looked at his face and saw Nate Hodges?

The softly rhythmical cadence of the surf as it swept over the shore lulled Cyn's ravaged nerves like the sweetest lullaby. Looking out at the ocean, she watched as wave after gentle wave covered the beach, then retreated, only to repeat the process, again and again.

Drawn by the night, the hypnotic lure of the ocean, the smell of the water and beach, the big, yellow moon and the romantic music coming from inside the house, Cyn stepped outside. The wind chilled her for a moment, then her body adjusted as she walked to the edge of the patio and took a step down. Just as she reached the final step, her bare feet encountering the sand, she saw him.

He was at least twenty feet away, standing alone on the beach. Noticing that he'd changed into cutoff jeans and a clean shirt, and the end of his short ponytail appeared damp, Cyn assumed he had returned home to bathe. Where was home for him? Surely, somewhere close by.

Had he, too, tried unsuccessfully to sleep? Somehow she

knew why he had come back, why he was on the beach taking a late-night stroll. He was seeking sanctuary from the demons that plagued him, and he was coming to her for the peace that could be found only in love. At the thought, she shuddered, wondering how on earth she knew that Nate Hodges was haunted by the past, that he was lonely and hurting, and in desperate need of her comforting arms. How could she possibly know such things about a total stranger?

He walked toward her, each step slow and deliberately measured, as if he were wary of her. She could feel his uncertainty, so strong was his apprehension. This big, dark and dangerous man was afraid of her. For some reason, he didn't want to be here right now, lured into coming to her as surely as some force beyond her understanding had guided her outside to wait for him.

Mesmerized, Cyn watched him approach. So tall. So big. So overwhelmingly male. Her mind told her to run, to escape the predatory look in his eyes, but her heart told her to open her arms to him, to take him into her comforting embrace and give him sanctuary. Cyn shivered with anxiety and with a need she didn't want to admit was sweeping her away, near the point of no return.

Nate moved closer, his gaze taking in every inch of her with undisguised hunger. So small and soft and alluring, she couldn't be real, he told himself. But she was. She was as real as the star-laden sky, the ancient ocean and the granules of sand beneath his feet. And she was his woman. The woman he'd dreamed about since he'd been eighteen. No matter how badly he wanted to deny it, he couldn't. A man whose life often depended on gut-level instincts, he knew, deep in his soul, that Cynthia Porter was the brown-eyed lover from his dreams, the woman destined to be his, the woman Ian Ryker would seek out and destroy.

And he knew he had no right to be here, on her beach, his soul reaching out for hers. Getting close to this woman would mean trouble for both of them.

Her waist-length blond hair hung in disarrayed waves, the

ends slightly moist as if she'd recently bathed. Her femininely round body was encased in aqua silk, the material as blue-green as the ocean and just as fluid where it clung to her curves.

He took a step forward, then waited. He could see the rapid rise and fall of her breasts, as if her breathing had become labored. He took another step. She stood, unmoving. Her lips parted, but she didn't speak. His next step put his body within inches of hers.

He looked into her eyes. The sight that met his gaze was like a welcome home, so familiar was the rich brown warmth.

Cyn couldn't move. She stood, transfixed, her gaze mating with his, the experience unbelievably erotic, as if they had often exchanged this visual love play many times while their bodies joined in life's most primeval dance.

Finally, he broke eye contact as he glanced downward at her breasts, her waist, her hips and legs. Cyn felt his gaze as it moved over her, making her nipples harden with desire, her knees weaken with longing and her femininity moisten with passion.

She had never known such raw, primitive feelings. This man, this big, savage beast of a man, made her long for things she had never experienced—except in her dreams.

Nate reached out, running the back of his fingers across Cyn's cheek. When she moaned, softly, sweetly, he felt his whole body tighten with arousal. God, he had never wanted anything so badly.

She leaned her face into his caressing hand. Suddenly, he shot his fingers into her hair, grasping a thick handful. She moaned again, tilting her head backward, arching her neck.

"You shouldn't be out here," he told her. "You shouldn't have been waiting for me."

"What...what makes you think I...I was waiting for you?" she asked as she felt him loosen his tenacious grip on her hair, allowing his fingers to cup her scalp. "After what happened tonight, I couldn't sleep. That's why I'm out here."

"You knew I'd be back." His moss-green eyes, eyes so dark

a green they appeared black, held her with their mesmerizing power.

"Where…where did you go, after you followed me here?"

"I went home. Like you, I've been trying to sleep and couldn't."

"Home? Where's home?"

"Didn't you know that I'm your neighbor? I bought the old house across the road." Using his gentle hold on her head, he brought her closer to him. Their bodies touched. Nate groaned when her soft breasts grazed his chest. Even through their clothes, he could feel her, his body reacting in a natural masculine fashion.

Cyn sucked in a deep breath, her head feeling light and slightly swimmy. "You bought Miss Carstairs's old place?" Dear God in heaven, Nate Hodges, the living, breathing embodiment of a ruthless warrior, was living in the old coquina house, built on the grounds where the Spanish mission had stood. Miss Carstairs had sworn that the storage rooms had been part of that original mission. And she had told Cyn the legend, time and again, of the ancient warrior and his Indian maiden whose spirits were doomed to wander this earth until a new warrior and his mate fulfilled the prophecy.

"The realtor told me that the owners didn't use this cottage in the winter months." Nate let his other hand roam downward, from Cyn's shoulder, over her arm, inward to her waist.

"It's spring," she whispered.

"You shouldn't be here," he said. "No one should be here. I need to be left alone."

"You've been alone for far too long." She wasn't sure how she knew that Nate Hodges was the loneliest man she'd ever met, that he'd spent a lifetime without the warmth of sharing. She just knew. Instinctively, she felt his loneliness, his pain. When he grabbed her hip and shoved her body into his, she didn't resist.

"Why now, Brown Eyes? Why now?" He took her mouth with the greed of a man starving, his lips feasting on the sweet surrender he found. It was just as he knew it would be, the feelings erupting from within him somehow familiar and yet more devastating than any he'd ever known.

She accepted the hard, relentless thrust of his tongue, the bruising force of his lips. No one had ever kissed her like this, no man had ever aroused such unrestrained longings within her. She couldn't understand why, but the very savagery of his lips on hers, his big hands raking her body, brought back memories of their wild matings. Memories from her dreams of him? she wondered, and then ceased to think at all.

She knew he'd opened her robe when the cool night air hit her chest a second before he covered her breast with his hand.

He wanted to lie her down, here in the sand, and take her. More than anything, he wanted to bury himself deep inside her, feel the shudders of her release, hear her cries of satisfaction. He touched her lips with his in a quick, light kiss before moving to her ear and nipping the lobe with his teeth. "I'm a dangerous man."

"I know." He didn't have to tell her how dangerous he was, didn't have to warn her that she should stay away from him. Her mind had already issued its own warnings, but her heart was incapable of heeding them.

He captured her in his arms, burying his face in her neck, groaning so low the sound was barely audible. Cyn threw her arms around him, letting her hands slide down his back, savoring the feel of his corded strength. He was so big, so powerful. Just touching him was ecstasy.

Her hands continued their downward trail until she reached his waist, then she felt it—the leather sheath attached to his belt. She ran her fingers over the warm, supple leather.

He's wearing a knife, she thought. The knife he had held at Lazarus Jones's neck? She stiffened, her whole body going rigid against him.

He knew her hand was on his knife sheath and realized she was afraid. He wasn't sure why she was reacting so strongly, but perhaps it was for the best. Neither of them seemed capable of resisting the other. Sexual attraction could be powerful. But no matter how much he wanted this woman or she him, now was the wrong time.

Ryker is coming for you, Nate reminded himself. If she's with you, anywhere near you, he'll use her. Get away from this woman and stay away or your recent dreams are likely to come true.

"I've killed men with that knife." For twenty years, from Nam to every cesspool in the world, he'd used his special skills to subdue the enemy, to achieve the goals of his superiors. At first, the killing had been difficult, but it had been a release for all the pent-up rage he'd felt as a kid. But eventually, the killing became easier. Until one day it became too easy, and Nate knew he had to get out—or lose what was left of his soul.

She dropped her hand from the sheath as if it were a burning coal. Trembling, she closed her eyes and gulped down a tortured sob.

Nate took her by the shoulders and gently shoved her back, an arm's length away from him. Gripping her soft flesh, he met her questioning gaze.

"I know every conceivable way there is to kill a man, and I've used my knowledge to teach others." He could feel her withdrawing. He wanted to beg her not to leave him, to understand, to accept the beast within him, to give his savage heart peace.

"You were a soldier?" She stepped backward.

He let his hands drop from her shoulders. "I'm proficient at using everything from a machine gun to a flamethrower. I've learned how to rig claymores, how to construct homemade booby traps and how to turn rope or piano wire into a deadly weapon."

He waited for her to run. She didn't. She stood there staring at him, tears misting her eyes.

"I was a navy SEAL for over twenty years," he said. "I make no apologies for who I am. Not even to you."

She didn't know what to say, how to respond. How could she ever explain to him that she had been having dreams about him for twenty years, that she had thought her dream lover was a gentle man, comforting and caring? How could she accept the fact that, after all this time, her green-eyed protector was actually a brutal warrior?

He saw the doubt and confusion in her eyes, and wished that she had never stepped out of his dreams into reality. When she had come to him in his dreams, she hadn't judged him, hadn't been appalled by the blood on his hands, hadn't cringed at the sight of the battle scars marring his body.

"I won't bother you again," he said, turning away from her.

She wanted to reach out, to call him back, but she couldn't. She was afraid. She stayed on the beach, watching him until he disappeared from sight. Hesitantly, she raised her fingers to her mouth, running them across her kiss-swollen lips. On a strangled cry of fear and remorse and unfulfilled longing, Cyn ran toward her cottage.

Nate Hodges needs you.

The ocean's gentle roar seemed to moan a premonitory message. She tried not to listen.

Chapter 4

Cyn placed the small wicker basket on the kitchen table as she debated with herself about the decision she'd made. Common sense told her to stay away from Nate Hodges. He was, by his own admission, a dangerous man. She didn't need a man, any man, least of all a troubled one. And she knew that Nate was a very troubled man.

If she'd learned anything from the tragedies she'd endured in recent years, it was the senseless waste that violence brought into the lives of both the perpetrators and the innocent alike.

Nate Hodges was no innocent. "I was a navy SEAL for over twenty years," he'd told her. "I make no apologies for who I am. Not even to you."

She kept reminding herself that a man like that didn't need anyone caring about him, worrying about him, wanting to be his friend. And, even if he did, she was hardly the right woman for him. He was a violent, dangerous man who carried a knife and was quite capable of using it. She abhorred violence of any kind, and the very thought of a knife brought back all the vivid memories of Evan's brutal murder.

The oven timer sounded. Cyn slipped her hand into the mitt, lifted the muffin tin from the stove and placed it on a wire rack to cool.

"Don't do this," she said aloud. "Be sensible, Cynthia Ellen. You can't take care of the whole world. You can't fix whatever's wrong in this man's life."

The whole time she was giving herself rational advice, she was searching the cabinets for a jar of Mimi's homemade orange marmalade. The delectable preserves would taste great spread atop the bran muffins.

She lined the basket with a soft, clean towel, then removed the muffins from the tin and placed them in the linen nest. Covering the muffins, she slid the small marmalade jar and a container of her favorite gourmet coffee inside the basket.

Taking a deep, confidence-boosting breath, Cyn picked up the basket and headed out the back door. She didn't want a sexual relationship with Nate Hodges, she told herself, despite the fact that no man had ever made her feel the way he'd made her feel last night. She had simply allowed her imagination to run rampant, she'd given herself over to the magic of moonlight, the power of an old legend and the potency of a virile man. In broad daylight, it would be different. He was a troubled human being; she was a woman long used to giving comfort to the troubled. Indeed, Cyn couldn't remember a time in her life when someone hadn't needed her, depended on her, expected her to take care of them.

Perhaps she was being foolish. Perhaps Nate would throw her offer of friendship back in her face. But, mother-to-the-world that she was, Cynthia Porter couldn't turn her back on the loneliness and pain she'd felt in Nate Hodges. She knew, on some instinctive level, that if ever anyone had needed her, he did.

Nate gulped down the last drops of strong, black coffee, then reached for the glass pot and poured his third cup for the morning. After less than three hours' sleep, he needed the caffeine boost.

His informative meeting with Nick Romero, the one-sided combat with Lazarus Jones and the ever-present knowledge that Ryker was alive and bent on revenge pumped adrenaline through Nate's body, preparing him for what lay ahead. A man long used to sleepless nights, Nate was surprised that he felt so lousy this morning. Hell, it was all her fault. That brown-eyed witch. He wasn't used to thinking about one specific woman, worrying about her, wanting her until he ached with frustration.

He had wanted her last night, more than he'd ever wanted anything in his life—and he could have taken her. Even though she'd been repulsed by the idea of his past, she had still wanted him. He knew she had felt exactly what he had. Life wasn't fair, he thought. It offered you the fulfillment of a dream, then changed that dream into a nightmare. He couldn't have Cyn Porter. Making her his woman would put her life in jeopardy.

Through the dense fog of his thoughts, Nate heard a loud rapping on his front door. Who the hell? No one knew where he was, except Romero and John Mason.

Within minutes he opened the heavy wooden door and glared at his unexpected visitor who, holding a small wicker basket in her hands, flashed him a brilliant, cheerful smile. Looking like springtime sunshine in her pale yellow slacks and matching cotton sweater, Cyn was beautiful—neat, clean and flowery-sweet. Her hair was knotted in a large loose bun at the nape of her neck, and a pair of tiny diamond studs glimmered at her ears.

"Good morning," Cyn said, reaching deep down inside herself to find the courage not to run from his scowling expression. *He needs you,* she reminded herself. *Just like the kids at To-morrow House. He's a wounded soul.* "It's a glorious day, isn't it?"

Nate stared at her, wondering why she was here and puzzled by her warm, friendly attitude. After last night, he had been fairly sure she'd never want to see him again. After all, he'd hardly gone out of his way to be charming.

When he didn't reply, she laughed, the sound a forced show

of bravado. "Aren't you going to invite me in?" she asked. "I've brought breakfast."

He gave her a quizzical look, then glanced down at the basket she held out in front of her. "You've brought—"

"Breakfast. I baked fresh bran muffins, and I've got some homemade orange marmalade." She took a tentative step forward, and when he didn't speak or make any attempt to allow her entrance into his home, she shoved the basket at his midsection. "Here, take this and show me to the kitchen. Have you made coffee yet? I've brought some vanilla nut coffee. It's a new blend I tried, and it's delicious."

Without thinking, Nate reached out and took the wicker basket, stepped backward, just enough for her to move past him, then turned to watch her prance into his home. Dammit, she was like a steamroller—a velvet steamroller, but a steamroller none the less. It was quite obvious that Cyn Porter was a woman used to taking charge, accustomed to issuing orders and expecting them to be obeyed. A hint of a smile curved the corner of his mouth as he thought that it was one thing they had in common.

"You haven't done much in here, have you?" Cyn wasn't sure what she had expected, but it certainly wasn't this dreary expanse of hallway. She glanced around at the open double doors on each side of the entrance. One room was empty, void of any furniture, and the windows were covered with dusty shutters that blocked out the vibrant morning sunshine.

"I've only been here a couple of months." He closed the front door. "The kitchen is straight back."

He wasn't sure what sort of game she was playing, but he'd indulge her for the time being. Maybe she was as hungry for him as he was for her. If she was looking for a quick tumble, he would, under ordinary circumstances, be more than interested. But his life was hardly his own at the present, and the last thing he needed was a woman in his life, a woman Ryker could use against him.

Cyn headed down the long, dark corridor, her sandaled feet making loud clip-clap noises as she walked along the stone floor. "You need to open this place up and air it out. It's awfully musty."

He followed her into the kitchen, set the basket down on the small wooden table in the center of the room, and pointed toward the drip coffee maker. "I've already made coffee. I'm afraid it's nothing special, just plain old high-octane java."

"Oh, that's all right. One cup won't hurt me. Pour us both a cup and I'll fix the muffins." Cyn glanced around the room, trying not to let her disgust show. The plastered walls probably had once been a soft yellow; now they were a putrid shade of tan. A small compact refrigerator sat in the corner, like a square white dwarf in the huge room. A long, wooden table placed against the back wall held a shiny new microwave, a rusty-looking hot plate, and a coffee machine. Two rickety wall shelves hung between the only window, an antiquated sink sat directly below. Sunshine sparkled off the metal faucets.

Nate wanted to ask her what she was doing here. Last night they had come close to making love. Then she'd discovered his knife sheath and had been unable to disguise her fear and disgust. "I'm pretty much baching it here. All I've got are some paper plates."

He looked over at her then, and his heart stopped for a split second. Her back was to the window and the radiant sunshine turned her hair to pale gold. She smiled at him, her brown eyes warm and inviting. Whether she knew it or not, she was offering him something he badly needed. She brought light into his darkness, giving solace to his pain, happiness to his sorrow, and matching his hard strength with a gentle strength equally as powerful.

"That's fine," she said, taking a step toward him. She had caught a glimmer of emotion in his dark green eyes, a glitch in his armor. "Get the paper plates and napkins. You do have some napkins, don't you?"

Nate shook is head. Damn, he hadn't planned on entertaining while he was here. "I've got some paper towels."

"Okay." Glancing around, she saw no chairs. "Where do you sit to eat?"

"In the den," he told her, handing her a couple of paper plates and a roll of towels. "It's the only other room in the house with furniture except for my bedroom."

While Nate poured coffee into two clean cups, ignoring his already filled mug, Cyn placed muffins on the paper plates and set the marmalade jar on the table. "I'll need a spoon or knife or something if you want some orange marmalade."

"I'll take my muffins plain," he said, handing her a cup of coffee, then picking up a plate. "Let's go in the den and sit down."

Cyn watched him carefully as he turned around and headed out of the kitchen. Wearing cutoff jeans and an unbuttoned shirt, he was every bit as big and savage-looking in broad daylight as he had been in moonlight. Maybe more so, with his long hair hanging loose, almost touching his massive shoulders.

She followed him back down the dark hallway, through a set of double doors and into a huge room. Well, he isn't a total barbarian, she thought as she surveyed Nate Hodges's den. The floors were wooden, the walls a faded white plaster, the arched, open-shuttered windows long and unadorned. Bright light filled every nook and cranny. Although sparsely decorated, the room held a leather sofa, three unmatched chairs, a desk, a small corner cabinet and several tables.

Her footsteps faltered, then stopped abruptly. She stood, frozen in the center of the room, her gaze riveted to the wall.

Nate realized immediately what was wrong. She was staring, transfixed, at part of his extensive knife collection hanging on the walls. Even though he'd known he would be living here only until his confrontation with Ryker, he hadn't been able to leave behind his highly prized knife collection at his house in St. Augustine. That was why the den had been the only room he'd bothered to fix up.

She trembled, sloshing the hot coffee around inside her mug. Acting quickly on instinct, Nate set his cup and plate on the desk, rushed over to her and grabbed her mug out of her hand. "Are you all right?" he asked.

"Yes. No. I..." Cyn felt numb. All her life she'd had an

aversion to violence, to guns and knives, weapons of any kind. But since Evan's brutal murder, the very sight of a knife sent shivers of fear spiraling through her.

"May…may I sit down?" she asked, her voice quivering.

Nate put her plate and her mug down on the wood-and-metal trunk in front of the sofa, then placed his arm around her, guiding her down and into the cool softness of the leather cushions. "Take it easy. Okay? Maybe I should have warned you."

"I…it was seeing all these knives…the swords." Cyn sat rigid, crossing her legs at the ankles, arching her back away from the sofa.

Nate ran a soothing hand across her shoulders. "Hey, Brown Eyes, I'm sorry. I knew you didn't like the feel of my knife last night, but… I'm sorry. I just wasn't thinking when I suggested we come in here."

She turned to face him, her cheeks flushed, her eyes overly bright. "My husband was stabbed to death." She took in a deep breath, then let out a long sigh, willing herself not to cry.

So, Nate thought, she hates my knives because some bastard used one to kill her husband. He was finding out just how different he and Cynthia Porter really were—opposites in every way. The more she found out about him, the more she was bound to dislike him. "I'm sorry about your husband."

"I apologize for overreacting." She forced herself to glance around the room. Knives, swords, sabers and daggers filled her line of vision.

"I've been collecting knives all my life. I'll bet you collect something. Most people do." He wanted to make her understand that his knife collection wasn't some deadly monster any more than he was. He wanted her to see past the superficial, past the obvious, for her to take a chance and reach his soul. He didn't know why it was so important that this woman accept him. He just knew that it was.

"I collect records from the fifties. I've got an extensive collection, and I've put most on cassette tapes." Her body's outward trembling subsided, but tremors still churned in her stomach. She knew he was trying to help her relax and adjust to the unfamiliarity of her surroundings. Somewhere beneath all that burly macho hardness, a touch of compassion existed in him.

He studied her intently, memorizing every line of her smooth, flawless face, every golden glimmer in her rich brown eyes.

He turned from her, uncertain what to say or do. How could he make a gentle woman understand the brutal life he'd led? How could he ask her to give his bitter existence her sweetness, to turn his anger into joy, to accept the man he was? He couldn't, even if he wanted to. If she was a part of his life, Ryker would find out and use her against him. Nate Hodges had no weaknesses. And God only knew he didn't need any now.

Seeing such an anguished look of desperation cross his face broke Cyn's heart. She didn't want to hurt him, for on some instinctive level, she knew he had already been hurt enough. What he needed, what he wanted, what his heart craved, was solace, compassion and…love. She had never turned from a fellow human being in need. But was it her motherly instinct that longed to comfort Nate Hodges, or her womanly instinct that longed to know him and care for him? She wasn't certain. All she knew was that, despite her better judgment, she couldn't desert this man.

Cyn reached out and placed her hand on his arm. He flinched. She squeezed his hard, smooth flesh. "I want to thank you for last night…for stepping in and…and subduing Lazarus Jones."

"I thought you were angry because I scared off your runaway boys." Nate looked down to where her small hand gripped his arm. He liked her touch—strong, yet gentle.

"I never should have gone to the Brazen Hussy. I acted irresponsibly." She squeezed his arm again, then released it. Reaching out, she retrieved her coffee mug from the trunk. "I wanted to help Bobby…and Casey, too. I did what I thought Evan would have done."

"Evan?"

"My husband." She held the mug in both hands, entwining her fingers.

"What happened to him?" Nate felt a twinge of something alien, an emotion he'd never known. It was foolish, but he couldn't help but think of Cyn's dead husband as a rival.

Cyn took several quick sips of coffee, thankful that it was still relatively hot. "Evan was a minister. After our marriage, he asked the church to assign him to Tomorrow House. The place had just opened, and we both knew we could make a contribution."

"Your husband was a minister?" Nate hadn't even realized he'd spoken the words aloud until he saw her nod her head. Nate wondered how he, a man waiting to kill or be killed, could compete with the memory of a saint?

"Evan was devoted to the kids, to trying to help them. It was his whole life, and it became mine, too." She didn't want to admit to Nate that there had been times when she had, self-ishly, envied those kids to whom her husband had given all his time and most of his love. "Four years ago, a young boy named Darren Kilbrew came to us. He was a drug addict."

Nate saw the torment in her eyes, could hear her quickened breathing. "If this is too painful—"

"I thought I had come to terms with what happened. I…I thought…"

"You don't have to tell me."

"Perhaps if I tell you, you'll understand why I feel the way I do."

Nate nodded his head, his gaze attentive, never once leaving her face.

"Darren stabbed Evan to death, then robbed him." Cyn bit her bottom lip, tightened her hold on her mug and turned to face Nate. "The last thing Evan said to me before he died was that he wanted me to continue his work at Tomorrow House."

Taking her mug from her, Nate placed it back on top of the trunk. He put his arms around her and pulled her into his embrace, the action as natural to him as breathing. As if he'd done it countless times.

She went to him, allowed him to enfold her within the strength of his big body. It felt so right, as if the place was familiar, as if he'd held and comforted her often.

Cyn could never remember feeling so safe, so protected. Relaxing against him, she absorbed his strength, somehow knowing that he understood how desperately she needed him. She waited for the tears, but they didn't come. Had she given all there was to give to Evan's memory? she wondered. Had the pain finally subsided enough where she could truly accept his death and the death of his killer?

"Darren, the boy who killed Evan, eluded the police and wasn't captured until last year," she told Nate, still safe within his arms. "He…he was killed in jail. By…by another inmate. Stabbed to death." The last words escaped her lips on a tortured sigh.

Nate hugged her to him, feeling fiercely protective, primitively possessive. He stroked her hair, letting his fingers lace through the long blond strands as he loosened the bun. "Scream if you want to, rant and rave and cry at the injustice. You don't have to be strong right now. Nothing's going to hurt you. I'm here. I'll take care of you."

The sobs that clogged her throat, almost choking her, erupted then, and tears filled her eyes. And for the first time since she'd been a small child, Cyn accepted comfort and strength from another, instead of giving it. They sat there on the tan leather sofa in Nate's brutally male den while Cyn cleansed her heart of a pain she'd been unable to wash away with four years of crying. Gradually, her breathing returned to normal, her ragged little cries silenced. She eased out of his arms, not allowing herself to look at him. If she saw his eyes, she would be lost— forever.

Wiping the remnants of moisture from her eyes and cheeks with the tips of her fingers, Cyn tried to smile. "You must think I'm a real crybaby. I'm usually in much better control."

"Maybe you keep too tight a control over your emotions," he said, reaching out to take her chin in his big hand.

"Normally, I'm a tower of strength." Even when he tilted

her face upward, she refused to look at him, cutting her eyes sideways, glancing over to the windows.

"Cyn?" He wanted her to look at him so that he could see what she was thinking. Her brown eyes were like windows to her soul, so expressive, so transparent.

She jerked away from him, stood up and began pacing around the room. "I haven't been down here to the cottage since last summer. I just came for a minivacation. I'll probably be returning to my apartment in Jacksonville in another week or so."

"Were you running away? Is that why you came to Sweet Haven?" he asked, then cursed himself.

Why was he taunting her about running away when that was the very thing he wanted her to do? He wanted her to run back to Jacksonville. And the sooner, the better. He didn't need the complications she could create in his life. If he had to worry about her safety, he wouldn't be as alert to protecting himself, and Ryker would use any advantage he could to win the up-coming battle.

Stopping by the table situated directly behind the sofa, Cyn ran her fingers over the array of cases that held an assortment of knives, and made a decision. "Yes, I suppose I was trying to run away. But now, I'm running back to the safety of what I know, of what I want to do with my life. Tomorrow, I'm going back to work. Half days."

"Are you sure it's what you want to do, or what you feel obligated to do for your late husband?" He stood up and moved around the sofa toward her.

She stared at him, puzzlement in her eyes. "What would make you ask such a question?"

"You said you had promised your husband."

"Tomorrow House was *our* dream, not just Evan's. You can't begin to imagine how many kids there are who need someone to care."

"Yeah, you're probably right. I haven't exactly spent my life helping the needy." He realized that she had no way of knowing that he had once been one of those kids who desperately needed someone, anyone, to care. He'd spent his whole life trying to escape from the past, not once confronting it or ever thinking about helping other kids with problems similar to his own.

"You said you were a navy SEAL, so you were helping others by serving your country." She had heard the self-condemnation in his words, the hidden pain masked behind his reply, and she couldn't bear to know he was hurting.

He was surprised to hear her defend him. He couldn't believe it. This woman who abhorred violence, who was scared of his knives, who condemned his brutality, was actually defending him. Damn, did she have any idea how that made him feel?

Nate came up behind her, gripped her by the shoulders and lowered his head so his lips were against her ear. "You're the most beautiful, desirable woman I've ever known." When he felt her trying to pull away, he tightened his hold. "Don't balk, Brown Eyes. I have no intention of ravishing you no matter how much I'd like to."

"I...I really should leave," she gasped, listening to the sound of her heartbeat roaring in her ears. When she tried to pull free, he let her go. She backed up several steps, then turned to face him.

He needs you, she reminded herself. *It's obvious he's never been friends with a woman.* The thought of exactly what he had been with other women unsettled Cyn. This man wasn't her type. He was nothing like Evan. So why was she so attracted to him? What was there about him that made her want to be with him? "I'll take care of you," he'd said, and in that moment, she had wanted his strength, had felt such relief in being allowed to lean on someone else.

"I don't want to be ravished...but if...if you need a friend..."

He looked at her, his eyes devoid of any emotion, his face a mask. She waited, wondering why he didn't say something, thinking perhaps she hadn't spoken the words aloud.

"We can never be just friends," he said.

"But Nate, I—"

"Go back to your cottage, Cynthia Porter, and stay away from me." He didn't want to send her away. He wanted to pick her up, carry her to his bed and spend the rest of the day and night making love to her. "I'm a dangerous man whose past is finally catching up with him."

"I don't understand."

"You don't have to understand. Just leave." Nate's voice was harsh. He'd meant it to be. He didn't dare let this woman become a part of his life. Not now. Not ever.

Cyn couldn't speak. She merely nodded in acquiescence, turned and ran out of the den. Stopping in the hallway, she leaned against the wall, gasping for air as she struggled to maintain control of her emotions. He didn't want her friendship. He'd made that abundantly clear.

"I...I won't bother you again," she said, not looking back as she moved hurriedly toward the front door.

It took all his willpower not to run after her, to ask her to stay, to demand that she take him into her loving arms and give his heart and soul the sanctuary he so desperately needed.

But he didn't. He let her go. For her sake, he had no other choice.

Nate aimed the Arkansas toothpick, the long, sharp blade gleaming like quicksilver in the afternoon sunlight. With expert ease, he threw the weapon toward its target, knowing, without looking, that the knife had hit its mark. In the past two months of daily practice, he had regained his once-renowned skill. But how much good would it do him in a fight with Ryker?

Ryker might demand a face-to-face confrontation, but he wouldn't fight fair. It wasn't his style. Nate had to be prepared, as battle-ready as he'd ever been in Nam or afterward on the numerous assignments he'd undertaken during his days as a SEAL. Ryker was as skilled, as ruthless, as prepared to die as Nate. They were equal opponents, except that Nate had been able to hang on to his sanity. Ryker hadn't.

Retrieving the knife, he returned to his designated spot by the cypress tree in the backyard, took deadly aim and sailed the dagger through the air. Once again it pierced the makeshift wooden dummy's heart.

What would Cynthia Porter think if she knew that many times he had killed victims by covering their mouth with his hand, jerking their head up, exposing their neck and then, with a quick diagonal slice, severing their carotid artery? A bloody, messy kill. But very effective.

She would be appalled, utterly disgusted. Even if the threat of Ryker's imminent arrival didn't stand between them, his Special Forces past would.

The faint, distant ring of the telephone drifted through the open windows. Nate pulled the knife out of the dummy, slipped it back into its sheath and walked quickly inside the house.

"Yeah?" He took several deep breaths.

"Are you busy?" Nick Romero asked.

"Sort of," Nate said.

"Not in the middle of entertaining your blond neighbor, are you?"

In no uncertain terms Nate told his friend what he could do to himself.

"Keep talking like that and I'll hang up without telling you why I called." Romero's chuckle vibrated over the phone lines.

"What's up?" Nate ran his hand through his loose hair.

"Just got off the phone with John."

"What happened?" Nate didn't want John involved, didn't want anyone else getting in the way, maybe getting themselves killed.

"Seems some strange guy approached John's wife Laurel at the local supermarket. Said a friend of his wanted to send a message to Nate Hodges."

"Damn! Where was her protection? I thought you said you had her and John covered."

"We do now. Our man was late getting in position," Romero said. "Mrs. Mason wasn't hurt. The guy didn't touch her. She told John that he was very courteous."

"Did she give John a description?" Nate wondered if Ryker had sent a colleague or had come himself.

"It wasn't Ryker."

Nate heard the hesitation in the other man's voice. "But?"

"This guy told Mrs. Mason to tell you that your old buddy Ian Ryker was on his way to St. Augustine and he'd be looking you up soon."

"Make sure nothing happens to Laurel and John," Nate said, then slammed down the phone.

Not all the horrors from his past had prepared him for his present torment. He'd seen buddies die—in Nam and other godforsaken countries around the world. But not once had a friend been in jeopardy because of him. Now anyone who was a friend or acquaintance was in danger. He had to keep Cyn Porter out of his life!

Chapter 5

What the hell is she doing? Nate slammed on the brakes, bringing his Jeep to a screeching halt a few feet away from Cyn Porter, who stood in the middle of the road.

He stuck his head out the open window. "Are you trying to get yourself killed, woman? I nearly ran over you."

Cyn cursed the fates that had thrown her together with Nate Hodges again. After their ill-fated breakfast ended yesterday, she'd sworn she'd never go near him again. By his less-than-friendly attitude, she could tell that he felt the same way.

Walking around to the driver's side of the Jeep, Cyn counted slowly to ten before replying. "I can assure you that I'm not suicidal. If you'd been driving at a normal speed on this dead-end dirt road, you would have had no problem stopping."

"What were you doing in the middle of the road?" he asked, trying not to notice how good Cynthia Porter looked in her jeans and sweater.

"Wasn't it obvious? I was trying to get your attention."

"There are other ways, you know."

"Don't get smart with me," she said, her voice growing

steadily louder and more agitated. "The deliveryman left a package at my house for you."

Nate tensed, every nerve in his body going deadly still. He hadn't been expecting a delivery. "Where's the package?"

"I just told you that it was at my house."

"Why didn't you just bring it out here?"

"Look, your swords are lying in the middle of my living room floor where they fell out of the package. I'd appreciate it if you'd come and get them." She flashed him a quick, phony smile, then turned on her heels and walked back toward her cottage.

Swords! Who the hell had sent him swords? And how had they wound up in the middle of Cynthia Porter's living room floor? Nate turned his Jeep into her drive. By the time he'd parked and gotten out, she was on her doorstep.

"Wait up," he called out, taking giant strides to reach her before she entered the house.

Turning on him just as he stepped up behind her, Cynthia blocked the doorway. "Just go in, get them and leave."

"What else did you think I'd do?" he asked.

"I didn't want you to think that I was inviting you to stay or anything after you made it perfectly clear yesterday that you neither want or need my friendship." *Stay angry,* she told herself. *If you stay angry, he can't get to you. And whatever you do, don't look into his eyes. You'll be offering him more than friendship if you see that passionate need he can't disguise.*

"Will you move out of the way, please?" he asked.

She moved inside. He followed. "There they are," she said, pointing toward the floor where a long box lay, one end open. Part of a heavy metal sword lay half in and half out of the box, and beside it was a matching sword, only a few inches of the tip still inside the box. Nate recognized the pieces immediately. They were excellent reproductions of Norman swords.

Who the hell had sent them? And why? Everyone who knew Nate knew about his collection. Even Ryker.

"I didn't open them," Cyn said. "When I walked in here

with the box, the bottom just came open and the swords fell out. I was so startled, I dropped them.''

"Have you touched them?" Maybe Romero could get some prints if the sender had been careless enough to leave any. If it had been Ryker, the swords would be clean.

"Most certainly not. The very sight of those things repulses me.'' What was wrong with him? Cyn wondered. For heaven's sake, the man collected knives, why was he so surprised that an order had arrived? "And I didn't touch the card, either.''

She nodded toward the floor, then tapped her foot beside the small envelope that had floated out of the box when it sprung open.

Nate hesitated no more than a second, but long enough for Cyn to notice. He acted almost afraid to touch the card. She shook her head to dislodge such a ridiculous notion. Nate Hodges afraid? Don't be ridiculous.

He glanced around the room. "I need to use your phone.''

"Is something wrong?''

"I want you to stay out of this.'' He made the mistake of grabbing her by the shoulders. The moment he touched her, he wanted to pull her closer, to tell her everything, to confess the danger he was in and the danger that would threaten her, too, if she became a part of his life.

"Nate, if something's wrong—''

"Why don't you go for a walk on the beach...or take a ride. Go somewhere until I can get this mess cleared up.'' Hell, he knew she wasn't about to leave. He hadn't given her an explanation, he'd just issued her an order.

"You forget, this is my house.'' She had sense enough to realize that Nate Hodges was in trouble whether or not he thought she was clever enough to figure it out. "You may not want me involved in this, whatever it is, but don't you think it's a little too late, now?''

"If you're smart, you'll pack your bags and go back to Jacksonville. Right now.''

Cyn walked around him and the weapons lying so deadly in their stillness on her living room floor. Sitting down on the couch, she crossed her arms over her chest. "Do whatever you need to do. I'm not leaving."

Nate uttered a few choice words under his breath. He wished he could order Cynthia Porter to leave, but he couldn't. For whatever reason, she was determined to stay. Hell, it was as if she honestly thought she could help him, and there was no way he could persuade her otherwise without telling her the truth. And he wasn't about to do that.

"Fine, sit there and behave," he told her. "But stay out of the way and don't ask any questions."

"The portable phone is right there on the coffee table."

Nate picked up the phone, punched out the numbers and waited. The moment he heard Romero's voice, he said, "I'm at Cynthia Porter's cottage. While I was out, a guy delivered a package containing two Norman swords. He left them here. They're lying in the middle of Ms. Porter's floor. There was a card enclosed."

"Has she touched anything?" Romero asked.

"Just the outside of the box."

"You think they're a gift from our friend Ryker?"

"That's my guess." Nate watched Cyn. She sat quietly on the sofa, her hands crossed in her lap, her chin tilted upward as she gazed at the ceiling.

"Probably no point in checking for prints, but I'll bring a guy with me. Just stay put."

Nate laid down the phone, then sat beside Cyn. "You remember my friend, Nick Romero, from the Brazen Hussy?"

She nodded, but didn't look at him.

"Well, he's coming over and bringing someone with him. Romero will probably ask you a few questions about the deliveryman—"

"Just who are you, Nate Hodges? And what sort of trouble are you mixed up in?" She uncrossed her arms, reached out and touched him, her hand covering his where it lay on his leg.

He pulled away from the warmth of her touch. It wouldn't be easy to open up, to tell her the truth, to share his past with her, but God in heaven, he wanted to. By choice, he'd been alone all his adult life. But he was tired of being alone, tired of being afraid to care.

"Nothing that needs to concern you, Cyn."

She felt as if he'd slammed a door in her face, the door to his life that was clearly marked Private. Why was he so afraid to let her help him? Didn't he know she was very good at taking care of others? "It'll be…interesting to see Mr. Romero again," she said, smiling, but still not looking directly at Nate. "He's very charming, isn't he?"

Nate gave her a harsh look. "You aren't interested in Romero, so don't bother pretending you are."

"What makes you think I'm not interested in Nick Romero?"

Reaching out, Nate cupped her chin in his hand, his grasp infinitely tender, his thumb and fingers biting gently into her flesh. "Because you're interested in me."

She looked at him then, unable to stop herself. What she saw in his eyes both frightened and excited her. "You need me," she said, her voice no more than a faint whisper.

More than you'll ever know, he said silently as he released her chin. "Don't try to use Romero to make me jealous. It won't work."

Nate hated to admit that he was jealous of his best friend, but he was. After Romero had sent the swords and note to the lab with another agent, Nate had done everything he could to persuade his old buddy to leave, but Romero had stayed. And, although Cyn hadn't deliberately flirted with Romero, she had been friendly and cooperative, answering his questions without asking him any in return. Nate would have already left, but Cyn had invited them to stay for lunch, and after Romero had accepted, what else could he have done but stay?

Now the three of them were sharing afternoon coffee on Cyn's patio. Romero was his usual charming, flattering Casanova self—as smooth as silk. His friend's way with the ladies had never bothered Nate before. Usually, he watched Romero's magic skills with amusement. But not today. Nate had never felt such gut-wrenching jealousy. Cyn Porter, whether he wanted her to be or not, had become important to him. She was more than just another woman, and she most certainly was not a woman he wanted to share.

When the phone rang, they all jumped. Cyn answered, then handed the phone to Romero. Nate glanced over at her just in time to catch her staring at him.

"Swords were clean. The note, too," Romero said. "Your guess about the gift-giver is probably right."

Nate merely nodded. The note had been typed. *For your collection*…the words as meaningful or as meaningless as anyone's personal interpretation.

"Fine," Nate said, having been reasonably certain that the gift had been from Ryker. Just his little way of letting Nate know that his whereabouts were no longer a secret. But it didn't mean Ryker was in town. On the contrary, the little gift was more than likely just another method of making Nate sweat. Maybe Ryker's business associate, Ramon Carranza, had arranged to have the swords delivered. After all, this guy Carranza lived close by, just a few miles away in St. Augustine.

"Would you care for some more coffee, Nick?" Cyn asked, trying to concentrate all her energies toward playing the perfect hostess while avoiding any eye contact with Nate. She had never deliberately tried to make one man jealous of another, and having done so today made her feel uncomfortable. But Nate had a way of making her act out of character. She had seldom met anyone, man, woman or child, who didn't respond to her loving and caring attitude. Nate had made it perfectly clear that he wasn't interested in being friends.

"I'd love to take you out for dinner tonight," Romero said. "I know this great seafood place down—"

"She can't go," Nate said.

"Sorry," Romero said, turning toward his friend. "I didn't realize you and Cyn had plans for tonight."

"We don't," Cyn said.

"Well, we do," Nate said at the same time Cyn spoke.

"Which is it?" Romero asked, grinning. "You do or you don't?"

Once again Cyn and Nate answered simultaneously.

"We don't."

"We do."

"Hey, I'm out of here," Romero said, standing. Taking Cyn's hand in his, he bestowed a gentlemanly kiss. "Looks like my friend has staked his claim."

Cyn decided the best course of action was to say and do nothing until Nick Romero left. After all, her problem wasn't with him. It was with Nate Hodges.

The moment she heard Romero's car start, she turned to Nate. "Do you want to tell me what's going on?"

"There's a guy who's been giving me some trouble. He probably sent the swords as some sort of joke. He's got a sick sense of humor." Nate noted that she didn't seem overly impressed with his explanation. The way she was staring at him made him wonder if she was getting ready to douse him with the contents of her cup. "Romero works for the government, and I knew he could get everything checked out."

"I'd ask more questions, but I doubt you'd answer them." Cyn stood, placed her cup on the concrete-and-glass table, then turned to Nate. "I don't know what sort of trouble you're in, and it's obvious you don't want me to know. So be it. But I wasn't referring to the swords or whatever mess you've gotten yourself into. I want to know why you told Nick that we have a date for dinner when we don't."

"I don't want you getting mixed up with Romero."

"Why not? He's a friend of yours, isn't he?"

"Hell, woman, he's got a thing for blondes." Nate jumped to his feet, his eyes dark with warning.

Cyn took several steps backward. "I like Nick."

"And he likes you. Romero likes all pretty blondes, and most of them like him." Didn't she understand that he cared about her, that he didn't want to see her harmed in any way. After all, if her safety wasn't uppermost on his mind, he'd have her in his bed right now, making slow, sweet love to her. "Stay away from Romero if you don't want to wind up just another number in his little black book.''

''Are we going out for dinner?'' she asked.

''What?''

''Are we going—''

''No.''

''Then leave.''

''What?'' he asked.

''I said leave.''

''Fine.'' He crashed his coffee cup against the top of the glass table, cracking the ceramic mug. ''Go back to Jacksonville and get out of my life.'' He stalked away.

Maybe he was right, she thought as she watched him disappear around the side of the house. She had come to Sweet Haven to rest, to get away from all her problems, from the memories. But being Nate Hodges's neighbor had simply created new problems—problems she had hoped she could handle by offering the man her friendship. She'd been a fool. There was something far stronger than friendship between them. Nate wanted to be her lover, but for reasons only he knew, he was determined to send her away. And for reasons only God knew, she was just as determined not to leave him.

Nate stood at a distance, watching her for a long time before pushing himself away from the tree and heading out onto the beach. He hadn't intended seeing her again, but he knew he had to get her to leave the cottage, return to Jacksonville, to the safety of her apartment. If Ryker came to Sweet Haven, Nate wanted Cynthia Porter long gone.

Cyn saw him approaching. She had noticed him a good while ago standing by the cypress, staring out at the ocean, occasionally glancing at her as she strolled along the beach. He looked remarkably handsome in his leisure attire. His cutoff jeans, his wrinkled shirt, his leather sandals. He'd combed his hair back and tied it with what looked like a shoe string.

''Hi,'' he said as he came up beside her, falling into step with her as she continued walking up the beach.

"Hi." She looked away quickly, not even momentarily slowing her stride.

"I'm sorry about the way I acted earlier. I've got a lot of problems in my life right now, and I took some of my frustration out on you." He had decided that somehow, some way, he had to get Cynthia out of his life, out of Sweet Haven and back to the safety of her Jacksonville apartment. But how was he ever going to get around to the subject of her leaving? He'd tried the hardball approach and it hadn't worked.

"I don't understand you, Nate. You're such a complex man. You can be so gentle, so understanding…and then you turn into a monster." What was he doing here, following her? She wanted an explanation. His apology just wasn't enough.

"I'm not used to women like you any more than you're accustomed to men like me. It's only natural that we'd have a difficult time understanding each other."

"You send out mixed signals," she said, slowing her pace so that she could look at him. "It's as if you're pulling me toward you with one hand and pushing me away with the other." She didn't miss the slight tightening of his jaw, the strained quiver.

"Like I told you, I've got some major problems in my life right now, problems I don't want to involve anyone else in." Could he make her understand without telling her about Ryker? If only he hadn't met her now when a relationship with her would mean putting her life on the line.

"You have problems. I want to help you." She stopped walking and turned to him, placing her hand on his arm. "I'm a good listener."

Damn, the last thing he needed was a caring woman. The touch of her small hand on his arm sent off alarm bells through his entire system. Cyn was a sweet temptation, one he was finding harder and harder to resist. "Look, Brown Eyes, I'm trouble with a capital T." He pulled away from her tender touch. "I'm a cynical, uncaring bastard with nothing to offer a woman like you except a scarred body, an unfeeling heart and a past that's filled with blood and violence."

"Another man, a lot like you, came to this beach once. Centuries ago. He even stayed in your house." She saw the bewilderment in Nate's eyes, and knew he'd never heard the legend. "I'd love to see inside the old mission again."

"The old mission?" He racked his brain trying to remember what the realtor had said about a mission. Something about a part of his house being hundreds of years old, dating back to the late sixteenth century. "Who was the man?"

"Obviously, you haven't heard the ancient legend. I can't believe the realtor didn't use it as a selling point," Cyn said, starting to walk again, moving toward the dirt road that separated their homes.

"She said something about part of the house dating back several centuries. The old storerooms, I think." Nate followed Cyn across the road. "I don't remember her saying anything about a legend." But then, he hadn't heard much of what the realtor had said about the house's history. All that had interested him had been the isolated location.

"I haven't been inside since Miss Carstairs died." Cyn stopped just short of Nate's porch. "Let me show you inside the storage rooms and I'll tell you the legend."

Nate followed her along the arched porch until they reached the area in question. What was he doing? he wondered. All he'd intended was to talk to her and try to persuade her to leave Sweet Haven. Now, here she was at his home, telling him some farfetched tale of an ancient warrior she said was a lot like him. And he was following along behind her like some doting puppy.

"Do you have a key?" Cyn held out her hand as she stepped up to the outside metal door of the vine-covered room.

"It isn't locked," he said. "Nothing in there but a bunch of old junk. I think the former owner used it as a storage shed."

Cyn took hold of the heavy metal door handle. The hinges creaked loudly when she gave the door a gentle nudge. As she opened the door fully, sunlight poured into the darkness, and minuscule motes of glittering dust danced in the air.

"I haven't been in here since I was a teenager and used to

come over and visit Miss Carstairs. She always kept this door locked.'' Cyn laughed, remembering the old woman who'd filled her head with stories of Florida's past, of numerous battles, countries fighting to claim this gloriously beautiful land as their own, of dark-skinned natives, of Spanish invaders—of a Timucuan maiden and a conquistador.

"Was she afraid someone would tote off some of this treasure?'' Nate asked as he stepped inside the large coquina room and looked around in the dreary gloom at moldy, cobweb-covered chairs, chests, crates, rotting boxes and a wooden bed.

"I don't think there was this much stuff in here back then, but Miss Carstairs wasn't worried about thieves. She was worried about ghosts. I never could understand how she thought a locked door would prevent spirits from entering if they wanted to."

Nate spied what looked like the remains of a meal, an aluminum drink can, a wrapper from a candy bar and the butt of a cigarette. "Looks like I've had company." Had Ryker sent a scout out ahead? One of Carranza's men? The thought that someone had been this close to him without his knowledge bothered Nate. Were his instincts that rusty? If they were, he was in big trouble.

Cyn spied the objects on the floor. "Probably just some vagrant taking shelter from the night. Or maybe even a runaway. I've found a couple of kids right over there on the beach."

Nate doubted that any of Ian Ryker's associates would have invaded this room and sat around eating candy and drinking a cola. More than likely Cyn's assessment was correct, and the vagrant or runaway was probably long gone by now. But there was always the possibility… "Who knows, maybe Miss Carstairs's ghosts like Hershey bars."

Cyn smiled at him, thinking what a marvelous sense of humor he had. "Did Spanish conquistadors eat Hershey bars?"

At the word conquistador, Nate flinched. Cyn noticed his reaction. "What's wrong?" she asked.

"Nothing." It had been years since anyone had called him that, not since he'd left the SEALs. Conquistador had been a nickname given in fun that had eventually become a hated symbol of everything from which Nate wanted to escape. "And no, I doubt the Spanish conquerors brought along any candy. Why did you ask? Was one of Miss Carstairs's ghosts a Spaniard?"

Cyn reached down, pulling a dusty box out from underneath a dilapidated chair. "Mm-mm. There are two ghosts," Cyn told him. "A man and a woman. He's a Spanish conquistador and she's a Timucuan Indian maiden."

"And how did Miss Carstairs know who her ghosts were?" Nate watched as Cyn rummaged around in the box, pulling out musty, moldy books. Already, he didn't like the sound of this old tale. Although the comparisons between himself and the ancient warrior were minuscule, the word conquistador was an undeniable bond. But he knew better than to tell Cyn about it.

Cyn stacked the books on the floor. "There's a legend about the ghosts who roam Sweet Haven's beach. Miss Carstairs told me she heard the legend when she was a child."

"Exactly what is the legend?" Nate asked, surprised that he was truly interested. It was this damned room, he thought. It piqued his curiosity.

"The maiden's and the conquistador's spirits are doomed to—" Suddenly and without warning, Cyn knew she had to escape. The feelings overwhelmed her. There was danger here in these rooms, danger and passion and death. The legend that had been so much a part of her life since childhood had now taken on a sinister aspect that frightened her.

She stood up, reached out and took Nate's hand. "Let's go back outside. You're right about this room. Nothing but junk here."

The warmth of her hand where it touched his spread through him like wildfire. He clasped her hand tightly and followed her outside into the daylight, away from the shadows, away from the panic that had claimed her. He knew fear when he saw it. It had been a part of his life for too many years for him not to recognize the signs. Cyn was scared, but he couldn't understand why. Was there something about the legend that seemed more real to her when she'd been in the storage rooms?

Pulling on his hand, Cyn began to run. He ran beside her. For some reason, she'd felt oddly chilled when she'd begun to tell him about the legend. It was as if an icy breeze had caressed her body. If those coquina walls could speak, she knew they would tell a story of great love and heartbreaking tragedy.

It was as if something or someone had been warning her. The fear she'd felt inside those cold ancient rooms had not been for the two long-dead lovers, but for Nate—and for herself. Nate was in danger, from something or someone who had the power to destroy him. She couldn't explain how she knew. She just did.

She slowed down near the cypress in the yard. Resting her back against the tree, she took a refreshing breath of ocean air, then smiled at him. How could she tell him about her fears without sounding like a complete idiot? Maybe she was. Maybe she'd let her imagination run amok. After all, she had convinced herself that there was a similarity between Nate and the conquistador who had died on this beach, his lover beside him.

Nate gripped her shoulder, his strength gentle yet commanding. "What's wrong? What happened in there?"

She covered his hand with hers, slowly pulling it away from her body to hold it to her cheek. "I'm not sure. I've always been fascinated by the legend, but I've never…never really believed it. Not the prophecy part, anyway."

"The prophecy?"

"I guess it's the fact that you're a warrior—"

"A former warrior."

"I suppose I associate the violence in the legend with the violence in your life."

"Tell me the legend," he said, taking her face in his hands, framing her cheekbones with his thumbs.

"The legend tells of a beautiful Timucuan maiden, with hair to her knees and a smile that enticed many a man. But she loved only one. A big Spanish conquistador. They came here to the mission to be married. You see, she had deserted her family's heathen ways and had converted to Catholicism. The priest married them.'' Cyn stopped talking. She didn't want to start crying. The legend, as beautifully romantic as it was, did not arouse all the feelings of magic and hope and love that it once had. Reality changed things. For the first time, she began to truly wonder what it had been like for those ancient lovers. What fear had they known? By whose violent hand had they died? And why?

''I take it that they didn't live happily ever after.'' Nate stepped toward her, his body leaning forward, almost touching hers.

''No. They were found dead, murdered, the morning after their marriage. Their bodies lay, naked and entwined, on the beach. The beach in front of my cottage.'' Tears escaped her eyes, trickling down her face, moistening the strands of her hair that curled around her ears. She wasn't crying for the lost lovers, but for herself and for Nate. There was a special bond forming between them, a physical attraction that drew them to each other. But they were such different people, with such opposing views on life. How could she ever love a man who'd made his living killing others? Could she ever reconcile herself to wanting a man to whom violence came as naturally as breathing?

Nate moved his body against hers, lowering his head until his lips hovered over her open mouth. ''Why do the ghosts haunt the beach?''

''The legend says that until another warrior and his maiden find eternal love on this beach and are united in a way the ancient lovers could never be, then the conquistador and his Timucuan maiden can never enter paradise.'' Cyn could feel his breath, hot and moist against her lips.

''The legend doesn't make any sense.'' he nipped at her bottom lip, then soothed it with the tip of his tongue. ''Surely the Spaniard and his bride had a wedding night. If they made love, then they were united.''

''Who knows,'' Cyn whispered, longing for his kiss.

''And who cares,'' Nate said. ''It's just a legend, isn't it?''

He took her mouth then, thrusting his tongue inside, tasting her sweetness. He ran his hands up and down her back, then crushed her to him, wanting to devour her, seeking out every inch of her flesh, needing to be a part of her.

She whimpered, then flung her arms around his shoulders. He moved his lips along her neck, into the hollow of her throat. She cried out his name. She wanted this man, wanted him here and now.

He jerked away from her, stepping backward, looking at her flushed cheeks and swollen lips? God, what was he doing? What was he thinking? He'd let some stupid tale of ancient lovers spin crazy dreams in his mind. He'd gone to find Cyn in the hopes of persuading her to leave Sweet Haven, and instead he'd lost his head and tried to make love to her.

"Nate?" She looked at him with those rich brown eyes, her gaze questioning him.

"Dammit, Cyn, I'm sorry." He took a tentative step toward her, then stopped. "I want you…I want you badly."

"I…I want you, too," she said, finally admitting the truth to him and to herself.

"Look, I don't have anything to offer you but a brief affair—"

"What if I said, all right?" The words escaped her mouth before thoughts of agreement had even reached her brain. She couldn't allow her heart to answer for her. If she did, she would be lost.

"No, it's not all right. If we'd met a year ago, then maybe. But not now."

"Why not now?"

He grabbed her by the shoulders. "Anyone close to me is in danger. I can't explain. The less you know, the better."

"But, Nate—"

"I can't risk it."

She reached out, touching his cheek with the palm of her hand. "Some things are worth the risk." Dropping her hand, she turned and walked away.

Nate let her go.

Chapter 6

Cyn stood outside Tomorrow House inspecting the faded metal sign, thinking how the weathered condition of the sign epitomized the shelter's money problems. Oh, the sign could be easily redone, probably the cheapest repair job needed. The building was another matter. The church paid the rent on the one-story brick structure and provided the services of Bruce Tomlinson, but everything else was paid for by donations, and all the workers were strictly volunteers. Except Mimi. The sixty-year old woman, widowed eight years ago, had no other source of income.

No one, not even Mimi, knew that Cyn paid her salary, but all the volunteers did know that Cynthia Wellington Porter lived quite comfortably off a sizable trust fund set up by her paternal grandfather the day she'd been born.

Opening the front door, Cyn walked inside and was immediately bathed in bright sunlight. A few feet away, a small crowd of teens stood staring up at the ceiling. Cyn's eyes followed their line of vision. She gasped when she saw the large ragged hole in the plaster ceiling, the rafters exposed like the weathered gray skeletons of a decayed carcass. Circular water stains dotted the ceiling in several places all around the open gap.

"What happened?" Cyn asked as she neared the group of gawking kids.

"I think a bomb exploded in the attic," one freckle-faced boy said.

"Naw," a black girl said, laughing, "I think Reverend Tomlinson cut that hole so his prayers could get past the ceiling."

Cyn clamped her teeth together in an effort not to laugh. Bruce Tomlinson was a very nice man, and quite dedicated to his work, but his overly pious attitude did little to endear him to the kids he encountered at Tomorrow House.

A tall, robust woman with graying red hair stepped out of a room at the end of the hall. Wiping her hands on her large purple apron, she grinned when she saw Cyn.

"Welcome back," Mimi Burnside said, giving Cyn a bear hug. "I see you've noticed our skylight. Lets in the sunshine, the moonlight, the cool breeze, and if it rains, it'll let that in, too. Of course a real bonus is that it's created an extra entrance for insects."

"When did this happen?" Cyn asked as she started toward her office, Mimi following.

"Yesterday. Luckily, nobody was standing directly in the line of fire, but we had one heck of a mess to clean up." Mimi closed Cyn's office door behind them.

Cyn picked up a stack of mail from the edge of her green metal desk, an army surplus purchase. "That roof has needed repairs for the past three years, but we simply haven't had the money. Has Bruce called someone to come out and give us an estimate?"

"What do you think?" Mimi settled her hefty frame onto one of the three metal folding chairs lined up across the back wall in the office.

"Let me guess." Cyn grabbed the back of her swivel chair, pulling it away from the desk. "He expects me to take care of it this morning. And he also expects me to come up with the money.''

''Right on both counts.'' Mimi cocked her head to one side and gave Cyn a long speculative look. ''You seem to be back to your normal self, but I sense something's wrong, Cynthia Ellen Porter. Are you sure you're ready to come back to work?''

''I'm fine.''

Mimi puckered her lips, squinted her hazel eyes and shook her head. ''No, you're not.''

''I haven't been sleeping much.''

''If you've been worrying about Bobby, then I can set your mind to rest. He came back last night.''

''Thank goodness.''

''He told me about what happened at the Brazen Hussy. He was worried about you.'' Mimi crossed her arms over her ample bosom. ''I assured him that you were fine.''

Cyn felt her cheeks sting with the beginnings of a blush. No doubt Bobby had told Mimi about Nate Hodges. ''I never should have gone to the Brazen Hussy.''

''Who was he, this one-man army that rescued you?''

''Nathan Hodges, a former navy SEAL, and…and my new neighbor.'' Cyn knew she might as well be honest with Mimi, because sooner or later the woman would worm every detail out of her.

''New neighbor?''

''He bought Miss Carstairs's old house.''

''Well, well.'' Mimi got up, rubbed her chin and walked to the door. ''So a warrior has finally come to the old mission, to the haunted beach.''

Cyn snapped her head around, her brown eyes focusing directly on Mimi's Cheshire cat grin. ''I should never have told you about that legend.''

''What's the matter? Something change your mind about how romantic that old legend is?''

''It was a beautiful story, tragically romantic…as long as it remained just an ancient legend. But now…''

"Now what?" Mimi asked, laughing. "Are you afraid you and your warrior are destined to fulfill the prophecy?"

"Sounds crazy, doesn't it?" Cyn had tried not to think about the parallel between the ancient lovers and Nate and herself. "Who's to say that Nate's the first warrior to come to the Sweet Haven beach? And I'm certainly no maiden."

"Nate, huh? Already on a first-name basis?" Mimi opened the door, hesitated momentarily, then turned around.

"We're so completely wrong for each other. His whole life is the total opposite of mine. For heaven's sake, Mimi, the man collects knives."

"If it's meant to be, there's nothing you or this Nate can do to stop it."

"We're never going to see each other again." Cyn raised her voice, wanting to make sure Mimi heard her, hoping her adamant tone would convince the other woman of her sincerity.

Mimi didn't turn around or acknowledge Cyn's remark in any way. *Dammit,* Cyn thought. *That's all I need, Mimi Burnside trying to pair me off with a man determined to keep me out of his life, a man who, by his own admission, isn't even interested in a brief affair.*

Nate heard the noise again. There was something in the storeroom, something making a whimpering sound. Could it be an injured animal that had taken shelter? Even though the door was closed, it was possible that a stray cat or dog could have crawled in through one of the partially boarded windows.

Nate opened the door and stepped inside, moving cautiously, just in case the animal might attack. It took a few minutes for his eyes to focus in the semidarkness. Glancing around, he noticed nothing changed from the day before, but then he heard the sound again. God, whatever it was, it sounded almost human.

Suddenly, a small dark shadow in the far corner moved. Nate took several tentative steps toward the movement. Without warning, a skinny kid hurled herself from behind a tall chest and, running past Nate, made a mad dash for the door.

"What the—" Turning quickly, Nate reached out, grabbing the little hooligan by the neck.

The child let out a frightened scream and began struggling. Thrashing arms and legs pelted Nate as he dragged the scrappy kid outside.

"I'm not going to hurt you," he said. "Stop your squirming!"

"Please…" Gradually, the child ceased struggling.

Nate took a good look at the intruder. Damn, it was a brown-eyed little girl with dirty, stringy black hair. Had this child been hiding in his storage rooms, eating candy and drinking cola? Probably. But that would hardly explain the cigarette butt.

"Hey, honey, it's all right." The child broke into tears. Nate released her, but kept a restraining hand on her back.

"I…I didn't do nothing wrong." She gulped and looked up at him, fear in her eyes.

That's when Nate noticed the fresh purple bruises on the side of her pretty face. His gaze traveled the length of the child's scrawny body, noting that her shorts and blouse were faded and dirty and that a line of fading bruises covered her left arm and the backs of both legs. Nausea rose in Nate's throat. If he could get his hands on the person who'd beaten this child, he would make sure that animal never touched her again.

"What's your name?" he asked.

She looked at him, her eyes wide and wild with fright. "Just let me go, okay? I didn't know somebody lived here."

"Did your mother or father do this to you?" Nate asked, pointing to her battered face.

"I won't go back. You can't make me," she screamed and started to balk.

Nate placed a restraining hand at her waist, then cursed himself when she cried out in pain. Dear God, he needed to get this child to the hospital. "Look, honey, I think we need to get you to a doctor."

"No!"

"You're hurt."

"It ain't so bad. I don't want no doctor, no police. They'll make me go back, and I'd rather die than go back." She curled up, dropping to her knees, her whole body trembling.

"No doctor. No police," Nate assured her. "I know a lady who helps kids like you. She works at a place called Tomorrow House in Jacksonville."

"She'll call the police."

"No. She'll help you. Give you a place to stay, some food and a doctor who won't report you to the police." Nate picked the child up in his arms. She trembled as if she were in the throes of a seizure.

This abused little girl needed help, and he intended to see that she got it. He also intended to make sure he got her away from Sweet Haven, away from him, as quickly as possible. She couldn't come back. If she did, she, too, would be in danger from Ryker. If the cigarette butt had been left by one of Ryker's cronies, then it was a miracle the child hadn't already been faced with the unspeakable. Dear God, what if she had? What if the bruises…? No, Ryker's type didn't just abuse, they killed. The Marquez family and Ramon Carranza were people who left behind no witnesses.

Nate headed toward Cyn's cottage, got halfway across the road, then remembered that she'd told him she was returning to work today. Making a hasty turn, he carried the little girl into his house. He eased her fragile body down on the sofa in his den.

"I promise that no one will hurt you. My friend is a nice lady. She'll take care of you."

Damn, this was one more complication he didn't need in his life. He was fast reaching the breaking point. And that's exactly what Ryker wanted. No doubt his old enemy was delaying the inevitable because he was enjoying the game, savoring each new torment, loving the idea of making Nate wait and watch and agonize.

Nate dug a ragged phone book from the desk drawer and searched through the tattered pages until he found the listing for Tomorrow House. Dialing the number, he watched the child, who had curled into a fetal position, her arms crossed over her chest.

"I need to speak to Cynthia Porter," he said. "And hurry, it's an emergency."

Nate had tried talking to the child on the drive from Sweet Haven to Jacksonville, but he'd finally given up when he realized she wasn't going to reply. She sat, huddled on the front seat of his Jeep, her eyes red and puffy, the bruises on her face vividly apparent in the bright Florida sun.

She couldn't possibly know how well he related to her, how completely he understood her withdrawal. How many times had he run from his abusive Uncle Collum? How many times had the police returned him to that vicious man's clutches?

God, how he wished there had been a Tomorrow House in his past, and a caring, giving woman like Cyn Porter. But there had been neither. No one had given a damn about a wild and rebellious boy. No one had wanted him, least of all his mother's older half brother. No one, except Uncle Sam. The U.S. Navy had wanted him, and they'd had him, body and soul, for twenty years. He'd given the SEALs the dedication and loyalty many men gave their families. The navy had been his salvation as surely as it had been his damnation.

The only decent thing Collum Hodges ever did for his nephew was sign the enlistment papers allowing him to join the navy at seventeen. He'd never forget his uncle's parting words.

"Maybe they'll ship your worthless butt off to Nam and let those gooks use you for target practice. God knows, you're no good for anything else."

Nate had never fully understood his uncle or the man's unrelenting hatred. Collum Hodges had been a bigoted, embittered man, and an ambitious one. His sister's illegitimate child had been a social embarrassment to him, and the fact that the boy quite obviously had Hispanic blood in him outraged Collum, whose conservative Anglo friends were less than accepting of Grace's mix-breed child.

Gripping the steering wheel tightly, Nate pulled his Jeep into the only empty parking space available, a half block down from Tomorrow House. He got out, walked around the car, opened the door and lifted his passenger up and into his arms.

Cyn stood in the open doorway, watching Nate walk up the sidewalk. He carried a small, unmoving child. When he'd told her that the little girl needed to see a doctor, Cyn had placed a call to her friend, Callie Reynolds, who did a great deal of volunteer work for the shelter. Callie, a successful St. Augustine pediatrician, promised to drive up on her lunch break.

Nate took the steps up to Tomorrow House's entrance two at a time. "Have you gotten in touch with a doctor?" he asked.

"One will be here around twelve-thirty." Cyn winced when she noticed the purple bruises on the child's face. Even though she'd seen this sort of thing more times than she cared to remember, she hadn't hardened herself to the reality that there were people in this world capable of brutalizing children. "Bring her on inside. Mimi has fixed her something to eat."

Nate followed Cyn down the hallway and into the kitchen. A big redheaded woman, busy stirring some delicious-smelling concoction in an enormous kettle atop an old stove, turned and smiled at him. He nodded an acknowledgment, then set the little girl down at the table.

The child stared at the bowl of cereal and the glasses of milk and orange juice, then looked up at Cyn with questioning eyes. "He said you wouldn't make me go back. You won't, will you?"

Cyn clutched the top of the chair opposite the one in which the child sat. "No one is going to make you do anything. All we want to do here at Tomorrow House is help you. Would you tell me your name?"

The little girl shook her head. "Can I still have the food, even if I don't tell you my name?"

With tears trapped in her throat, Cyn couldn't respond immediately. She glanced over at Mimi.

"You eat up, honey child," Mimi said. "And if you're still

hungry, it won't be long until lunch. I'm working on some good old chicken stew.''

The child picked up her spoon, dug into the cereal and ate as if she were starving. After finishing the last bite, she gulped down the orange juice.

''Mimi, would you let our young visitor keep you company here in the kitchen while I give Nate a tour of Tomorrow House?'' Cyn asked.

''You ain't calling the police, are you?'' The little girl jumped up, her eyes wide with fear.

''No,'' Nate told her. ''Stay here and help Miss Mimi with lunch and I'll come say goodbye before I leave.''

''I'll see if Bobby wants to come give me a hand, too,'' Mimi said. ''That boy's good at helping.''

''Who's Bobby?'' the little girl asked.

Cyn and Nate left the kitchen. He followed her into the hallway. Children of various ages, sexes and races moved freely around the building, some passing Cyn and Nate in the hall, others busy watching television, playing Nintendo and shooting pool, as well as sweeping, mopping and dusting.

''You said on the phone that you found her in the old mission.'' Cyn nodded to several smiling youngsters.

''The storage room,'' Nate said. ''And yeah, she's probably the one who left the cola can and candy bar that we found yesterday.''

''How about the cigarette butt?''

''Possibly. But I doubt it.'' He knew the chances were good that the cigarette butt had been left by one of Ryker's friends, but there was no point in trying to explain that to Cyn. ''What can you do for the kid? She doesn't look a day over eight or nine.'' Nate glanced around at the boy who stood in an open doorway across the hall. Recognizing him, Nate nodded. Bobby slipped back into the game room, silently disappearing.

''He came back last night.'' Cyn nodded toward where the boy had been standing. ''More than likely, he's afraid of you after seeing your macho demonstration at the Brazen Hussy.'' She reached out, placing her hand on Nate's arm. ''Why don't we go into my office and I'll tell you what our options are as far as your little waif is concerned.''

The moment she touched him, he wanted to drag her out of this place and back to the beach. He wanted to be alone with her, to explore where that one simple touch could lead.

He followed her the few yards to her office, but just as they started in, a short, stocky man, wearing a suit and tie, approached them.

"Hello, Cyn. I'm sorry I wasn't here to greet you on your return this morning, but I had a breakfast appointment with the Reverend Lockwood," Bruce Tomlinson said, placing his hand on Cyn's shoulder.

The moment the other man touched her, Nate wanted to knock his pale, immaculately clean hand off her. He wanted to issue a warning. But he didn't. Instead, he glared at the man.

"Bruce, I'd like you to meet Nate Hodges. He found a badly beaten little girl this morning and brought her to us." Cyn squeezed Nate's arm, smiling at him.

"Unfortunate. Unfortunate." Bruce made a tsk-tsk sound with his tongue against his teeth and shook his head.

"Nate, this is Tomorrow House's director, Reverend Bruce Tomlinson." Cyn wasn't surprised at the tension she felt as she introduced the two men. It was only natural that two such opposite extremes of the male species would be wary of each other. The gentle, weak, condescending Bruce and the fierce, strong, proud Nate.

Bruce, ever the gentleman, held out his hand. Nate merely nodded, completely ignoring the other man's cordial gesture. "Mr. Hodges, I wonder if you'd mind giving me a few minutes alone with Mrs. Porter. I have an urgent business matter to discuss with her."

Beneath her hand, she felt Nate's arm tense. She couldn't take a chance on what response he might make. "Bruce, if you want to ask me if I've done anything about the ceiling, then I can tell you that a roofer will be here tomorrow." Cyn pointed toward the hole in the ceiling near the front entrance.

Nate's gaze wandered over the gaping hollow. "What happened?"

"An old roof, rotting wood and too much rain this past winter," Cyn said. "We've needed a new roof for years, but just couldn't afford one."

"Then how are we going to pay a roofer now?" Bruce asked. "We don't even have enough money to pay this month's bills. Reverend Lockwood is very concerned. He says that it's a real possibility that the church will have to close us down."

"They've been saying that for the last six months," Cyn reminded him. "Look, Bruce, I'll find a way to cover the cost of roof repair, even if I have to pay for it myself."

"Oh, my dear girl, we couldn't allow it. You do too much already. Working here without a salary, donating everything for the game room—"

"Hush, Bruce! Go…go do some paperwork, and quit worrying so much. Everything will work out. Remember, the Lord helps those who help themselves. And I have every intention of finding a way to help us."

"Very well." Bruce gave Nate a cold, silent look. "Goodbye, Mr. Hodges." Then he walked away.

"Prissy little guy," Nate said, laughing. "I don't think he likes me."

"Probably not. Did you like him?" Cyn pulled on Nate's arm. "Let's go in my office so none of the kids will overhear more than they already have."

Nate followed her into the surprisingly pleasant room. All the furniture was old, the metal desk, file cabinets and chairs were an army green. The walls had been painted a lighter shade of green, a very soothing hue. Open blinds covered the long narrow windows facing the street.

"Have a seat." Cyn pointed to one of the metal chairs.

Nate sat down, never once taking his eyes off Cyn. "How can you afford to work here without pay and to donate equipment for a game room?"

Cyn seated herself behind her desk. Not knowing how he'd

take the news that she was independently wealthy, she hesitated. "Well, I—"

"Your husband leave you a bundle?" Nate asked. "What were you two doing with this place, playing social workers?"

Cyn straightened in her chair, took a calming breath and placed her clasped hands on top of her desk. "My husband wasn't wealthy. He was a dedicated man of God, a man who gave all his time and love to Tomorrow House."

"That must have been difficult for you, being the wife of a man who put you second in his life." Nate watched as her face paled, and knew he had struck a nerve.

Damn him! Cyn thought. But as much as she wanted to lash out at him and deny his accusations, she couldn't deny the truth. She decided it was best to make no comment on her marriage to Evan. "I was born into a wealthy family. My father is Senator Denton Wellington of Georgia. My mother was a St. Augustine Phillips. My grandfather provided me with a substantial trust fund."

"La-di-da." He should have known. A woman didn't have the poise and strength and self-assurance Cyn Porter possessed without having had it bred into her. She had the kind of classy looks and dominating personality that only comes from having been raised with money. "Did your rich parents give you your nickname?"

"I beg your pardon?" Cyn glared at him.

"Oh, it's a cute nickname, but I just wondered if your family thought it suitable for someone so…so pure and sweet and virtuous. I mean, how many ministers' wives do you think are called Cyn? And how many work at a church shelter?"

"For your information, my younger brother gave me the nickname when he was only three and couldn't pronounce Cynthia. My rich parents thought the name was adorable. And my minister husband found it a constant source of amusement. Evan had a wonderful sense of humor."

"I imagine Evan was just about perfect in every way."

"I think we should confine our discussion to the little girl you brought here. Otherwise we're liable to exchange blows…verbal blows.'' Cyn leaned back in her chair, praying that her voice sounded more composed than she felt. She had no intention of discussing Evan with this man. She would not allow him to force her to admit that her marriage had been less than perfect, that often she had longed for a husband as dedicated to her as he'd been to his work—that she had needed a man with whom she could share life's burdens and not try to shoulder them all by herself.

''I'm listening.'' Nate decided right then and there that the sooner he could get the hell away from Cyn and her blasted shelter full of emotionally starved kids, the better off he'd be. He didn't need to care about this woman or her damned bunch of hooligans. So what if his body craved her the way an alcoholic craves liquor. So what if he felt the deepest empathy for these kids because he'd once been one of them.

''A friend of mine, Dr. Reynolds, will check the child and see if she needs medical treatment. I can offer her a place to stay, get our volunteer psychologist to talk to her, try to persuade her to let us locate her parents.''

''No police, remember,'' Nate said. ''She'll run like hell if you push her too hard.''

''I know. Believe me, we'll do all that we can to help her, but in the end, we can only do so much.''

''Yeah.'' He stood up, walked to the door, then turned and faced her. ''How much longer are you going to be staying at your family's cottage?''

''Eager to get rid of your only neighbor?'' she asked.

''Look, Cyn, this thing between us can't go any further.'' He grasped the doorknob in his big hand.

''Exactly what is between us?'' She stood up, meeting his stare head-on.

''Cut the act, lady. We want each other. Badly.'' He noted that her cheeks were turning pink. ''Now isn't the right time for me. I've never had anyone special, never wanted or needed anyone, and I sure as hell don't want to get involved with you, especially not now.''

"Why not now?" she asked, then averted her gaze from his perusal, glancing down at the wooden floor.

"Like I've told you, I'm a dangerous man," he said, wishing that he didn't have to frighten her away. "And I have dangerous friends."

"You're not a criminal, are you?" she blurted out before thinking how the question would sound.

"No, Brown Eyes, believe it or not, I've always considered myself one of the good guys."

Cyn walked around the desk, moving quickly toward Nate. Just as he opened the door, she placed her hand on his arm. His muscles hardened under her touch. "Nate?"

"Look, honey, if you're so hungry to get laid, why don't you ask Bruce? I'm sure he'd be delighted. Me, I don't have time to play house." He saw the startled expression on her face change to one of hurt, and he hated himself for having to say something so totally demeaning to her. But he had to make her stay away from him.

She dropped her hand from his arm and stood staring at him, willing herself not to cry as he turned and walked away. Suddenly tears gathered in her eyes. With the tips of her fingers, she swatted at them as if they were pesky flies.

While Cyn was trying to curb her tears and make some sense out of Nate's brutally insulting statement, she heard footsteps. Turning, she saw Nate's little ragamuffin coming toward her.

"Did he hurt you?" the child asked.

"Who, honey? What are you talking about?"

"That man. Nate. Did he hurt you? You're crying." The child walked over to Cyn, looking up at her with sympathy in her eyes.

"Oh, no, honey, he didn't hurt me." Cyn dropped to her knees, longing to reach out, take the child in her arms and offer her comfort.

"But you're crying." She reached out and wiped away a tear from Cyn's eye.

"We had a little disagreement, and he said something that hurt my feelings. That's all." That wasn't all, Cyn thought.

Nate Hodges had been deliberately cruel. He'd wanted to make sure she left him alone. His ploy had been so obvious, she'd have to be an utter fool to think he'd meant what he'd said. Something bad was going on in Nate's life, something so horrible that he didn't want Cyn involved. Didn't he realize that she was already involved, whether she wanted to be or not? Didn't he have sense enough to know that neither of them had any control over the way they felt?

The little girl stroked Cyn's cheek. "My name is Aleta."

Cyn smiled, reached out and gave Aleta a gentle hug. The child hugged her back. "Well, Aleta, how about lunch? I think I smell Mimi's apple cobbler."

She took Aleta's hand, led her toward the dining hall, then sat down beside her. Within a few minutes the room filled with children from the smallest eight-year-old to the biggest eighteen-year-old. Bruce joined them, said a prayer, then retreated to his office to eat lunch alone. Cyn knew that if Nate had stayed, he would have shared lunch with the kids.

Oh, Nathan Hodges, if you think you've seen the last of me, then you'd better think again. On some instinctive level, Cyn realized that no matter how hard she and Nate might fight the attraction they felt for each other, neither of them could control it.

Chapter 7

Cyn sat at her desk, absentmindedly rubbing a pencil back and forth between her hands. Three days after returning to work half days, here she was still at Tomorrow House at three-thirty in the afternoon. Although there was more work to do than time to accomplish it all, she should have been out of here by noon, but she hadn't been able to concentrate all morning. Indeed, she'd had difficulty keeping her mind on her job since her last unpleasant confrontation with Nate.

Mimi had offered a motherly shoulder to cry on, but even talking to Mimi hadn't solved her problem. She'd gone and fallen in love with a man totally unsuitable for her, a man who epitomized the one element she despised most in this world—violence. If she knew what was good for her, she would listen to Nate's warnings to stay away from him.

How had she allowed something like this to happen? She wasn't the type to do stupid, irresponsible things like falling in love with a man she barely knew. Of course, she had to admit that she had always been susceptible to romantic fantasies—a real sucker for legends and myths and fairy tales. But, dear

Lord in heaven, Nate Hodges was hardly a romantic hero. Far from it. He was no Sir Lancelot. No Romeo. And certainly no Cary Grant, Robert Redford or Kevin Costner. He was more the Genghis Khan-Jesse James type. A man like the bad-guy heroes so often portrayed by Humphrey Bogart, Clint Eastwood and Charles Bronson.

Damn! Stop thinking about him. Cyn threw the pencil down on her desk, scooted back her chair and stood up. Gazing outside, she watched as people scurried along the sidewalks and the beginnings of afternoon work traffic clogged the street. Momentarily closing her eyes, she listened to the soft, constant drizzle that dampened the cool April day.

Soon the view outside blurred as Cyn's mind focused on her memories of Nate Hodges, of the sight of him running along the beach. Every day for the past three days, she'd stood on her patio and watched him, waiting and hoping he would stop and talk to her. Once, on the first day, she had run out to him, calling his name. He'd stopped briefly, given her a hard look, and left her standing on the beach, feeling like an utter fool.

If he didn't want her, then why was she so certain that he did? She knew that Nate needed her, more than anyone had ever needed her. Why wouldn't he let her love him?

Don't do this to yourself. Concentrate on Tomorrow House, on the kids who so desperately need you. Think about Bobby and Aleta and the dozens of others who depend on you.

She wasn't sure what would become of Bobby. Since his return to Tomorrow House, he'd spent only one night, the other two he'd spent on the streets, doing God only knew what with boys like Casey. She'd tried everything she knew. Nothing worked. He was a good kid in a bad situation.

Aleta. Poor little Aleta. She was twelve years old, but didn't look it. She was a small, frail child, a little girl afraid of everything and everyone. After Callie had examined Aleta and assured Cyn that there was no permanent damage and her outward wounds would heal in a few days, Cyn's relief was short-lived. What on earth was she going to do with Aleta? If she called the police, Aleta would only run away again, so great was her fear of being returned to her abusive mother, a woman, Aleta had confided in Cyn, who stayed drunk almost all the time.

Tomorrow House was only a temporary solution to the ever-growing problem of runaway children. The institution had been founded to provide temporary food, shelter and assistance to the boys and girls who had no other place to go, no other safe haven, no other sanctuary from the horrid existence found on the streets.

A slight knock sounded on her door seconds before Bruce Tomlinson entered, a forlorn expression on his round face.

"I need to speak to you," he said. "I'm afraid the news isn't good."

"Then sit down, Bruce, and tell me what's wrong." Cyn motioned toward one of the folding chairs.

"No, no. Sit down if you'd like, but I'd rather stand." He moved nervously around the room, wringing his hands together as his round head bobbed up and down. "Cyn, I just got off the phone with Reverend Lockwood. The council met this morning and…and, well, things don't look good for Tomorrow House."

She knew what he was going to say, had known it was inevitable and had been dreading this day. "How bad is it?"

"Church funds are limited. They can't give us an increase of any kind this year. If…if we can't raise enough to cover the deficit, then the church will close Tomorrow House." Beads of perspiration dotted his pink forehead.

"How long?"

"If we can't raise enough to cover expenses for the next six months, the church will officially close Tomorrow House at the end of May." Bruce shook his head. "It's a terrible shame, Cyn. I know how much this place means to you, how much work and love you and Evan put into it."

Cyn leaned back against her desk, resting her hip on the edge. "Evan and I came here as newlyweds. Tomorrow House had just opened. Evan was the very first director."

Bruce came over and put a comforting arm around Cyn's

shoulders. "Do you want to tell Mimi and the volunteers, or do you want me to? And what about the kids?"

She straightened her shoulders, tilted up her chin and gave Bruce a defiant look. "I'll explain the situation to Mimi and the others, but I don't want one word of this getting back to the kids. I'm not going to let the church close us down. I've invested ten years of my life in this shelter."

"But how on earth do you think you can raise that kind of money in a little over a month?" Bruce gave her a quick hug, then released her.

Cyn moved around her desk, sat down and began rummaging through the bottom drawer. "More donations. We've got some millionaires who've contributed big money to this place. I'll just make a few phone calls and see if they don't want to be even more generous."

"Cyn, I think you're kidding yourself."

"Why don't you go on and do whatever it is you do this time of day," Cyn said. "And leave this problem to me. I promise you that Tomorrow House is not going to close its doors at the end of May or the end of this year or any other year."

"Very well." Bruce walked to the door. "If there's anything I can do to help, you'll let me know?"

"Of course." Wimp! Cyn thought, then chastised herself for expecting more from Bruce than he was capable of giving. How often in the past four years had she wished that Bruce Tomlinson was half the man Evan Porter had been? If Evan was here, he'd be fighting the church's callous decision. Evan would have found a way to keep Tomorrow House open. But Evan wasn't here, so it was up to her to keep his dream alive.

"What's the matter with Brucie?" Mimi Burnside asked as she walked into the office carrying a tray, which she placed on Cyn's desk. "Expecting you to come up with the solutions to all our problems here at Tomorrow House?"

Cyn retrieved a thin manila folder from the bottom drawer, slammed the drawer shut and sat up in her chair, clutching the folder in her right hand. "Close the door, will you, Mimi?"

The big redhead walked over, closed the door, then pulled a folding chair up to the desk. "This is serious, isn't it? Mary Alice told me Bruce had been on the phone with Reverend Lockwood. Money problems again, huh?"

"Unless we can come up with enough money to cover the next six months' expenses, the church plans to close Tomorrow House at the end of May." Cyn laid the folder down on her desk. "I've got to come up with some pretty hefty donations. And soon."

"I've seen this coming." Mimi handed Cyn a cup from the tray. "Here, drink some tea and we'll talk. And eat that sandwich. You didn't even take time out to have lunch today, and that's not like you. You usually have a healthy appetite."

"Too healthy." Cyn accepted the cup of tea. "I've had a lot on my mind today. Besides, I've been raiding the refrigerator too much at night lately."

"Well, it must be bad, whatever it is, to make you turn to food. Dare I tell you what I think you should do?"

"What are you babbling about?" Cyn sipped the tea, enjoying the warm sweet taste.

"That man, that Nate Hodges, he's got you running around in circles, honey child. And I say, if you want him, then go get him."

"Oh, for heaven's sake, Mimi, that man is a total barbarian. He's…he's in some kind of terrible trouble. All he wants is for me to stay away from him, and, believe me, that's just what I intend to do." Cyn knew she had lied to Mimi, but she couldn't lie to herself. If Nate Hodges called her this very minute, she would go to him.

"Easier said than done. 'Cause I think this thing is bigger than the both of you. I think it's completely out of your hands." Mimi picked up her cup of tea and took a healthy swallow.

"You're being ridiculous."

"Am I? Look, honey child, I've lived a lot of years and known my share of men. Lust and love are two things folks just don't have no control over."

Cyn crinkled up her nose as if she'd suddenly smelled something unpleasant. "He isn't the sort of man I could build a future with. He's too…too—"

"Too much of a man?" Mimi asked. "Not the sweet, gentle, turn-the-other-cheek type you're so used to. But my guess is that when a man like Nate Hodges loves a woman, she's the most important thing in his life."

Groaning, Cyn cast her gaze heavenward. "Why did I ever trust you with so many of my deepest, darkest secrets? I should have known you'd use them against me when I was at my weakest. You're the only person I ever told about my jealousy of Evan's dedication to Tomorrow House."

Mimi took another hearty sip of tea, then set her cup down on the tray. "Because, like you, I'm the mother-to-the-world type. Even strangers tell us their problems. Besides, we're friends who can trust each other. There's nothing wrong with a woman wanting to come first in her man's life. We all need to be loved."

"Even Nate?" Cyn asked, clutching her cup in both hands.

"That man definitely needs you, honey child."

"He thinks he doesn't need anyone. He's so strong, so capable of taking care of himself. Maybe he doesn't need me. Besides, it doesn't matter. We're all wrong for each other. He's nothing like Evan."

"I like him," Mimi said. "He's more man than Evan ever was. Just the kind of man a strong, caring woman like you needs. I'd say you two are perfect for each other."

"Mimi—"

"He's gone wanting for a long time. It shows in his eyes. He's like the kids that come here. Ain't nobody ever loved him the way he needs to be loved. And you, Cynthia Ellen Porter, have got the kind of heart that could heal that man's soul."

Cyn didn't like the thoughts that Mimi's words created in her mind. The legend said that someday a warrior in need of peace would come to the beach, to the old mission, and would find solace in the arms of a woman, the only woman on earth capable of giving his heart and soul sanctuary.

"I want to change the subject. I don't have time to try to figure out why Nate and I met now, when he's involved in something he won't talk about and I've got Evan's dream to save."

Puckering her lips into a frown, Mimi grunted. "What can I do to help?"

"Just keep being my friend. Keep putting up with me." Cyn tapped her slender fingers on the manila folder.

"What have you got there?" Mimi asked.

"A list of all our contributors." Cyn opened the file folder. "I plan to see each one of our major contributors and ask for…no…beg them for another donation."

"I suppose you plan to hit your father up first thing?"

"I know I can count on Daddy." Cyn lifted the list from the folder and scanned the pages quickly, reading out the names of the people who'd donated over a thousand dollars.

Cyn's eyes focused on one name. She didn't remember ever meeting the man, but she knew that for the past five years he had been Tomorrow House's largest contributor. "This is who I'll contact first. He's donated ten thousand dollars every year for the past five years."

"Who in the world has that kind of money to give away?"

"Ramon Carranza. I'm going to call and try to set up an appointment with him."

"I've heard of that guy," Mimi said, thumping her cheek with her index finger. "My friend Georgia, who lives in my apartment building, has a nephew who works for this Carranza. Waylon is the gardener, and he told Georgia that his boss was a very wealthy man. Got money invested in just about everything, and he's involved in a casino out in Vegas and another in Atlantic City. And the dog tracks."

"He's probably a millionaire and needs the tax write-off large donations can provide for him."

"Rumors are that he was once a very big man in Miami, back when the Cubans ran things, before the Colombians took over."

"My goodness, Mimi, you sound like an expert on Florida crime," Cyn said.

"Naw, I'm just an old woman who likes to gossip. People like this Carranza guy make for interesting conversation."

"Well, at this point I'm willing to give Ramon Carranza the benefit of the doubt. No one knows for sure how he made his money. We don't really know that he's a crime boss, do we? And in a way it's only fitting that bad money should do some good."

"My guess is the old man is trying to soothe his conscience before he dies. Probably thinks he can buy his way into heaven."

"He's an old man?" Cyn asked. "How old?"

"Nearly eighty. Waylon told Georgia that he ain't got nobody. No children, and his wife died years ago."

"He lives alone?"

"Except for the servants and his bodyguard," Mimi said.

"Bodyguard?"

"Well, he is very rich."

"I suppose you're right. I just hope I can persuade him to share those riches with us."

When she exited Interstate 1 directly behind the big black limousine, Cyn wondered who would be visiting Sweet Haven in such opulent style. Her curiosity peaked when she noted that the limo turned off onto the beachfront road. As she followed the huge, slow-moving Caddy, Cyn's puzzlement increased when the vehicle passed her cottage and pulled up in front of Nate's house.

Cyn parked in her drive and got out, balancing the paper grocery bag on one hip and her briefcase and purse on the other. She couldn't help but stare across the road at the enormous man getting out of the driver's side of the limo. She didn't think she'd seen such a mountain of a man except on TV wrestling. The stranger wasn't wearing a chauffeur uniform however, but a tailored, dove-gray, three-piece suit. Even at this distance, she could make out the man's strong Hispanic features.

Stepping up on the front porch, she readjusted the grocery bag, then inserted her door key in the lock. As soon as she heard the opening click, she glanced again across the road. The gargantuan man stood at Nate's front door. Who on earth was he? And why had he come to see Nate? Could this man possibly be the dangerous enemy of whom Nate had spoken?

Giving the door a push with her hip, Cyn stepped inside, dropping her purse, key ring and briefcase on the nearest chair. Clutching the paper bag in her hand, she started toward the kitchen, stopped dead still, turned around and walked back to the open door. Peering outside, she took one more look across the street.

Nate stood on his porch talking to the big stranger. She was too far away to hear even the sound of their voices, and she couldn't make out the expression on either man's face. Suddenly, Nate shoved his front door open and waited until his guest entered before returning inside.

Cyn slammed the door and made her way to the kitchen. She placed the paper bag on the table and rummaged through it, removing the perishable items first. All the while she put away her groceries, Cyn kept thinking about Nate's visitor.

Enough already! she told herself. *You've got better things to do than worry about your unfriendly neighbor.* And unfriendly was exactly what Nate had been the last three days.

After a light supper of tuna salad, Cyn poured herself another glass of iced tea, put on a Patti Page tape and settled down on the over-stuffed chintz sofa in the living room. Picking up the manila folder, she pulled out the contributors list, her gaze immediately focusing on the name she'd circled in red. Memorizing the number, Cyn dialed her portable phone.

A female voice answered. "Ramon Carranza's residence. May I help you?"

"Yes, this is Cynthia Porter. I'd like to speak to Mr. Carranza about Tomorrow House in Jacksonville."

"Very well, Ms. Porter. Please hold."

Cyn gave a silent prayer of thanks that she'd had no trouble getting through to Ramon Carranza. She waited and waited and waited. Finally she began tapping her fingers on the sofa's armrest, patting her foot to the gentle rhythm of the music and even humming along with the tune.

"Hello, Señora Porter. This is Ramon Carranza. How may I help you?" The voice was strong and deep and only slightly accented.

"Mr. Carranza," Cyn said, her own voice breathless. "I'm the assistant director at Tomorrow House in Jacksonville."

"I'm very familiar with Tomorrow House. I wholly support your efforts to help young runaways."

"That's wonderful, Mr. Carranza, and we're extremely grateful for your generous yearly donations." Take it slow and easy, she cautioned herself. Just use your feminine charm and don't push so hard.

"But surely you are calling for more than to thank me." The tone of his voice had grown lighter, less formal.

"As a matter of fact, I am. You see, if we can't raise a substantial amount of money before the end of May, the church plans to close us down, and I simply can't let that happen. I know it's presumptuous of me to be pleading with someone who's already been more than generous—"

"Señora Porter, I would like to invite you to have brunch with me tomorrow, here at my home. I would be delighted if you can find the time to accept my offer."

"Delighted...lunch...tomorrow...at your home?" God, she knew she was babbling, but his invitation had been so unexpected, so totally out of the blue.

"May I take that as a yes?" he asked, amusement clearly in his voice.

"You most certainly may," Cyn said. "What time?"

"Shall we say around ten-thirty?"

"Ten-thirty would be fine."

"Will you need the services of my chauffeur?"

"No, thank you." For a split second her mind wandered to the limo parked across the road. Did Ramon Carranza's chauffeur drive a big, black Caddy, too? "I'll drive myself. And…thank you for agreeing to see me."

"It would be no problem for my chauffeur to come for you. Just give me your address."

"I'm staying at my family's beach house in Sweet Haven right now, Señor Carranza. It's on the other side of nowhere. The only two cottages out here are mine and Nate Hodges's across the road."

"Living in such isolation, I hope your neighbor…this Señor Hodges…is a man you can count on for assistance?"

Clearly his comment was a question, and Cyn found his fatherly concern endearing. "Oh, believe me, Nate is definitely a man I could turn to if I were in trouble."

"Nate? Then he is a friend of long acquaintance, yes?"

"Actually, no. We only met recently. He just moved into the house across the road a few months ago."

"It is always good to make new friends."

"Yes," Cyn said with a sigh, thinking how she would hardly describe her relationship with Nate as friendship. "It was kind of you to offer to send your chauffeur for me, but it will be easier all around for me to just drive myself."

"Very well, then. I'll be looking forward to meeting you, Señora Porter."

"Yes. Thank you, thank you so much." Cyn punched the off button on the telephone, held it up against her cheek and smiled. She had a lunch date with a man who could solve all of the shelter's problems. Somehow, some way, she was going to make a good impression on Ramon Carranza and sweet-talk him into becoming Tomorrow House's savior.

Now, if she could only figure out a way to solve her other problem, she thought as the tossed the phone onto the sofa and got up to walk over to the front windows. The limo was still parked at Nate's house. Dammit, why had that infuriating man come into her life? Even if he were willing for them to explore their feelings for each other, he'd made it perfectly clear that he wasn't interested in a permanent relationship with a woman. Well, if she could charm thousands of dollars from a man rumored to be a former Miami crime boss, then who was to say she couldn't teach a hardened warrior how to love?

Nate stood in the middle of his den eyeing the man standing directly across from him. Hell, he hadn't seen a man that big since Sonny Rorie, a survival instructor from his days at Coronado, that do-or-die time when he'd been a SEAL recruit.

"You said you had news of Ryker?" Nate asked, wondering just who the hell this guy was, one of Ryker's front men or some agent he didn't know. From the looks of him, Nate's first guess would have been a sumo wrestler.

"I do," the man said, his voice laced with a slight Spanish accent.

"Who are you?"

"Emilio Rivera."

Nate widened his almond-shaped eyes, a questioning frown wrinkling his smooth forehead. So, he thought, this is Ramon Carranza's bodyguard. "Where did you get your information?"

"My employer has his sources," Emilio said.

"And just who is your boss?" Nate asked.

"I am sure that your friend, Señor Romero, has already informed you of my employer's identity."

"Maybe you should inform me."

"Very well. Ramon Carranza has sent me to tell you that your enemy, Ian Ryker, has left Miami and is en route to St. Augustine."

"I've been expecting him, so this really isn't such urgent news." Nate noticed the big man flinch, his jaw tighten.

"Ryker already knows your exact location. We estimate that in approximately three days, he will make his move on you."

"Just what is Carranza's stake in all this? And why the hell should I believe anything you tell me?" Nate didn't like puzzles, especially not ones that involved his life.

"Señor Carranza is a very wealthy and powerful man. He has instructed me to tell you that everything he has is at your disposal if you wish to simply *disappear*. Ryker has signed your death warrant, Nathan Hodges. If you stay here, one of you will die.''

Why would Ramon Carranza offer him the means by which to escape Ryker? Nate wondered. The man obviously had something to gain. Or perhaps it was all some elaborate trap. Maybe Carranza liked to play games as much as Ryker did. ''What is your boss's interest in me and Ryker? What possible reason would he have to want to help me?''

''If you wish to start a new life in another country, with a new identity, of course, we can arrange for the woman to join you,'' Emilio said.

''What did you say?'' The tension in Nate's stomach wound tighter and tighter until it spread through his whole body.

''Señora Porter. If you wish for her to join you—''

Moving with the speed of an attacking leopard, Nate pulled his knife to the other man's throat.

Emilio, seemingly undisturbed by Nate's aggressive response, stood perfectly still. ''You can put your knife away, Señor Hodges, I mean you no harm. But you must know that if we found out about Señora Porter, Ryker will find out about her, too.''

''There is nothing to find out about. She's my neighbor. I hardly know her.'' Hell, how had this happened? Nate asked himself. The one thing he hadn't wanted was to involve Cyn in his sordid battle with Ryker. ''Tell your boss that I don't run from a fight, that I'm ready for Ryker.''

''And Ryker is ready for you,'' Rivera said. ''A smart man would accept my employer's offer.''

''Tell Señor Carranza, thanks, but no thanks. I'll take care of my problems, my way.'' Nate had no idea what Carranza's stake in all this was, but there was no way he would trust any acquaintance of the Marquez family. Carranza was his enemy as surely as Ryker was. Nate had no doubts about that.

''Very well. We thought as much.'' Emilio stared down at the knife Nate still held at his throat. ''Would you mind?''

Slowly, cautiously, Nate lowered the knife. ''You still haven't told me why your boss is so interested in me.''

"I'm afraid I can't answer that."

"Can't or won't?" Nate asked.

"There is no need for either you or Ryker to die," Rivera said.

"Is that what this is all about?" Nate asked. "Carranza is so afraid that I'll kill Ryker, he's willing to send me on a little all-expenses-paid vacation? Ryker must be very important to your boss, or perhaps to some of your boss's friends."

"If you change your mind, feel free to contact me." Emilio Rivera smiled, the expression softening his tough, lived-in face. He handed Nate a business card. "I'll tell Señor Carranza of your decision."

"You do that." Nate watched his uninvited guest leave, not bothering to follow him to the front door.

Just what the hell was that all about? Nate wondered. Something was damned screwy here. Something just didn't add up. What connection did a retired Cuban *businessman* have with the new Colombian regime? Birds of a feather? Or did Carranza's connection to Ryker supercede his old enemy's association with the Marquez family? And why had Emilio's powerful employer kept tabs on Nate since his days in Nam? As a favor to Ryker?

Nate walked over to the desk, picked up the phone and dialed. While he listened to the ringing, Nate looked at the card in his hand. The name and address of a local restaurant was printed on the front. He flipped the card over. Scrawled in heavy black ink was a St. Augustine phone number.

"Yeah?" Nick Romero answered, his voice loud and clearly agitated.

"I've got a news bulletin for you," Nate said.

"What?"

"Guess who just paid me a visit."

Chapter 8

Nate sat in the cool stillness of his den, with only the sound of his own breathing to keep him company. He caressed the smooth blade of the straight razor he held. It was old, he knew, but exactly how old, he wasn't sure. Old enough to have belonged to his grandfather.

Closing the blade, he cradled the razor in his palm, then clutched it tightly. Had his knife collection started the day his mother had given this to him? he wondered. She'd placed it in his hand the last time he'd seen her, pale and weak in her hospital bed.

"This was my father's," she'd told him. "It belonged to his father, and he would have wanted you, his only grandson, to have it."

Nate tossed the razor down on the metal trunk in front of the sofa as he stood up. He didn't think about his mother often, nor did he let his mind dwell on his tortured childhood, his abusive uncle. But when he did, the hatred festered inside him, feeding the loneliness and bitterness from which he couldn't escape.

In the thirty-six years since his mother died, Nate had been alone and unloved. A boy always on the outside looking in. A man whose untamed life had taught him brutal lessons about the dark side of humanity. But there was light in this world, something pure and good shining through all the dark horror. He had seen a glimpse of that light in his mother, and he saw it in Cynthia Porter. She was truly light to his darkness, joy to his pain, sweetness to his bitterness. She held the key that could unchain the heavy bonds holding him prisoner in a cold, bleak and lonely existence.

After a lifetime of waiting for her, and not even realizing he was waiting, she had finally materialized. From out of his dreams, Cyn had entered his world, igniting the fires of a passion he had known only in the shadows of his fantasies. She was real, not some imaginary lover who had haunted him for so long. She was flesh and blood, and he wanted her as he had never wanted anything in his life.

But she could never be his. He didn't dare risk letting her into his heart. As long as Ryker lived, anyone close to Nate would be in danger.

Restless, anxiety and longing frazzling his nerves, Nate paced the floor, finally throwing open the door and walking around the yard. In the distance, the ocean's steady heartbeat and the cries of an occasional gull echoed in his ears, creating a tune that blended perfectly with the vivid portrait of an isolated Florida beach, warm and damp after spring rain.

He knew he had to find a way to get Cyn to move out of her cottage, to leave Sweet Haven and return to Jacksonville. After what Emilio Rivera had told him, he knew that Cyn's life was already in danger if she stayed here. If Carranza knew about Cyn, then no doubt Ryker would soon learn of her existence. He had to make sure that Ryker understood the woman meant nothing to him. He couldn't allow Cyn to be caught in the terror from his past.

He had to talk to Cyn, maybe even tell her just enough to persuade her to cooperate. She was proving to be a very stubborn woman. It had taken every ounce of his willpower the last three days to stay away from her. And the day she'd run to him on the beach, he had wanted nothing more than to lie her down in the sand and take her. Instead, he had given her a stern, disapproving look, then run away.

God, what it took for a man to reject a woman like Cyn! Maybe she didn't want to want him, but she did. He saw it in her eyes, those warm, rich brown eyes. Every time she looked at him, she told him she wanted him.

Would it be so wrong, he asked himself, to spend one day with her? It might be all they ever had, the only chance for him to find, even momentarily, an escape from the pain that ruled his heart. He could go to her now, ask her to be with him, and later, when he had absorbed some of her light into his dark soul, he would make her understand that, for her own sake, she would have to leave Sweet Haven.

Cyn tapped her bottom teeth with the tip of her long finger-nail as she scanned the pages of the paperback novel. Although she was having difficulty concentrating on the story, she was determined to finish the book. Reading was great escapism, and it had usually worked in the past to take her mind off her problems, but it wasn't working this evening.

She couldn't stop thinking about Nate Hodges, about the black limousine and the mysterious danger surrounding the man she longed to help. Slapping the book closed and tossing it down beside her on the couch, Cyn clinched her teeth, re-leased a loud huffing breath and balled her hands into fists.

"Damn. Stop doing this to yourself." Jumping up from the couch, she headed toward the kitchen. If a good book didn't work, then maybe food would.

"Why won't he let me help him?" Cyn asked herself aloud. "He's so alone and in so much pain, and yet he keeps shutting me out."

She placed her hand on the refrigerator handle, but before she could open it, she heard several loud knocks coming from her front door. With her heart racing and her stomach swirling,

Cyn rushed to the door, knowing before she saw him that Nate Hodges had come to her.

She swung open the door. His gaze met hers, his moss-green eyes pleading silently. She smiled. He looked so good, so very, very good. His jeans were old and faded but clean, and they fit his lean, muscular hips and legs like a snug, well-worn glove. His khaki-green cotton shirt encased his broad shoulders and chest tightly, then billowed out around his flat stomach and narrow waist. He had tied his hair back into the familiar ponytail. He looked big, rugged and dangerous. But in his eyes, she saw his soul, a dark, hungry soul in desperate need of light and nourishment.

"Nate."

He thought he'd never heard anything as beautiful as his name on her lips, and he knew he'd never seen anything as lovely as Cynthia Porter. Wearing a sheer yellow cotton blouse and skirt, with her golden-blond hair spilling freely to her waist and her flesh tanned to a tawny cream, she looked like a sunbeam—strong and bright and life-giving.

He wanted to bask in the warmth of her brown eyes, to reach out and draw her shimmering sweetness into his bitter heart.

"I need to talk to you," he said, thankful that she hadn't slammed the door in his face. Of course, he'd known she wouldn't. His heart had assured him that she would welcome him.

"Come in." She stepped aside to allow him the space to enter her living room.

He hesitated. "Look, we both know that there's something pretty strong going on between us, and…and I realize we can't just keep ignoring it."

"You're the one who's been trying to ignore it."

"Brown Eyes, I'd like nothing more than to make love to you, to explore the way I feel about you." He leaned toward her, placing one big hand on the doorframe. "But my life is complicated, too complicated to involve a woman like you."

"Then why are you here?" she asked, trying to disguise the catch in her voice, the disappointment in her heart.

"We can have this evening. That's all I can give you." He reached out and ran the back of his hand across her cheek, down her neck and chest to where her blouse covered her breasts. He wanted to say let me love you, let me drink my fill from your cup of life, let me find sanctuary in your arms.

"I don't understand." Her breath caught in her throat when his hand moved lower, down the front of her blouse, his knuckles raking across the small pearl buttons. "You keep...keep contradicting yourself. You say one thing, then do the opposite. You keep changing your mind."

He stopped his hand just below her left breast, spread open his palm and clutched her waist, pulling her toward him very slowly. "Come home with me. Give us this evening, and I'll try to explain."

She would never understand it in any logical fashion afterward, but her reaction to his request had nothing to do with rational thought. She swayed toward him, allowing him to enfold her in his embrace. She slipped her arms up and around his neck, standing on tiptoe to reach the band around his hair. With trembling fingers, she snapped the band, allowing his hair to fall freely down his neck and around his face.

He saw the hunger he felt reflected in her warm brown eyes, and he longed to take her mouth, to ravish her lips. But he didn't. He had to muster all his self-control. If he kissed her now, he'd be lost.

Rubbing her cheek with his, he held her to him, savoring the feel of her soft, womanly body. "Do you like steak?" he asked.

She cocked her head to one side, looked up at him and smiled. "See what I mean about saying and doing totally opposite things?"

"No contradictions," he said, loosening his hold on her. "My actions have been telling you that I want you, and what I'm trying to do with words is ask you for a date."

Cyn laughed, the sound deep and real and sweet. Her laughter filled his heart, warming the coldness, softening the hardness. "Are you inviting me to your house for a steak dinner?"

"Sort of." He released her completely, except for one slender hand that he held tightly. "I'm not much of a cook, but I can grill a steak, if you'll help with the potatoes and salad—"

"Do you like ice cream?" she asked, her whole body swimming with giddiness. She felt like shouting and singing and dancing around and around. She was going to spend the evening with Nate Hodges. They were going to have a date—a real, honest-to-goodness date. Maybe there was hope for them, after all.

"Love it," he said. "Why?"

Tugging on his hand, she pulled him inside her house and led him to the kitchen. "I'll pack a basket of goodies to take over to your house. We'll fix ourselves a banquet."

He wanted to tell her that she was the banquet, a true feast for his lonely heart and tortured soul. And he *would* tell her—tonight.

Nate sat on one end of the tan leather sofa, and Cyn sat on the other end. She had curled her feet up underneath her skirt; he had stretched his long legs out on top of the metal trunk. One of her Patti Page cassettes played on his stereo, the music and lyrics of "What'll I Do?" filled the ultra-masculine room.

They had shared a delicious meal, after-dinner drinks and discussions on subjects ranging from the weather to politics. They'd even broached the subject of his boating business in St. Augustine, from which he'd said he was taking a leave of absence.

More than once she'd tried to steer the conversation around to his past, and every time he'd artfully dodged her questions. Finally she gave up and began entertaining him with stories of how her father had disapproved of practically every boy she'd ever dated.

"Once I realized that no matter how perfect a boy was, my father was going to find something wrong with him, I figured out a way to make him appreciate the fine young man I'd been bringing home."

"And just how did you do that?"

"I started dating the absolutely worst boys in school."

"Who were the worst boys in school?"

"Oh, you know, the ones who rode motorcycles, wore an earring and had hair down to their shoulders." Playfully she reached out and flipped the end of his ponytail.

"Did your strategy work?"

"Of course. And it only took two perfectly awful dates before Daddy was asking about 'that nice young man' I'd dated a few weeks earlier."

"Such a manipulative female." He laughed, a genuine chuckle from deep inside. She made him feel good. Damned good!

"Not manipulative, just smart."

"And did you enjoy being a bad girl?"

"I've never been bad. I've always been a good girl. Ask anyone who's ever known me." She sat up straight, easing her legs out from beneath her skirt, inching them slowly toward Nate's where they lay stretched out on the trunk. "Cynthia Ellen Wellington Porter has always been a strong, sensible, levelheaded girl who could shoulder any burden, overcome any tragedy, and take care of anyone and everyone who needs her."

"And who takes care of Cynthia Ellen?" The moment he felt her leg touch his, he wanted to pull her close, entwining their legs in a sensual braid while their bodies joined in a passion neither could hide.

Cyn rested one of her legs atop his, the other cuddling beside it. "I take care of myself and everyone else. I have ever since my mother was killed in a plane crash when I was fifteen. I'm a take-charge person. I've been that way for so long, I can't be any other way."

"Didn't your husband take care of you?" Nate asked, wondering how a man could possess such a woman and not protect her as fiercely as he would the world's greatest treasure.

"Evan was a good man, but he was too busy taking care of all the kids at Tomorrow House to take care of me." Her eyes glazed over momentarily with a faraway pain, then brightened to their normal rich warmth. She felt as if she were betraying Evan's memory to criticize him in any way. It hadn't been his fault that he had never been able to give her the kind of possessive passion she had so desperately wanted.

Noticing Nate staring at her with a mixture of suspicion and understanding in his eyes, she tried to smile at him. "Besides, I didn't need taking care of. Haven't you guessed by now that I'm a mother-to-the-world type of person?"

"Mothers, even mothers-to-the-world, need husbands to take care of them." His own mother had desperately needed his father. She had been strong, strong enough to have and keep an illegitimate child in the morally judgmental fifties. But Grace Hodges had been so alone, so in need of—

"Nate, what's wrong?" Cyn asked, reaching out to take his hand, squeezing it tenderly.

"What?" He looked at her, his moss-green eyes slightly dazed.

"You looked so sad."

"I was thinking about my mother." He brought Cyn's hand to his lips, kissing it softly once, twice, three times. "She was a strong woman like you, but she needed someone to take care of her sometimes and there was no one there for her."

"Your father?" Cyn felt his pain. It filled his eyes.

It marred his handsome face. He made a sound somewhere between a groan and a snort. "I never had a father. I don't even know who he was. Anyway, it doesn't much matter. He's dead. He died before I was born."

"Oh, Nate, I'm so sorry." She held his hand even tighter, longing to take him in her arms and give him comfort. But she wasn't sure he would accept it, not right now when the pain was so great.

"All he ever gave her was me." Nate pulled away from Cyn's hold and stood up, his back to her. "A bastard child of uncertain heritage who never fit into her blue-blooded Anglo family."

Nate began to walk around the room as if movement alone would ease the tension from his big body. "His name was Rafael. She told me that much. I guess she had to, since she named me after him."

"Nathan Rafael." Cyn thought how well the name suited him, how perfectly it blended his mixed heritage.

"She said I looked like him, and I guess I must. I sure don't resemble anyone in her family, except for my green Anglo eyes."

"Your eyes?" Cyn asked as she stood up and went to him. "You have green eyes like your mother?" She touched his face with tenderness.

"Don't feel sorry for me." He stepped back, away from her touch. "I don't want your pity."

"What *do* you want from me?" she asked, her voice quietly pleading.

"Nothing. Everything. Too much. More than any woman could ever give." He couldn't stand seeing the look in her eyes, the pure, undisguised love. He turned away, moving toward the windows. Didn't she know that if he took what she was offering, he would destroy her? Even if Ryker didn't pose an immediate threat, Nate knew he would still be the wrong man for Cyn. She was so gentle and caring, so filled with love for the whole world. And he was a man filled with bitterness, a man who had spent a lifetime fighting the realities of a brutal world far removed from Cynthia Porter's awareness.

Following him, she placed her hand on his shoulder. She wanted to tell him that she was willing to give him everything, all that was her, every beat of her heart, every fiber of her being, the very essence of her soul. Didn't he know she already belonged to him?

"Take a walk with me," she said. "Show me the old mission again before it gets too dark to see inside." She wasn't quite sure why she'd made the suggestion, but somehow she knew it was the right thing to do.

Without turning around, he nodded. "No one knows for sure those old storage rooms were once part of a mission." Then he turned around, his face a mask of calm, hiding the emotions he was fighting to conquer. "Inside the sensible, levelheaded Cyn Porter is the soul of a romantic."

"Who, me?" She breathed a sigh of relief, knowing she

could handle a cordial Nate much easier than a brooding man in pain. "Just because I love fairy tales and myths and want to believe in legends, you call me a romantic."

"Come on, Persephone. Go with me into the darkness." He held out his hand.

Cyn felt the instant chill, the shuddering anxiety that claimed her. His words held a meaning he had not intended. She reached out and took his hand, knowing that she would follow this man anywhere, even into the jaws of death—and beyond, to the depths of Hades or through the gates of heaven.

Twilight shadows fell across the earth while the fading colors of dusk painted the sky with muted tones of pink and lavender. A gentle evening breeze murmured through the trees and bushes, its cool breath caressing Cyn and Nate the moment they stepped outside.

"Is there no entrance to the mission inside the house?" Cyn asked when they stood in front of the arched doorway.

"I think there used to be, but someone plastered over it years ago. Probably long before your Miss Carstairs lived here."

Nate shoved the heavy door open, standing aside to allow Cyn to enter first. Even though he didn't believe in ancient legends and certainly not in ghosts, Nate felt the same curiosity here that he'd felt the first time he'd come to these rooms with Cyn. He couldn't quite pinpoint the source of his uncertainty, but he knew there was something here waiting for him, something he wasn't yet ready to accept.

Cyn stepped inside and stopped abruptly, hesitating until her eyesight adjusted to the darkness. Faint evening light seeped through the boarded windows and crept in from the open doorway. Slowly, cautious in her movements, Cyn walked inside, glancing around, searching for something, for anything, that could explain why this place drew her like a magnet. She'd felt it the time before when she'd come here with Nate.

She wasn't sure how she knew, she simply knew that once, long ago, something wonderful had happened here and something horrible. She trembled.

"Are you cold?" Nate asked.

"Don't you feel it?" she asked. "The joy. The pain."

Damn this place to hell and damn his crazy imagination. She'd asked if he felt it. Yes, hell, yes, he could feel it, but he didn't want to. "This is a damp, dark, musty old building. You're letting that stupid legend make you imagine things."

She moved around the room, quickly, almost frantically, her breath coming in quick, ragged spurts. "They were married here, you know. The priest married them."

What was wrong with her? Nate wondered. She was staring at the back wall as if she saw more than moss-coated shell rock partially obscured by a stack of battered furniture and decaying cardboard boxes. He reached out, grabbing her by the wrist. "Come on, Cyn, let's get out of here. Let's go for a walk along the beach."

"They died here," she cried. "He killed them both in this very room and dragged their bodies out onto the beach." Cyn fell against the wall, her hot, flushed face seeking comfort on the cool stone surface.

Just as her knees buckled and she began to sway, Nate caught her up in his arms and rushed outside. Deeply inhaling the clean evening air, he felt his chest rising and falling with the heaviness of his breathing. The moment she'd said *they died here,* he'd known the ancient lovers had been killed in the mission—the Timucuan maiden and her Spanish conquistador. But the images that had flashed through his mind had not been of long-dead lovers, but of Cyn and himself. And Ryker.

"Oh, Nate, you felt it, too, didn't you?" She clung to him, her slender arms draped around his neck, her fingers threaded through his hair.

"Cyn, don't do this to yourself." He carried her across the road and onto the beach.

"Are you saying you didn't feel them, feel their joy, share their pain?" she asked as he lowered her to her feet, allowing her body to slide down his slowly, sensuously.

"I'm saying that we both can't let our imaginations run wild." He wanted her. Now. His body was hard, pulsating, throbbing with desire. How could he answer her, how could he admit that even now, the passion flowing through his veins like an untamed river was more than one man's passion? How could he tell her, without sounding insane, that he wanted to make love to her again, to find the fulfillment he had found only in her body, to come home to her arms and find the sanctuary his soul had sought for so long?

"It's as if we've been together before," she whispered, clinging to him, her lips pressed against his chest where she was unbuttoning his shirt. "Oh, Nate, I'm scared."

"It's all right, Cyn. I'll never let anything or anyone hurt you." Tonight is all you'll have with her, he told himself. Take her, only if you're sure you can let her go afterward.

"It's not just the legend. There's more." She breathed in the deeply masculine smell of the big man holding her so protectively in his arms. "I'm not afraid for them. They died hundreds of years ago."

"Don't think about it, Brown Eyes." He lowered his mouth, brushing the top of her head with tender kisses.

"It's us. You and me and the mission. And this beach. Oh, Nate, tell me what kind of trouble you're in. You need me. I can help you."

He took her mouth with the savagery of a man pushed beyond the limits of his control. Holding her close, Nate conquered her lips with unrelenting pressure, impaling her soft moistness with his tongue. Without really knowing anything, she already knew too much. She had sensed the truth as surely as he had. If he couldn't find a way to prevent it, Ryker would kill them both inside the old mission and drag their bodies onto the beach...the way the ancient conquistador's enemy had done.

Was that how the ancient legend's prophecy would be fulfilled? he wondered, his heart aching with some unknown emotion, his body suffering the tortures of the damned. His need for this woman went beyond any normal desire he'd ever felt, and he seemed powerless to stop himself from devouring her whole.

She moaned as her body quivered with response, pushing,

clawing, straining for closer contact. How could she endure much more? she asked herself. Never had such overwhelming desire consumed her. If she didn't mate with this man soon, she would die from the insatiable hunger.

They drank the sweetness of each other's lips, their tongues dipping, licking, thrusting in a parody of a more intimate act. He moved his hands over her in a frenzied exploration, savoring each new curve, and yet remembering the feel of her as if he'd touched her a hundred times. She clung to him, her fingers in his hair, her nails scratching at his neck, his back, his shoulders.

Together they sank to the ground, their knees cradled in the gritty sand. He yanked open her blouse, popping the buttons in his haste. Lowering his head, he took one tight nipple into his mouth, sucking her through the sheer yellow lace of her bra. She arched her back and moaned from the sweet ecstasy that was building between her thighs.

Still kissing her, Nate shoved her onto the ground, straddling her, looking down at her, dying with the need to be inside her.

Cyn felt lost in a world of dreams, so often had she seen those moss-green eyes staring down at her, felt the throbbing pressure of this special man needing to mate with her and her alone. But this was no dream, this was reality and he had promised her tonight, only tonight. No matter how precious this one night could be, would it be enough? Could she give herself to him and walk away as if nothing had happened? Could he?

"Nate," she whispered, her hands braced against his chest. She could feel the strong, powerful thud of his heart under her fingers.

"I want you," he said, his voice ragged with desire.

"Only for tonight?" she asked, unsure where she'd gained the strength to question their future.

Stunned by her inquiry in the midst of their lovemaking, Nate hesitated. Still straddling her, he gazed down into her warm brown eyes. "I'll want you forever," he told her truthfully. "But all we'll ever have is tonight. There's no future for us."

How could he tell her that soon, very soon, he would fight the last battle of his life with an opponent as skilled and deadly as he himself was? If he allowed her to stay with him, to become a part of him, then she would die as surely as she had in his dreams.

"I want you, Nate. I…I love you." She saw the fires ignite and burn in his eyes when she told him that she loved him. "But I want more. I want you to trust me enough to share your problems with me. I want you to let me help you."

Nate jumped up, grabbed her hands and jerked her up beside him. He reached out, taking her by the back of the neck, bringing her close. Bending over, he kissed her forehead. "Go away, Brown Eyes. You want more than I can give you."

She stared at him, not knowing what to say or do. More than anything she wanted to tell him to make love with her, that tomorrow didn't matter, that nothing but the two of them and this moment mattered. But she couldn't.

He released her. "You'll find someone else, someone like your Evan. A man who owns his own soul." He turned and walked away.

"Nate…"

He didn't slow his stride, even though she kept calling his name over and over again.

Cyn stood in her open front door looking across the road at the coquina-and-wooden house. The late-night rain had washed the earth, leaving the world outside coated with fresh moisture. Overhead, streaks of gold-kissed pink hinted at the dawn sunlight still hidden on the other side of the universe.

She hadn't slept even though she'd gone to bed. After hours of thinking and crying and praying, she'd gotten up. For the past thirty minutes she'd been staring across the road at Nate's house, wondering where he was and what he was doing. Was he sleeping? She doubted it. If he was hurting as badly as she, he was probably wide-awake and cursing the day he'd met her.

Her fearless warrior had reached out to her last night, and she, in her weak need for permanence and fear of the unknown,

had turned him away. She'd been a fool. She should have accepted what he offered, no questions asked, and had one perfect
night to remember for the rest of her life.

Was it too late? she asked herself. If she went to him now,
would he reject her?

Cyn tied the belt around her aqua silk robe, walked outside
and closed the door behind her. With her heart in her throat,
the rapid beat roaring in her ears, she crossed the road.

Lifting the heavy metal door knocker, she announced her
presence. No answer. Again and again she beat the knocker
against the wooden door. Finally, she turned away, but couldn't
bring herself to leave. With slow, purposeful strides, she moved
along the arched portico to the back of the house. The first
tentative rays of dawn light fell across the earth, kissing awake
the lush, unkempt vegetation in Nate's garden.

She saw him, and sucked in her breath. He stood on the rock
walkway in the garden, only a few feet from the house. The
early morning breeze caressed his hair like a lover's hand, the
long black threads whipping his cheeks. He was naked, only
the wind and the morning sun touching his flesh as she longed
to touch it.

His body held the scars of a warrior many times wounded
in battle, but she knew that the deepest, most painful scars lay
buried in his heart, and that unhealed wounds marred his soul.

Shivers of fear and longing swirled inside her, growing,
moving, increasing in strength, as she stood silently in the dawn
of a new day and brought the sight of Nathan Hodges, standing
boldly, arrogantly naked, into her heart and into her soul. His
body was big and bronzed, corded with thick, tight muscles,
and it gleamed like polished metal, damp from the rain, slick
and sleek. The only hair on his body was nestled around his
powerful maleness, and its color matched the midnight black
of the long tresses that touched his shoulders.

Never had she seen anything as beautiful as the man who
stood before her, his very maleness beckoning to her, his masculinity calling to her to come to him, to give herself as a
sacrifice to his desires, to match him thrust for thrust, hard

strength to soft strength, man to woman, in a mating ritual that would join their souls forever.

Moving almost as if in a trance, Cyn went to him. Nate knew she was there moments before he actually saw her. He had felt her. Already, she had become a part of him. He waited while she moved forward, stopping an arm's length away. Never letting her gaze falter, she stared up at him.

After hours of restless tossing, he had gotten out of bed and come outside. He'd been waiting for her, knowing in his soul that she would come to him. The sensible, levelheaded Cynthia Porter wouldn't want to come, but romantic Cyn, who believed in fairy tales and myths, would be unable to resist the unearthly magnetism that had claimed them. They were doomed. Whether caught in the spell of some ancient legend or simply overwhelmed by their own sexual needs, Nate didn't know. But he did know that Cyn was his, she had always been his and she would be his forever. As surely as he needed air to breathe, he needed her.

He watched, transfixed by her beauty, while she untied her belt and slipped out of her robe, letting it fall to the rock walkway beneath her feet. The breeze tousled her hair around her face and shoulders and molded her thin, aqua gown to her round curves. Without saying a word, she reached up and lowered the straps of her gown, one at a time. They dropped down onto her shoulders. Her breasts swelled above the silky material, her nipples pressing against the softness.

When she reached up to tug on the bodice of her fitted gown, Nate stepped forward, pushing her hand away, replacing it with his own. With a slow, gentle tug, he pulled the gown down to her waist, baring her full, rounded breasts. He ran the tips of his fingers down the length of her body, from neck to waist, letting his hand still momentarily when he touched her breast.

She moaned when he flicked her tight nipple with his fingernail. He jerked her to him, crushing her swollen, throbbing breasts against his chest. She felt him, all of him, hard and hot and pulsating.

He was so big, so primitively male, that she shuddered with

a maiden's fear of conquest, knowing that soon her body would accept the wild thrusts of his huge body.

He ran one hand down her hip, over her buttocks, kneading softly, clutching her soft flesh in his callused hand, bunching the silky fabric of her gown. With his other hand, he grasped her head, spearing his fingers through her golden hair, letting it ripple over his hand, his bare shoulder and arm.

Easing his hand lower and lower, he edged her gown higher and higher, until he was able to slip his hand beneath and touch her naked skin.

She ached with emptiness, her femininity pulsing painfully with a need only this man could appease. "Please," she whispered, her lips parting on a sigh as his hand moved between her legs to caress her inner thigh.

"Tell me what you want." He maneuvered his fingers between her closed thighs, dipping inside her damp, sweet body. Her thighs parted, her knees melting.

"Make love to me." She struggled for breath, then lost it completely when he circled her throbbing need with his thumb and forefinger.

With one agile move, he jerked her gown down her hips, letting it puddle around her feet like a pale aqua pool. He could smell her heat, thick, heavy, female moistness waiting for him to lay claim to it. It was all he could do not to take her where they stood, not to plunge into her with all the violent need commanding his male body.

He kissed her then, his lips tenderly loving at first as he tried to control the desire raging inside him. She was everything he'd ever longed for—and more. Deepening the kiss, his tongue boldly lunged and was met by the equally powerful drive of her tongue. Challenged by her forceful response, the seeds of a long dormant passion blossoming with an untamed fury, he lowered her down, down, down onto the soft, wet grass. With his knees straddling her hips, he gazed at her naked beauty, devouring her, drinking in the sight of her womanliness. Then he looked into her eyes—warm, rich, brown eyes that had haunted his dreams for twenty-five years.

He shook with desire, wanting her, needing her as he had never needed anything. He wanted to take her with all the savage wildness he barely controlled, but knew he mustn't allow himself that pleasure. No matter how strong a woman Cyn Porter was, she was also small and fragile and hadn't known a man's possession in a long time.

Nate prayed for the strength to take her gently, but the moment she touched him and called out his name, he knew he was lost.

She let her hand rest on his stomach, longing to lower it and take him within her grasp. "Nate...Nate..."

In one swift, perfectly coordinated move, he entered her, his thrust hard and demanding, calling forth all the unleashed passion in her soul. She cried out, so great was the pleasure of their joining, such pure, unforgettable rapture. She arched her body, lifting her hips to meet each vigorous lunge, a shattering crescendo of sensation taking over her body, spiraling out from her core, spreading into every nerve ending, every cell.

He lowered his head, his black hair caressing one breast while his mouth suckled the other. Tiny fissions of undiluted ecstasy exploded within her. She writhed beneath him, arching higher and higher, seeking a closer joining.

Taking her hips into his hands, he lifted her against him and increased the tempo of their lovemaking. "You want more?" he asked, his voice thick with desire.

"Yes...more." She clung to his back, her nails scoring his bronzed flesh with love trails.

"Deeper. Faster." His thrusts grew wilder, hotter, more intense.

"Yes!" she screamed. "Harder...harder..."

And he obeyed her command, giving her the depth of his hardness. Suddenly she cried out, tears of joy cascading down her cheeks. He listened to her moans of fulfillment, taking them into his mouth, savoring their sweet, undisguised surrender. She was his once again, as she had been in his dreams, only the reality far excelled the dreams. He felt her shuddering release, her body tightening, clenching him like a tight fist. With one final, brutal stab, he fell headlong into climatic fulfillment. His groans echoed in the stillness of the early morning, their guttural eruption the sounds of a healthy male animal who had claimed his mate.

Cyn had never known such total wonder, such complete and utter satisfaction. Nothing in her life had prepared her for Nate Hodges's possession.

His big body lay over her, damp and hot and heavy. He raised himself onto his elbows, looking down into her dazed brown eyes. "Did I hurt you?" He knew he'd taken her with savage force, seeking his own pleasure while trying to give the same to her.

"No," she said, reaching up to touch his face, a face so dear to her. "But I am lying here in the wet grass and I'm getting cold."

He smiled. Standing, he pulled her to her feet and picked her up. She shivered, partly from the cool morning breeze on her damp flesh and partly as an aftershock from such unequaled fulfillment.

"Stay with me a few more hours." Holding her naked body against his, he stepped inside the house.

"Will you send me away then?" she asked, knowing the answer before he replied.

"I'll have to," he said.

"Let me help you. Let me stand by you through whatever trouble you're in." She kissed his neck as her fingers laced themselves through his long hair.

"I don't want to talk about it. Not now. I want to make love to you again while I still can." He carried her down the long, dark corridor, kicked open his bedroom door and placed her on his rumpled sheets.

She opened her arms, taking him into her body, giving her lover, her fierce and lonely warrior, the safety he could find only within her embrace.

Nate took all she had to give, knowing he would never get enough. But for now, he was satisfied. For now he had found a sanctuary for his heart and soul.

Later, he would have to send her away. Even if these precious moments were all they would ever have, he could survive as long as he knew she was alive and safe. But if anything ever happened to her, if Ryker harmed her, then Nate knew he would be eternally lost. Cynthia Ellen Porter was his very soul.

Chapter 9

Cyn sat on the edge of the bed in Nate's sparsely decorated bedroom. She pulled the lapels of her aqua robe across her breasts, then tightened the belt. When she had awakened, she'd found her gown and robe on the wooden chair beside the bed. Nate, dressed in nothing but his cutoff jeans, had been standing by the window looking outside.

They hadn't spoken as their gazes met, and the hot passion that had existed between them in the previous hours ignited once again. She'd been shocked by her own primitive need to have him touch her.

When he had approached her, she'd held up the sheet that barely covered her naked body.

"We need to talk before you leave," he had said. "I brought in your gown and robe from the garden. Put them on while I fix coffee."

He'd left her alone then, giving her time to think about what she had done and what she was going to do now. She loved Nate Hodges. That and that alone was the only clear fact in her mind. She had come to him last night, throwing caution to the wind, forgetting everything except the passionate need to become his woman.

And now, he was going to send her away.

Common sense told her that she should go, leave him and find a way to overcome the overwhelming desire she felt for him. After all, he was hardly the kind of man she would have chosen for herself. He had spent almost all of his adult life as a navy SEAL, a professional warrior, a trained and highly skillful killer. By his very nature, Nate was a violent man. How could she ever reconcile herself to loving a man capable of destroying another human being with his bare hands?

And yet, how could she keep from loving him when every feminine instinct she possessed told her that Nate Hodges needed her, more than he had ever needed anyone or anything in his life?

Nate entered the bedroom. He handed her a mug filled with freshly brewed coffee. "Sugar and milk," he said.

Accepting the mug, she smiled. "Thanks."

He sat down in the wooden chair beside the bed. Their knees almost touched. Cyn readjusted her sitting position, moving her legs away from Nate's.

"Should I apologize for what happened?" he asked, looking at her, trying to gauge her reaction.

She stared down into the creamy brown coffee. "What happened between us was a mutual decision. I…I came to you because I couldn't stay away. And…and you—"

"Took you because I couldn't stop myself."

Jerking her head up, she glared at him, wondering if he regretted making love to her. "You make me feel vulnerable, Nate, and I don't like feeling that way. For as long as I can remember, I've always been the one in charge, the strong one, the one others came to for help, depended on to solve their problems."

"You can't help me, Cyn."

"So you keep telling me." She took a sip of her coffee, then circled the warm mug with both hands. "But knowing you don't want my help doesn't stop me from wanting to give it to you."

"For once in your life, let someone else take care of you. Let me make sure you're safe." He bent over slightly in the chair, dropping his hands between his spread knees. "I can't allow you to become important to me. It would put you in danger."

"I don't understand."

"The less you know, the safer you'll be."

Cyn jumped up, the contents of her mug splashing onto her silk robe, staining the aqua material with wet tan splotches. She flung the mug, coffee and all, across the room. With a splintering crash, the ceramic cup broke into pieces and the muddy liquid splattered the wall, then spread down onto the floor.

"It's too late to shut me out of your life. Haven't you got sense enough to realize that?" She stood in front of him, her intent gaze fixed on his startled face. "I'm in love with you. Whether I want to be or not. Do you think I go around sleeping with men I don't love?"

Nate stood up. When he tried to touch her, she shoved against his chest. "Of course I don't think you—"

"Maybe what we shared didn't mean anything to you. Maybe you can just send me away and go on with your life." Cyn sucked in the soft inner flesh of her mouth, closing her teeth downward in an effort to keep herself from crying. "I hate your damned knife collection." She jabbed her index finger into his chest. "I despise the fact that you spent twenty years in the SEALs, doing God only knows what." She jabbed him again. "You're a man who uses violence to settle his disputes. I've seen you in action. You're a deadly weapon."

Her words wounded Nate more surely than any knife in his extensive collection could have. Her every accusation was right on target. How could he defend himself to a woman as loving as Cyn? Why should he even try?

He grabbed her by the shoulders so quickly that she didn't

have time to evade his capture. She struggled momentarily, then stopped trying to pull away from him.

She met his fierce stare head-on. "Loving a man like you goes against everything I've ever believed in, and yet I can't change the way I feel. Something inside me tells me that you need me, and yet you keep trying to send me away. I think I have a right to know why."

Tightening his hold on her shoulders, he pulled her closer, so close her breasts brushed his naked chest. She trembled with desire from the intimate contact. Heat spread through his body. "I don't need you, Brown Eyes. Not the way you think." Hell, he knew he was lying to her, but he couldn't lie to himself. He needed Cyn Porter as surely as he needed air to breathe, but the last thing she needed was him—a man who could bring danger and death into her life.

Cyn took in quick, ragged breaths as she stared at Nate, love and longing in her eyes. "Am I making a fool of myself?" she asked, her voice trembly with tears.

"We're both fools," he told her, his own voice deliberately hard and controlled. He dropped his hands from her shoulders. "We've allowed our hormones to get us into a dangerous situation."

"There's more between us than overactive hormones." Stepping away from him, she tilted her head slightly, then stuck out her chin, a defiant, determined look on her face. "What we shared went beyond good sex."

Nate fought the urge to take her in his arms, the overwhelming desire to admit to Cyn that what he felt for her went beyond anything he'd ever experienced, even in his dreams. "The sex was good, wasn't it?"

"Don't do this, Nate. Don't try to alienate me by playing the chauvinist male."

"But that's exactly what I am. I'm no Prince Charming, no answer to a maiden's prayers. You said yourself that loving me goes against everything you've ever believed in."

"What kind of trouble are you in?" she asked, taking a

tentative step toward him, knowing that he was deliberately trying to be insulting enough to make her run.

He held out a restraining hand, a visible reminder that he didn't want her to touch him. "There's a man I knew years ago. In Nam." Nate walked across the room, wanting to put physical space between him and the woman who was so determined to help him. Dear God, how much he wanted to accept what she was offering. But he couldn't.

"A part of your violent past?" Somehow she knew that whatever danger he faced, he intended to confront it by calling upon his skills as a warrior. *Live by the sword, die by the sword* flashed through Cyn's mind.

"Yeah," Nate said, hating the look of condemnation he saw in her eyes. "Something happened between me and this man, something you don't need to know about." How could he ever tell Cyn the whole story and expect her to understand? Without knowing any specific details of his past, she was already repulsed. If she knew the bloody facts, she would hate herself for loving him.

"You can tell me anything. I'll understand." She went up behind him, wanting to put her arms around him, longing to ease the pain she heard in his voice, saw in his slumped shoulders. If only she could help him put his violent past behind him, and teach him how to live in peace. Surely he could change. All he needed was for her to show him how. Violence didn't solve anything; it only destroyed life.

"The less you know, the better," he said.

"Then tell me what I need to know." She reached out, allowing her hand to hover in mid-air, almost touching his tense back.

"This man, Ryker, swore he'd kill me someday, swore revenge. For the past five years, I've thought he was dead, that I didn't have to be constantly looking over my shoulder, waiting for the day of reckoning." Nate turned, facing her. "He's alive. He's on his way to St. Augustine, and when he finds me, he's going to try to kill me."

She touched him then, unable to stop herself. He grabbed

her hand where it caressed his cheek, and buried his mouth in her open palm.

"Oh, Nate. Nate…" Tears gathered in the corners of her eyes, spilling over onto her cheeks.

Suddenly he pulled her into his arms, nuzzling her neck, whispering her name. "If you were my woman, you'd be in danger. I can't let that happen." He wouldn't allow anything to happen to Cyn. He knew as surely as he knew the sun rose in the east that this woman was his soul. If she died because of him, he would be eternally lost.

"I think it's too late, Nathan Hodges. I'm already your woman, and we both know it." She held on to him with the fierce protectiveness of a mother lion safeguarding her cubs, of a strong female willing to go the limit to take care of her mate.

"But Ryker doesn't know it. He must never know. You have to get out of my life and stay out. For both our sakes." Nate remembered that Ramon Carranza had found out. How could he hope to keep her safe from Ryker when he had such powerful and ruthless friends? Nate released her, and when she refused to let him go, he pulled away.

"Can't the police help you? Surely they won't allow a man to just hunt another man down like an animal."

"Brown Eyes, you don't understand, you couldn't even begin to imagine. We're talking about jungle warfare here. We're talking about two trained killers who are evenly matched. This has nothing to do with any kind of civilized law you know."

The blood ran cold in her veins. No, she had never known anything about that kind of world, those kind of men, and yet, somewhere deep inside of her, she understood. "Two warriors who will fight to the death."

The look in her eyes ripped into his gut. He wanted to take her back into his arms, to reassure her that if he came out of this alive, he'd come for her. But he knew better than to promise anything. "What do I have to say or do to make you understand that if Ryker finds out about you, he'll use you to get to me?" A kaleidoscope of images flashed quickly through

Nate's mind. Ryker's icy blue eye. His triumphant grin. Cyn's lifeless body in Ryker's arms.

"Nate…" She reached out for him.

"I'm sorry, Brown Eyes, sorrier than you'll ever know."

Although she longed to touch him, to reassure him with her embrace, she realized he wanted her to stay at arm's length, that he was fighting the desire to keep her with him.

"You're approaching this problem the wrong way," she said. "Violence can't be the only solution. This man, this Ryker, can't fight you if you're not willing. If what he's seeking is a confrontation, then don't give it to him."

"Dammit, woman, do you think all I've got to do is tell him I don't want to fight? When a man is intent on killing you, you have only one choice, and that's to defend yourself."

"Let the police take care of Ryker. That's their job. Protecting law-abiding citizens from criminals." She clenched her fists at her sides in an effort to keep from touching him.

"The way they protected your husband?" Nate asked, knowing full well that his words would hurt her, but determined to make her realize the naiveté of her thinking. "And what about the boy who killed Evan? There are times when a man has to take care of himself."

A knot of unshed tears lodged in her throat. Her hands jerked. She balled her fingers tightly against her palms, her nails cutting into the soft flesh. "Damn you, Nate Hodges. You know Evan was nothing like you. His situation and yours have nothing in common. He didn't seek out violence, it was thrust upon him."

Didn't she realize, Nate wondered, that despite his brutal past, he wasn't seeking danger; it was seeking him. "Your husband chose to try to help a boy addicted to drugs. He put himself and you in danger by doing that."

"No." She placed her hands over her ears and turned from Nate as tears escaped her eyes, falling in thin, warm streams down her cheeks. As quickly as she had shunned the sight of him, Cyn spun around, her damp eyes glaring. "Evan was the most gentle man I've ever known, the most caring. He always

put the needs of others before his own. He…he was as opposed
to violence as I am. He didn't realize he was in danger, that
he was putting me… Darren Kilbrew brought violence into our
lives. His whole life had been filled with it, just like yours has
been.''

''I didn't spend twenty years as a criminal, killing innocent
people. I was one of the good guys, dammit. I worked for the
government, defending this country. Just like the police, my
job was protecting others, the people of this country.'' He saw
the look of disbelief in her eyes, the lack of understanding.
Could he ever make her realize that countries, as well as in-
dividuals, often had little choice in choosing violence over
peace. ''When danger threatens, when violence is thrust upon
you, then you have to fight in order to survive. Ian Ryker will
give me no choice.''

''I don't think you want one,'' Cyn told him.

''That's not true.''

''Then let me help you.'' She watched him carefully, praying
for some sign of agreement. ''Together we can find a way.
You don't have to meet him on a field of battle. You don't
have to fight a duel to the death.''

''You don't understand,'' Nate said. Cyn, in her innocence,
had no knowledge of a man like Ryker. Despite the fact that
her husband had been brutally murdered, she didn't know anything about professional killers. ''Darren Kilbrew was a kid
half out of his mind on drugs. The drug was as much Evan's
murderer as that boy was. Ian Ryker is different. He kills for
the sheer pleasure of it, and the longer he can make his victim
suffer, the better he likes it.''

''What about Nick Romero?'' Cyn asked. ''He's some sort
of government agent, isn't he? Let him or whatever agency he
works for take care of Ryker.''

''Romero is already involved, but that's not going to solve
my problem. Ryker wants me. I can't let someone else fight
my battle.''

''You don't want to.''

''All right,'' he admitted, ''I don't want someone to fight

for me, to die for me. This is between Ryker and me. I don't want any innocent bystanders getting in the way."

"Is that what I am, an innocent bystander?"

Hell, how did he answer that question? he wondered. Of course she was more than a bystander. She was his woman, and more than anyone else, she was in danger. "Yeah, Brown Eyes, that's exactly what you are."

She tried to see beyond the words, past the cool, unemotional statement, but his expression gave away nothing. He seemed totally unmoved by her tears, her offer of help and her profession of love.

"I have a ten-thirty appointment this morning," she said as she walked past him, not giving in to the impulse to take one final look at him in the hopes that some emotion would show on his face.

By the time she reached the front door, she realized he wasn't following her. And she was glad, she told herself. She had fallen in love with a man incapable of loving her in return. Not once, not even when they had shared the most passionate intimacies, had Nate told her he loved her. She had allowed her own sexual desire and the fantasy spell of an ancient legend to overrule her common sense.

Nate was right. She should get out of his life and stay out. For both their sakes.

Cyn opened the front door. Just as she stepped outside, she heard him coming up behind her. Hesitating momentarily, she waited for him to touch her or to say something to her. He did neither. Turning her head, she caught a glimpse of him in the doorway. Their gazes met for one brief instant before he closed the door.

Cyn jumped out of her van, glanced down at her watch and groaned. She was fifteen minutes late for her brunch date with Ramon Carranza. She hoped the wealthy Cuban was lenient with tardy guests.

Standing on the stone walkway, she scrutinized the Spanish-style mansion. It was exactly what she had expected. A two-story cream stucco house with a red tile roof, arched windows and doors, and a lawn filled with palm trees.

Stepping up, she hesitated briefly as she studied the beautifully carved wooden door. She had to make a good impression. She had to convince this man to help Tomorrow House. Of course, he wasn't her last hope, but he was her best chance. A man with enough money to donate ten thousand dollars a year to a small shelter for runaway teens had enough money to solve her problems, at least temporarily.

Cyn rang the doorbell. Instantly, a young woman opened the door and smiled a friendly greeting.

"Señora Porter?"

"Yes." Cyn walked inside the enormous foyer. If she hadn't been raised in her father's ancestral home in Savannah, she would have been awestruck by the grandeur of Ramon Carranza's home. But Cyn was quite accustomed to fine antiques, impeccable decorating, homes with museum-style quality.

"Please follow me," the maid said in slightly accented English as she led Cyn down the hallway and out onto a back patio.

Spring flowers, in large concrete pots, surrounded the wide expanse of open courtyard just beyond the patio. A glass table had been set with pristine white linen, sparkling china and heavy crystal.

"Please be seated," the maid said. "Señor Carranza received an important telephone call only moments ago. He will join you shortly."

"Thank you." Cyn sat down when the maid went back into the house.

She was grateful to the person who had called Ramon Carranza. Perhaps he wouldn't even be aware that she had arrived late.

The day was beautiful, she decided, looking up at the clear blue sky. Everything was fresh and crisp and caressed with Florida sunshine. The day should be perfect, but it wasn't. Not for her. She was in love with a man who didn't love her, a man totally unsuitable for her.

She remembered the first time she had awakened this morning. Nate had been awake and lying beside her, propped on his elbow while he watched her. He had kissed her, held her, and made slow, sweet love to her. How could a man give of himself to a woman the way Nate had given to her and not love her?

"Señora Porter," a deep, throaty voice said. "I hope you don't mind eating outside. I know it is only the first day of May, but after last night's rain, the world is so clean and fresh and bathed in the sun's warmth."

Cyn glanced up at the tall, elegantly dressed man who had just stepped out onto the patio.

He took her hand, kissing it with Continental flair. "You are even more beautiful than I had imagined."

"Why, thank you, Señor Carranza. I'm flattered." Cyn felt awed at the sight of the elderly gentleman. She wasn't quite sure what she had expected, but it certainly hadn't been this handsome man, so tall, so broad-shouldered, so incredibly suave with his mane of white hair and his thick white mustache. His black eyes sparkled with intelligence and curiosity.

"You must call me Ramon, as all my friends do." He sat, taking the chair opposite her. "And you and I are going to be good friends, *si?*"

"Yes, I hope so." Cyn thought there was something familiar about this man. Perhaps she had seen his picture in the paper.

"I hope you like seafood, Señora Porter." Ramon waved his hand, and as if on cue, a plump, dark-haired woman appeared carrying a huge serving tray.

"I love seafood." Cyn's mouth watered at the sight of the scrumptious shrimp cocktail the woman set before her. "And please call me Cyn."

When he widened his eyes in surprise, an amused look on his face, Cyn laughed, then said, "My name is Cynthia, but all *my* friends call me Cyn."

"What a perfectly delightful nickname."

All through brunch, they discussed a variety of things. Everything from music to wine, but somehow the discussion kept coming back around to the fact that Cyn was living alone in

Sweet Haven with only one close neighbor. It seemed of great interest to Ramon Carranza that Nate Hodges was a man Cyn could count on for protection. She simply didn't understand Señor Carranza's interest in her personal life.

"I came here to ask you for money, and yet we seem to have discussed everything except Tomorrow House." Cyn had enjoyed her meal and the charming old man's company, but there was something in his persistent questions about Nate that bothered her. Something she couldn't quite put her finger on.

"Ah, but it is a foregone conclusion that I will give you the money you need. I will give you a check to cover the expenses of your shelter for the next six months." Ramon sipped his wine, eyeing Cyn over the rim of his crystal glass.

"You will?" Cyn gasped. "But…but how did you know that I needed enough money for six months' expenses?"

With a toss of his hand, indicating that it was nothing for him to know the closest, most-guarded secrets of others, he smiled at Cyn. "I am sure you are aware of the fact that not only am I a very rich man, I am a powerful man with many powerful friends. My friends know many things, and what I want to know, they find out for me."

A cold chill raced along Cyn's spine, reminding her that no matter how charming Ramon Carranza was now at nearly eighty, it was reputed that he had once been a part of the Cuban mafia.

"Why does my shelter interest you so much, Señor Car… Ramon?"

He took another sip of his wine. "May I be perfectly honest with you, Cyn?" His wide smile displayed his sparkling teeth against the background of his white mustache and leathery brown skin.

Uncertain how to reply, she simply nodded as she returned his smile. A tight knot formed in the pit of Cyn's stomach, as niggling little doubts wafted through her mind.

"I could say that it is because I consider myself a philanthropist, but I am not. I could say that I was once a boy without a home who needed a place like Tomorrow House, but it would be a lie.'' His smile widened. ''You have heard rumors about me, have you not?''

How was she supposed to answer a question like that? she wondered. ''People always like to gossip about the wealthy.''

Ramon laughed hardily, the sound deep and husky. ''Such a diplomatic reply. But I would expect no less from a politician's daughter.''

''You know who my father is?''

''Senator Denton Wellington of Georgia.''

''But how—''

''I give to charity, my dear little Cyn, for two reasons. As a tax write-off, first and foremost. And, I am an old man, reared in the Catholic faith. In case there is a hereafter, it would not hurt for me to make some small recompense before I die.'' He looked down into his almost empty wine-glass as if it were a pool reflecting his past.

''Do you know my father?'' She couldn't shake the notion that perhaps Ramon Carranza was generous to Tomorrow House in particular because he was one of her father's acquaintances. But surely her father wasn't foolish enough to accept campaign contributions from a reputed crime boss.

''Do not worry yourself.'' He tilted the glass to his lips and swallowed the last drops of wine, then set the goblet on the table. ''Your father and I have never met. He is not indebted to me in any way.''

Cyn hoped the relief she felt wasn't visible on her face. As debonairly charming as Ramon Carranza was, there was something about the man that disturbed her. There had to be a reason why he'd gathered so much information about her personal life, why he seemed so interested in the fact that she was living alone in Sweet Haven. ''I enjoyed brunch very much, Señor Carranza—'' When he widened his eyes as a reminder, she quickly corrected herself, ''Ramon. I'm very grateful for your offer to help us. I simply can't let the church close down Tomorrow House. You are aware of how much money it will take?''

''The check is already written.'' He reached inside the breast pocket of his coat and pulled out a long white envelope, then handed it to Cyn. "Please make sure it is the correct amount."

With trembling fingers, Cyn opened the envelope and peeped inside. She sucked in her breath. The amount was thousands of dollars over the desperately needed amount. "Señor Car... Ramon, how can I ever thank you?"

When she looked across the table at the elderly Cuban gentleman, she saw that he was watching her intently, the fierceness of his scrutiny frightening. Then suddenly his expression softened, and he smiled again. "There is no need for thanks. My motives are selfish."

Cyn scooted back her chair, dropped her napkin on the table and stood. "Thank you again...for everything. I should be going. There's never enough hours in the day at Tomorrow House."

Ramon stood, regally commanding with the wide breadth of his shoulders and his towering height. He took her hand, kissed it, but did not immediately release it. "I ask a favor, my dear little Cyn. One that should be no problem for you."

Her heart accelerated. She knew she had nothing to fear from this man, and yet he frightened her. She tried to smile. The corners of her mouth turned up slightly. She tried again, opening her mouth for a more friendly appearance. "Certainly, Ramon."

"Your only neighbor...a Señor Hodges I believe you said. Please give him a message from me."

When she tried to pull her hand away, he tightened his hold briefly, then released her. "You want me to give...a message to Nate?" Cyn could feel the heat rising from her chest, covering her throat, suffusing her face.

"Tell this Señor Nate Hodges that he should keep close watch on such a beautiful neighbor. Anything could happen to a lovely woman living all alone. Perhaps I am just an old-fashioned man, but I believe a woman should have a protector."

Cyn laughed, the sound halfway between a cry and giggle. Why was he so interested in her safety? "It's so kind of you to be concerned about me, Ramon, but I can assure you that women today are quite capable of taking care of themselves.''

"Ah, yes. The modern woman." Ramon made a circular motion with his hand, a gesture of acceptance. "But you will pass along my message to your neighbor all the same, will you not?"

"The next time I see him," Cyn said, knowing that she had no intention of seeing Nate Hodges anytime in the near future.

Chapter 10

Mimi met her at the door the minute Cyn entered Tomorrow House. The place was a riot of confusion, with kids lining up in the hallway for lunch, a crew of workmen banging away on the roof, while two dirty, bearded men worked inside to repair the ceiling. From the game room, the noise of a loud advertisement for a foreign car competed with the screeching of a hot new hard-rock group blaring from the radio.

Rushing out of his office, Reverend Bruce Tomlinson, his eyes wide, his forehead dotted with perspiration, came barreling toward Cyn.

"Things are pretty wild around here," Mimi said, placing a motherly arm around Cyn's shoulder, guiding her toward her office and away from Bruce's inevitable approach.

"Noisy, too, huh?" Cyn laughed, allowing Mimi to herd her into her office.

"I gotta talk fast because Brucie's going to be in here any minute. Look, you got a tall, dark, good-looking visitor and Brucie ain't liking it a bit."

"Nate's here?" What was he doing here at Tomorrow

House? After the way they had parted this morning, she'd been certain that he wouldn't seek her out again. After all, he'd made it perfectly clear that he didn't want her in his life.

"Did you know he was coming?" Mimi asked, leaning against the door when she heard Bruce take hold of the doorknob. "Bobby has told Bruce all about the Brazen Hussy, and Bruce thinks our Nate is a bad influence on the kids. You know what a jerk Brucie can be. Besides, I think he's a mite jealous. He's been sweet on you for a long time."

"I set him straight about that over a year ago, Mimi."

"Well, I know you did, but the fact is he's being downright unfriendly to Nate. You won't let Bruce run our man off, will you?"

Cyn dropped her purse and briefcase on top of her desk, then straightened the pleats in her navy skirt. "Move out of the way and let Bruce in before he wears himself out shoving on the door."

Mimi stepped aside and Reverend Tomlinson came bounding into the room, practically falling over his own feet. "You need to see about that door, Cyn," he said. "It's sticking again. I thought I'd never get it open."

"Oh, I think Mimi can take care of the problem," Cyn said, trying not to smile. "Come on in, Bruce. Did you want to see me about something important?"

"That man is here." Bruce puffed out his basset hound jaws, took a monogrammed handkerchief from his coat pocket and wiped the perspiration from his upper lip.

"If you're referring to Mr. Hodges, then I think you should know that he's here as my guest. We have some business to discuss." Cyn removed her white cashmere sweater and hung it on the back of her chair. She had no idea why Nate had come to Tomorrow House, but whatever the reason, it was certainly none of Bruce's business.

"Bobby told me all about the Brazen Hussy, how Mr. Hodges carries a knife, how he single-handedly subdued that boy," Bruce said. "What sort of business could you possibly have to discuss with a man like that?"

"Personal business, you ninny." Mimi stood in the doorway. "I'll be in the lunchroom if you need me," she said to Cyn before leaving.

"That woman's behavior is outrageous!" Bruce stuffed his handkerchief back into his pocket.

"Mimi is the heart of Tomorrow House. The kids love her." It was on the tip of Cyn's tongue to tell him that Mimi's contributions to the shelter far outweighed his. "And my business with Mr. Hodges is none of your concern. Like Mimi said, it's personal."

"I see."

"Look, Bruce, we have something more important to discuss than your misgivings about Mimi and Na—Mr. Hodges." Picking up her purse, Cyn unsnapped the catch, pulled out a white envelope and waved it around in the air. "I have here a check that will more than cover the expense of running Tomorrow House for the next six months. Call Reverend Lockwood and tell him that we have a patron saint."

"My word, Cyn, is this true?" Bruce shuffled nervously like a child trying to postpone a trip to the bathroom.

"Quite true."

"Who?" he asked, then gave Cyn a puzzled look.

"Ramon Carranza." Cyn smiled as she remembered her unusual brunch with the elderly Cuban gentleman.

"The name sounds familiar."

"He's a retired businessman. No family. A charming and generous man." Cyn asked God to forgive her for the little white lie she'd just told Bruce. After all, it was for a good reason and for a good cause. Although she had some misgivings about taking money from a man with Ramon Carranza's reputation, she knew Bruce would absolutely refuse. Where she was able to see life in various shades of gray, Bruce saw it only in black and white. Considering the fact that Tomorrow House would close without Señor Carranza's generosity, Cyn figured that what Bruce didn't know wouldn't hurt any of them.

"I'll call Reverend Lockwood immediately." Bruce turned to go, then stopped short. "Cyn, I don't think Mr. Hodges is the kind of role model the boys need. Bobby seems in awe of the man."

"I thought Bobby might be a little bit afraid of—"

"Well, if he was, he no longer is," Bruce said. "The two of them have been playing pool for the last hour. I still don't wholly approve of you putting that pool table in the game room."

Cyn slumped down on the edge of her desk, crossing her arm over her waist and resting her chin on the knuckles of her other hand. Watching Bruce walk out of her office, she sighed and shook her head. How could two men as different as Evan Porter and Bruce Tomlinson both have been ordained by the same church and placed in the same position as director of Tomorrow House?

After locking Ramon Carranza's check in the small safety box in her desk, Cyn went in search of Nate Hodges. As much as she wanted to see him, she dreaded facing him. Somehow, she knew he hadn't come to profess his undying love for her.

She found him in the game room, standing back and watching Bobby as the boy studied the pool table, contemplating his next shot.

Nate saw her the minute she walked in. Sunshine. That's what he thought of every time he saw her. Pure, clean, bright light. No dark places, no hidden shadows. A woman as honest and good and loving as this old world could create.

He had talked to Romero after Cyn had left this morning, asking if there was any way to get protection for her. Romero had said it was doubtful, but he'd see what he could do. Nate knew that Cynthia Porter's best protection was staying away from him. But just in case it was already too late, just in case Carranza was Ryker's comrade, then Nate had to make sure she was kept safe. He'd placed a call to Sam Dundee right after his conversation with Romero. Dundee was the best bodyguard in the business, and as long as Romero couldn't come up with federal protection, then a hired gun would have to suffice. Of course, he wasn't sure how Cyn would feel about having a bodyguard. That's why he'd come to Tomorrow House—to tell her about his decision to hire Sam Dundee. He just hoped he could persuade her to agree.

"Lunchtime, guys," Cyn said as she walked into the game room.

Bobby laid his pool cue on the table. Smiling, he pointed to Nate. "He's winning, anyway. Man, Cyn, he's good at everything. You should see him playing Nintendo."

"Won't you join us for lunch?" she asked, her eyes filled with questions as she looked at Nate. "Bobby, you go ahead and save us a couple of seats."

"Thanks, I'd like to join you." Nate hung the cue sticks on the wall holder and restacked the fifteen balls.

The lunchroom was crowded and noisy, but the food was hot and delicious. Nate sat beside Cyn, aware that she was doing her level best to avoid any eye contact with him. She had every reason to be angry about this morning. After all, he'd spent hours making love to her and then had sent her packing. He had tried to explain, but she hadn't bought his explanation.

"Did you make your ten-thirty appointment?" Nate asked.

"Yes." Cyn picked up her glass of iced tea and sipped slowly.

"Mimi said you had a brunch date with some millionaire you were hoping would make a large donation to Tomorrow House." Nate cut into the slice of chocolate cake with his fork.

"That's right."

"Did you get the money?"

"As a matter of fact, Señor Carranza gave me a check to cover all the expenses for the next six months." Hearing Nate choke, then cough, she turned quickly to him. He glared at her. "Are you all right?" she asked.

Nate's stomach knotted tightly. He could hear the roar of his heartbeat in his ears. She had lunch with Ramon Carranza? Damnation! How the hell had Carranza gotten to Cyn so quickly?

"How did you meet Ramon Carranza?" Nate asked.

"Do you know Ramon?"

"I've heard of him." Just who the hell was this Carranza? Nate had been turning the question over in his mind for days now and had asked Romero to dig a little deeper into the mysterious Cuban's background. Regardless of what Romero found out, Nate knew one thing for certain. Ramon Carranza meant trouble for him.

"I suppose everyone in Florida knows about his reputation," Cyn admitted, trying not to allow her conscience to bother her about taking money from such a man. Possibly dirty money—even blood money.

"Then if you know about his criminal past, why did you agree to meet with him?"

"He's been contributing ten thousand dollars a year to Tomorrow House for the past several years. He was the logical person to contact when I needed more money." She didn't like the tone of Nate's voice or the accusation she heard in his words. How dare he, of all people, condemn her. "Besides, I found him to be a very charming man."

"Did you indeed?"

"Will you kindly lower your voice. Everyone is staring at us."

"Then let's finish this conversation in private." Dropping the paper napkin he held in his hand, Nate stood up abruptly, grabbing Cyn by the arm and jerking her up beside him.

"Good idea," she said. "I happen to have a few questions I want to ask you."

It took them fifteen minutes to finally get away from the kids, from Bruce's reappearance to tell her that he'd spoken to Reverend Lockwood, and to settle a squabble between the inside and outside repairmen.

The minute the door of Cyn's office closed behind them, Cyn placed her hands on her hips and swirled around to face Nate. "Why are you here?"

"Your questions will have to wait a few minutes. We're not through discussing Ramon Carranza and why the hell you took money from a damned crime boss."

"Reputed crime boss. Señor Carranza has never been convicted of a crime," Cyn said, her breath huffy. "I think we should give him the benefit of the doubt, don't you?"

"No, I don't. Reputed crime boss, my rear end. He was a top dog in Cuba back in the forties and fifties and moved his operations to Miami when Castro took over."

"You seem to know an awful lot about Señor Carranza. Why is that?"

Hell! He'd opened his big mouth and said more than he should have. "Word gets around." Nate reached out, grabbing her shoulders. When she tried to pull away, he tightened his hold. "The point is this—stay away from Carranza. He's bad news."

"I won't have you dictating whom I should and should not see. I don't need a protector despite what you and Ramon Carranza might think." Cyn struggled to free herself from Nate's tenacious grip.

"Be still." His words were low and deep and commanding. "What did you mean when you said that Carranza thinks you need a protector?"

"Will you let go of me?"

"What did Carranza say to you?"

"It was no big deal." Nate was frightening her, more than Ramon had. Was there some connection between the two men? No, please, Lord. No.

"Tell me, anyway."

"I just happened to mention to Señor Carranza that I was staying in Sweet Haven and you were my nearest neighbor."

Nate's curse word stung Cyn's ears.

"What's the matter with you?" Cyn tried to push some bothersome, half-formed doubts out of her mind. Now was not the time to let her imagination run wild. "It was no big deal. Señor Carranza simply asked if you were someone I could count on if I needed help."

Nate squeezed her shoulders so forcefully that she let out a yelp of pain. He released her immediately. "Is that all?"

"Well, he said I should give you a message."

Hot coals filled Nate's stomach, burning through his insides.

Carranza had sent him a message—a warning? And he had used Cyn as his messenger. "What was the message?"

"Aren't you taking this a little too seriously?" Cyn asked, puzzled by Nate's attitude, and yet bothered by the shadowy suspicions she couldn't escape.

"He said to tell you to keep a close eye on me, because anything could happen to a woman living all alone."

Nate turned from her, afraid she would see the fear in his eyes and discern for herself the danger their relationship had put her in. Under his breath, he let out a string of rather crude curses. Carranza was sending him a warning, all right. There was no doubt in Nate's mind that the old Cuban knew Ryker and was working with him.

"You've got to move back to Jacksonville, to your apartment." He wasn't going to tell her that Nick Romero was working on getting her some government protection. It would be hard enough to explain why he wanted to hire a private bodyguard for her. That news alone would probably scare her to death. But what choice did he have, especially since Carranza had issued his warning?

"I don't want to leave Sweet Haven, not yet. Don't you think you're overreacting?"

"You're going back to Jacksonville," Nate said. "And I'm hiring someone to protect you."

"You're what?"

"Ryker could show up in a few days. Maybe even tomorrow. I don't want you anywhere around me when he does show."

"I...I'll go back to Jacksonville tomorrow if that's what you want, but I will not have some...some guy watching my every move."

"Not just some guy. A private bodyguard. Romero recommended him. He used to be a DEA agent."

"No."

"Yes. I've already put a call in. He can be in Sweet Haven today, and he'll help you move your things back to Jacksonville and keep you—"

"I can't leave yet," Cyn said.

"Yes, you can and you will."

"We're having a picnic at the beach this evening. Mimi is already making preparations for the food. Bruce has borrowed a bus from the church. The kids are expecting to spend May Day at my beach house."

Nate slammed his big fist into his open palm. Cyn jumped at the unexpected noise. "If you can't cancel the picnic, then you'll have to leave when it's over and not come back until you hear from me…or Romero."

"I'll go, but I refuse to have a bodyguard."

"We'll see."

"No bodyguard!"

"What do I have to say or do to make you understand that if Ryker finds out about you, he'll use you to get to me."

"Nate…" She reached out for him.

He turned and walked out of her office, not once looking back.

Sitting down in her swivel chair, Cyn huddled over her desk and buried her face in her hands. She cried then, for Nate, for herself and for two ancient lovers. Someone had murdered the Timucuan maiden and her conquistador. A man named Ryker wanted to kill Nate, and if he knew she was Nate's woman, he would kill her, too.

Nate spotted the black Cadillac limousine the minute he stepped out of Tomorrow House and onto the sidewalk. Emilio had parked across the street, almost a block away, but in this neighborhood, a limousine stuck out like a sore thumb. Undoubtedly, the man wasn't trying to hide.

Jaywalking, Nate crossed the street. When he reached the black Caddy, he leaned over and pecked on the side window. Emilio Rivera opened the door and stepped out, his six-foot-eight, three-hundred-pound body towering over a six-foot-two, two-hundred-pound Nate.

"Has your boss got you following me?" Nate asked, slipping on his aviator sunglasses.

"I'm keeping an eye on Señora Porter." Emilio glanced across the street, nodding toward the one-story building that housed Cyn's shelter.

"Tell your boss that I got his message."

"Ryker is in St. Augustine. Señora Porter will soon be in danger."

Nate felt the blood run hot in his veins, fear and anger heating it to the boiling point. "Tell Carranza that I will hold him personally responsible if anything happens to Cyn Porter."

"Such a fierce protector," Emilio said. "Señor Carranza said you would be."

"Carranza can go straight to hell for all I care."

Nate thought he saw the corners of Emilio's mouth turn up slightly as if he were about to smile and caught himself. "*Si*, I will tell him how you feel."

Nate stood on the street watching the black Cadillac until it was out of sight. As soon as he could get to a telephone, he was calling Sam Dundee. Like it or not, Cyn was going to have a bodyguard.

Cyn handed Bruce the plastic bag filled with damp bathing suits, then turned to pick up a basket of leftovers from the late-afternoon picnic.

"I think that's got it," Bruce said. "We'd better be on our way, it's past six now."

"You go on," Mimi Burnside told him. "I'll be there in a minute." The big redhead grabbed Cyn by the arm and pulled her away from the open bus door. "Why are you moving back to your apartment tonight? I didn't think you were a quitter."

Cyn looked away from Mimi, waving at some of the kids who were hanging out open bus windows. Deliberately avoiding direct eye contact, Cyn tried to explain her reasons without revealing too much. "Nate has some personal problems that he has to work out before we can even think about a future together."

"And just why can't you stay here and help him work out

those problems?'' Mimi scowled at Bruce, who stood on the first step of the bus entrance, motioning for her to hurry.

"Nate doesn't want me here," Cyn said.

"Hogwash."

"Thanks for caring so much." Cyn hugged Mimi, as a child might seek comfort from her mother. "I love you, but don't push me on this. Please take my word that I'm not giving up on Nate, I'm just doing what's best for both of us for the time being."

"Well, if you ask me—"

"Mimi." Cyn gave her friend a pleading look.

"You know where to find me, day and night, if you need to talk." Mimi gave Cyn a bear hug, turned around and walked toward the bus. "I'm coming, I'm coming," she said to Bruce, whose round face was lobster-red from the heat and his agitated state of mind.

Cyn stood at the edge of the road, watching the bus until the red taillights disappeared. She let her gaze stray across the road, knowing that Nate was home, waiting—waiting to send her away.

She couldn't bring herself to turn around and go inside. The desire to run to Nate overwhelmed her. Her legs ached with the pressure she exerted to keep them from moving toward his house.

Reminding herself that she still had to pack before her long drive back to her Jacksonville apartment tonight, Cyn began to turn, the effort taking all her willpower. And then she saw him. He stepped out onto his front walkway, stopping abruptly when he glanced in her direction. He threw up his hand and waved. Stunned, she simply gazed back at him, watching while he moved toward her, down the walkway, across the yard and then the road.

She thought he looked as breathtakingly male as a man could look, all six-foot-two inches of hard, lean muscles and bronze flesh. He moved quickly, with the swift, sure stride of a jungle animal. Quiet. Deadly.

When he was within a few feet of her, she could see him

plainly in the bright outdoor lighting she'd turned on for the picnickers. His expensive clothes gave him an air of elegance, but the unbuttoned shirt, worn without a tie, and the short black ponytail proclaimed him a rebel, a man who lived by his own rules.

"Cyn, we need to talk." He took several slow, tentative steps, stopping within arm's reach of her. She seemed wary, almost afraid. The last thing on earth he wanted was for her to be afraid of him.

"You didn't have to come over to remind me to leave. I was just going in to pack. I'm returning to Jacksonville tonight, and I won't come back to the cottage until you tell me it's all right." She turned around, hoping he wouldn't see the tears forming in her eyes.

He reached out and took her by the shoulders, pulling her back up against his chest. Feeling the tremors that racked her body made him curse the fates that had decreed the two of them should meet now when all he could offer her was danger.

"Before you leave, we have to talk." God, she felt so good. Soft, warm and all woman. He wanted nothing more than to lift her into his arms, lower her to the ground and take her quickly, spilling himself into her while listening to her feminine cries.

"I thought we'd already said all there was to say this afternoon." Belligerently, Cyn tried to pull away, but he held fast, tightening his big hands on her shoulders.

"Let's go inside." How was he going to be alone with her long enough to explain everything she needed to know and not succumb to the desire raging within him? The last thing he wanted was to send this woman away.

"This afternoon you said it was dangerous for me to be with you. Has that changed?" Cyn gave in to the longing to lean back against him, to absorb the power and strength of his big, hard body.

Lowering his head, he nuzzled the side of her neck, his lips savoring the taste of her sunshine-fresh hair as he kissed the golden strands. Loosening his tenacious hold, he ran his hands up and down her arms. "No, that hasn't changed." He felt her stiffen, knew she was already withdrawing from him. "I've arranged for a bodyguard, and I don't want any arguments."

She whirled around, her brown eyes wide, her soft lips parted on her indrawn breath. "I don't want… Oh, Nate, is it really necessary?"

"Sam Dundee is waiting for you in Sweet Haven. He's going to follow you home tonight. He'll keep an eye on you until Nick Romero can arrange protection."

"Protection? More than a bodyguard?"

Taking her hands into his large ones, he pulled her toward him. "Government protection. Ryker works for the Marquez family, the leading drug dealers in Florida. Romero and the DEA are involved, at least, unofficially."

"Why must I…why…?"

"Because I can't protect you and keep you away from me at the same time."

"I could stay with you," she said hopefully, gazing up at him with such love in her eyes that he thought he'd die from the pleasure-pain that her fearless devotion gave him.

"No, Brown Eyes. I want you far away when I meet Ryker." He turned her hands palm up, and lavished hungry kisses across her tender flesh. "I want you to promise me to be careful. Allow Sam Dundee to do his job. I'll call when Nick has a man in place so you'll know the change has been made."

"When will I see you again?" she asked, breathless from his nearness. She ached to hold him, to take him into her arms and into her body and find again that hot, sweet, secret place where they had gone together in the moments of total fulfillment.

"Not until it's all over. One way or the other."

"Nate, I don't understand any of this, especially Ramon Carranza's involvement." Before Nate could reply, Cyn gave him a warning look. "Don't try to deny that there's something going on between you and Señor Carranza."

"I'm not sure about Carranza. That's something else I'll

have to deal with once I've eliminated Ryker.'' When he felt her cringe at his choice of words, he regretted his bluntness.

When she tugged on her hands, he released her. "Do I *have* to leave you tonight?" she asked.

No, his heart screamed. *Stay. Stay with me forever,* his soul cried. "Yes," he said.

She slipped her arms beneath his jacket and around his waist, hugging him tightly. She ran her fingers over the smooth leather sheath that held his knife. She willed herself not to tremble, not to be repulsed by the deadly weapon strapped to his body. "I don't want to leave you."

He grabbed her, lifting her off her feet. "Do you think I want you to go?" He took her mouth with all the savage hunger within him, longing to devour her sweetness, desperate to know again the pure pleasure that her loving heart and body could provide.

She accepted his marauding lips, the conquering pillage of his thrusting tongue as she returned, full force, the power and passion with which he took her. The world around her seemed to fade into a haze of swirling darkness, a sea of brown, edged with pale light. This man, his virile energy, his intense masculinity, surrounded her. She could feel him drawing her into his body, consuming her femininity, taking strength from her womanly power.

Nate trembled. Dear God, he had to let her go! No matter how much he wanted her or how badly he needed her, he had to send her away. To keep her safe.

Slowly, reluctantly, he eased her down the hard, muscular length of his body, allowing her softness to slide over every inch of his pulsating manhood. She clung to him, her slender arms draping his neck, her lips parted on a sigh of pure pleasure as their bodies caressed each other's.

"You have to leave," he told her, but his big hands still lingered around her waist.

She didn't say a word, only looked at him, her eyes speaking for her heart, pleading with him. It might be the wrong time and the wrong place, but the feelings were right. Nate had never been so sure of anything in his life. He had never truly needed anyone. He'd made sure of that. He had spent a lifetime protecting himself from the weaknesses that dominated other men's lives. No one had ever broken through the protective shell Nathan Rafael Hodges had constructed around his heart, a barrier of solitude and indifference that kept him safely apart from the emotional attachments to which most men succumbed.

But Cynthia Porter had done what no other woman had ever done. She had put a crack in Nate's defensive armor. She meant more to him than she should. If he allowed his selfish need to overcome his common sense, he would be putting her life in danger. But her life was already in danger, he reminded himself.

He swooped her up into his arms, leaving her breathless and clinging to him with all her might as he carried her inside her cottage. Kicking open the slightly ajar front door, Nate entered the living room. Without hesitation, he lowered her onto the chintz sofa and covered her body with his own.

"I need you," he breathed into her ear, his mouth moist and hot against the side of her neck. "I need this." He ground his hips against hers, crushing her trembling body deeper into the sofa.

"Yes." She would have refused him nothing, so powerful was her desire, so overwhelming her love. Even knowing that he would send her away afterward, she still wanted to give herself to him.

He kissed her, his lips masterful in their seduction. Moving his fingers to the hem of her cotton pullover sweater, he jerked it up and under her arms, revealing her lace-covered breasts. Lowering his head, he took one nipple into his mouth, sucking greedily through the lacy barrier.

"I want you naked," he told her, lifting her up to remove her sweater. Quickly, he unsnapped her bra, removed it and tossed it to the floor.

He buried his face between her breasts, allowing his tongue to paint an erotic trail from one erect nipple to the other. She arched against him, thrusting upward against his throbbing arousal.

"Oh, Nate, I want you so much." Her voice sounded strange to her own ears, distant and haunting.

He grasped the elastic waistband of her slacks, tugging downward until he encountered her bikini briefs. Slipping his fingers inside the top of her panties, he lowered both underwear and slacks down and off.

When she fumbled with the buttons on his shirt, Nate lifted himself off her and removed his jacket, tossing it toward a nearby chair. In his haste to rid himself of his shirt, he popped several buttons.

"I want to feel you against me." Lowering his body back down onto her, he rubbed his broad, smooth chest over her breasts, the action tightening her nipples to diamond-hard points. "Woman...woman...you make me crazy."

"I want you so much, I'm hurting." She reached out, trying to undo his belt and was startled when he pushed her hands away. "Nate?"

"I want you aching even more." He ran his hand between her thighs, delving his fingers through the tight blond curls and between her moist folds. "I want you so wet and hot and throbbing that you'd do anything to have me inside you."

She moaned, squirming beneath the knowledgeable strokes of his fingers as he fondled and petted her sensitive flesh. Beginning at her breasts, Nate aroused her to a fever pitch with the repeated licking and sucking motions of his mouth and tongue as they created a fiery path downward. He eased her legs further apart, his kisses coating the inside of her thighs.

She writhed beneath him, her body responding to his every touch as if it had never known a man. And indeed, Cyn thought, her mind dazzled by torrid sensations, every time with Nate was like the first time. Powerful. Hungry. Lustful.

His mouth covered her intimately. She groaned.

He tortured her, bringing her close to the edge, then retreating, returning to bring her to the edge again.

She grabbed handfuls of his shiny black hair, trying to pull his marauding mouth away. "Please...please..."

Raising his head, he looked at her, satisfied by the wild look in her eyes, the passion-drugged expression on her face. Inch by inch, he edged his body upward until he covered her, then he raised himself on his elbows, lowered his head and took one peaked nipple between his teeth.

Cyn cried out from the pleasure. Her body was so sensitized that a mere touch shot through her with aching intensity. "Now!" she cried out, gripping his buttocks in her hands, clutching the soft fabric of his trousers.

Nate jerked his zipper open, shoved his slacks and briefs down below his hips and rammed into her with shocking force. He felt her buck beneath him, heard her loud moans, and smelled the strong, heady aroma of her womanly scent. He wanted to ask if he was being too rough, but he was too far gone to be capable of speech. The world condensed to include nothing except the two of them—her body, his body, the fast hard thrusts of his manhood, the answering undulating rhythm of her femininity.

Sweat-slick and passion-hot, they mated, with the hard, heavy needs within them ruling their every move until one final lunge propelled them through the timeless ecstasy of fulfillment. She shook with a release so strong she thought she might never recover from the forceful shudders that continued claiming her when his life force emptied into her. His groaning cries of fulfillment echoed in the stillness of the cottage as his body trembled.

Her man, stronger and more powerful than most, lay weak and drained in the arms of the woman who loved him. Loved him enough to die for him. Even enough to kill for him. The thought of loving someone so deeply and completely frightened her. She had known Nate Hodges for such a short period of time, and yet it seemed that she had known him always, that he had been a part of her from the day she'd been born.

With their bodies still joined, Cyn snuggled against him, caressing his back, whispering love words to him. He claimed her mouth for a leisurely kiss. She felt his sex hardening within her as his tongue slipped inside her mouth.

"One more time, Brown Eyes," he said, and began again the ancient dance that bound them together eternally.

Chapter 11

Nate lifted her suitcases into the van, slammed the door and stepped away. He couldn't touch her again. If he did, he'd be lost—he'd never be able to let her go.

"I'll follow you to the gas station," he said. "Sam Dundee is waiting there. He'll be as inconspicuous as possible so you can go on about your life as usual. No one should notice his presence if he's as good as Romero says he is."

The moonlight cast honeyed shadows across her face, and the night breeze stirred the loose tendrils of her long hair. He knew she was close to tears, and if he prolonged their goodbye, she would be crying soon.

"I'll let you know when Romero gets someone to replace Dundee." He took one last long look at Cyn before getting behind the wheel of his Jeep Cherokee, which he'd parked beside her van.

Feeling numb, Cyn started the engine and maneuvered the minivan out of the driveway, and onto the deserted road. Within five minutes, she slowed down in front of the closed gas station. A tall, broad-shouldered man stepped out of a compact car. Cyn pulled the van to a stop, but remembering Nate's instructions, didn't get out. She watched as Nate drove in beside her, jumped out of his Jeep and went over to speak to the man he'd hired to protect her.

She could hardly believe her life had come to this—that she had to live in fear that some madman would use her to get even with Nate. Never once had she sought out violence, but it had come to her, ripping her life apart. Why, dear God, why? Was Nate right? Did you have to face violence when it was thrust upon you and fight for your own salvation? And for the safety of those you loved?

Cyn sat quietly but impatiently until Nate and the other man approached her. When the two neared, she got a close-up look at her bodyguard. He was big and blond, with a hard, weathered-looking face and a muscular body that seemed to be in prime condition.

"This is Dundee," Nate told her, then gave the other man a warning stare. "Make sure nothing happens to her." With that said, Nate got in his Jeep and drove away, not once looking back.

Cyn tried to open the van door, wanting to run after Nate, needing to cry out to him for one final word of goodbye, but Dundee's big body pressed against the door. "It's time to leave for Jacksonville, Ms. Porter."

Clinging to the last shreds of her composure, Cyn nodded her head, silently agreeing. Perhaps it was best not to be allowed a farewell look, a final touch.

As Cyn made the journey from Sweet Haven to her Jacksonville apartment, she remembered the last moments she had shared with Nate. They had made love twice, each time a passionate sharing, an eternal bonding that transcended the merely physical act that brought them both so much pleasure.

After they had showered together and redressed, he had set her down at the kitchen table and told her about Ian Ryker. She knew he hadn't told her everything, that he had spared her all but the necessary facts.

"I knew Ryker in Viet Nam. We hated each other," Nate

had told her. ''Ryker was a mercenary, and it was a known fact that he was supplying drugs to Uncle Sam's boys. Although American by birth, Ryker's loyalties were questionable, and his morals nonexistent.''

Cyn had listened patiently while Nate explained the reasons Ryker held such a deadly grudge against him. ''On an assignment deep into Vietcong-held territory to capture a hamlet chief that we hoped could give us specific information about enemy supplies and movements, Ryker and I met face-to-face.

''Ryker was involved with the village chief's daughter and had sold out to the NVA. During the Vietcong chief's capture, his daughter was accidently killed in the crossfire when she ran to Ryker for protection. I have no idea whose fire actually killed the girl, only that in the split second that it took Ryker to react to his lover's death, I opened fire on him. My SEAL team barely escaped with our lives and our prisoner.''

Cyn realized how difficult it was for Nate to tell her about what had happened so long ago, in a country halfway around the world. In those moments while he shared a painful part of his past with her, Cyn began to understand what had made Nate Hodges the hard and lonely man he was today. And it made her love him all the more.

''For several years after the incident, I thought Ryker was dead, but then he showed up, out of the blue, missing a hand and an eye and warning me that, one day, he'd get even with me.

''I didn't live in fear, but I dreaded the day he'd make good on his threats,'' Nate had told her, while he sat tall and rigid at her kitchen table, his face solemn, his eyes haunted with tormented memories. ''I stayed in the SEALs. Spent twenty years in the navy, and I always kept vigil, waiting for Ryker.''

''Oh, Nate.'' When she had reached across the table and tried to take hold of Nate's hands, he'd pulled away.

''Five years ago, reports came in from South America that Ryker had been imprisoned for smuggling and had been killed in a prison fight. The reports were wrong. He reappeared a few months ago. I knew then that it was only a matter of time.''

Cyn pulled into the parking area of her apartment complex. Leaving her suitcases inside, she locked the van and looked around, searching for Dundee. He parked and got out of his car. Dear God, how could her life have changed so drastically in so short a period of time? Although violence had marred her safe existence when Evan had been brutally murdered, Cyn lived her daily life on a fairly normal, safe routine. Violence had lain on the outskirts of her civilized life.

But Nate Hodges had changed all that. Loving a warrior had thrown her into harm's way. Filled with all of mankind's imperfections, this earth fell far short of paradise, but Cyn wanted this life and the love of the man her heart and soul had been waiting to find. Eternity's perfection could wait. All she had ever wanted was within her grasp. The man of her dreams was here with her in this imperfect world—here, this side of heaven.

Morning sunlight brightened Nate's den, shimmering on the wall-mounted swords and reflecting off the numerous glass cases. Nate snapped the lid on the suede-lined case and placed his prized Gurkha hunting dagger alongside several other cases containing many precious treasures. A loner by choice, Nate was attached to few people and even fewer things. But his extensive knife collection meant a great deal to him.

He would never forget Cyn's reaction to this room filled with the acquisitions of a lifetime. She hated knives as much as Nate loved them. For he did, indeed, love knives. He loved the look and feel of them. And he loved their capabilities. In the right hands, a knife was a tool of endless diversity.

But Cyn's husband had been stabbed to death, and erroneously, she blamed the weapon as well as its user. Damn, how had this happened to him? How had he allowed himself to become involved with a woman as gentle and loving as Cynthia Porter? She offered him her heart and her body, freely, but he knew loving her could cost him dearly. He had found with Cyn something he'd only dreamed about, something he didn't believe existed. She had given his soul the sanctuary it craved. Her pure, sweet goodness had enveloped the cold darkness within him, bringing him warmth. She filled his world with light. But he would have to keep his past from destroying her before he could accept what she offered.

The loud pounding noise aroused Nate from his thoughts. When he opened the front door, Nick Romero rushed inside.

"What the hell are you doing here?" Nate asked. "If you've got a man to cover Cyn, you could have called."

"I'm still working on that." Nick ran his fingers through his curly black hair. "Dammit, man, why did you have to pick now to finally get seriously involved with a woman?"

"What the hell's the matter with you?" Nate knew something was bothering Romero, more than having to twist a few arms and call in some favors to get protection from the agency for Cyn.

"I could use a cup of coffee. I haven't had time for even a taste this morning." Romero didn't look directly at Nate.

"In the kitchen. Come on."

Nate led Romero into his makeshift kitchen, poured him a cup of hot coffee and led him outside to the patio. A sky filled with soft clouds and morning sunshine promised the warmth of an early spring day.

"So, what's up?" Nate asked.

Romero took several hefty swigs from the coffee, then, looking out at the overgrown garden, he said, "John is all right, but there was an explosion aboard one of your cruisers early this morning."

Cold fear chilled Nate's body and coated his mouth with a metallic flavor. "Where's John?"

"He's been with the police all morning, trying to answer questions without telling them the complete truth." Romero took another deep swallow of coffee. "There's nothing left of the boat, and one of your employees, a guy named Wickman, got hit with some of the debris. He was on the pier."

"How is he?"

"Emergency room's already released him."

"I need to see John," Nate said.

"No, you don't." Romero finished the last sips of his coffee, and, clutching the empty cup in one hand, he placed his other hand on Nate's shoulder. "John is taking his wife and son home to Alabama to stay with her family until this thing with Ryker is settled. He wanted me to tell you. He said you'd understand."

"Hell, yes, I understand." Nate shrugged off Romero's hand as he paced up and down the long archway that led from the patio to the wraparound porch. "His first priority is to protect the woman he loves and their child."

"Ryker is in St. Augustine," Romero said. "The bomb explosion was just his way of announcing his arrival. We both know that."

"Looks like my time has just about run out."

Cyn flipped through the television channels, hoping to find something interesting enough to grab her attention. Alone and restless after a full day's work at Tomorrow House, she longed to forget that a hired bodyguard stood watch outside her apartment, that miles away Nate might be engaged in battle with his enemy, that she was powerless to change the inevitable.

"National Geographic" was on the educational channel, and under normal circumstances, the program would have piqued her curiosity about the subject, but tonight she didn't care about the plight of any species. All she could think about was Nate, alone and in danger.

Rational thought told her that he was better off without her, that her presence would have harmed him far more than it would have helped him. But her irrational heart told her that he needed her, that a woman should stand by her man and face the enemy with him. She was beginning to understand that there were times in one's life when turning the other cheek meant certain death. *When violence is thrust upon you...*

She flipped off the television, dropping the remote control on the plaid colonial sofa. Well, what was she going to do? She had already eaten a late dinner, cleaned the kitchen, done a load of laundry and taken a bubble bath. She had tried reading, doing a crossword puzzle and watching TV. Nothing worked. Nothing had taken her mind off Nate. They had been apart less than twenty-four hours, and already she was miserable without him. If only he were safe. If only this nightmare would end. If only he would come to her and stay with her forever.

Cyn went into her compact kitchen and opened the refrigerator. Resisting the urge to devour a quart of chocolate ice cream, she reached for the diet cola and poured herself a tall glass.

Maybe she could play solitaire until she got sleepy. Where had she put that deck of playing cards? she wondered. Remembering that she and Mimi had played poker several months ago right here at the kitchen table, Cyn figured she had put the cards in one of the nearby cabinets. Before she had a chance to search for the missing deck, the telephone rang.

She removed the receiver from the wall phone. "Hello."

"Cynthia Porter." The voice on the other end was distinctly male, deeply baritone.

"Yes." She felt an irrational uncertainty creep through her like a slowly spreading plague.

"You have made a fatal mistake," he said, enunciating each word with precise deliberation.

"Who is this?" She knew, dammit, she knew. If he had found her, he had found Nate.

"You signed your own death warrant when you became the Conquistador's woman."

"What?" Cyn cried out. The dial tone sang in her ear.

She dropped the phone. It hit the floor with a resounding clatter. Stepping back, she stared at the dangling cord, her mind reeling with panic. Taking several deep breaths, Cyn hunched over and covered her face with her hands. Stay calm, she told herself. Think. Think.

Reaching down, she picked up the telephone and dialed Nate's number. The phone rang and rang and rang. Where are you? *Answer, please answer. I need you.*

"Hello," Nate said.

"Oh, thank God, Nate."

"Cyn, what's wrong?"

"Please, tell me that you're all right." She leaned against the wall, clutching the phone tightly in both hands.

"I'm fine. Do you hear me? I'm all right. Tell me what's wrong. What happened?"

"He…he called."

"Who called?"

"Ryker."

"Did he tell you who he was?" Nate asked.

Pressing her hand into her mouth, Cyn bit down on her fist trying to curb the flow of tears.

"Cyn!" Nate's voice was loud and insistent.

"He said…he said that I had signed my own death warrant…when…when I became the Conquistador's woman."

"Listen to me very carefully," Nate told her. "Go outside and get Dundee. Tell him that I said for him to stay inside with you until I get there."

"But Nate—"

"Do what I told you. I'll be there as quick as I can."

"Nate, why did he call me?"

"Because he's playing a game," Nate told her. "It's called 'Let's make Nate sweat.' He wants me to know that he's aware that you're important to me, that he knows where you live and how to get to you."

After she'd spoken to Nate, Cyn calmed down considerably and fixed a fresh pot of coffee for Dundee and her. They were both on their third cup when the doorbell rang.

Dundee pulled a Magnum from his shoulder holster and stood to the side of the door, his big hand hovering over the doorknob.

"Ask who it is," he instructed her in a whisper.

"Who is it?" she asked, her voice so tight and highly pitched she barely recognized it as her own.

"Nate. Open the damned door!"

Releasing the safety latch, she opened the door and flung herself into Nate's waiting arms. He lifted her off the floor in his protective embrace. God, he hated himself for allowing this

woman to become so important to him. Until she had come
into his life, he'd never had a weakness, and now he had a
major one, just at a time when he needed to be strong and
invulnerable.

Half walking her, half carrying her, Nate guided Cyn to the
sofa. Dundee closed the door behind them.

Cyn ran her fingers over Nate's face, stroking his flesh, cher-
ishing the sight of him, alive and safe in her arms. "I was so
afraid that he'd found you...that—"

Nate covered her moving lips with his index finger, momentarily silencing her babbling. He looked over her head where
it rested on his chest and saw that Dundee held a Magnum in
his right hand.

"Go check around outside. Scout out the area," Nate said.
"I'm going to take her to a friend's house, and I want to make
sure we aren't followed."

"Sure thing," Dundee said. "I'm glad you're here. I
couldn't convince her that you were all right."

The moment Dundee left, Nate took Cyn's face in his hands,
stared at her tear-filled eyes, then released her. Why her? he
asked himself, and why now? The last thing he needed was to
have to worry about her safety when his own life was on the
line. Ryker must be laughing his fool head off, Nate thought.
The minute Carranza told Ryker about Cyn, he probably realized that using her to destroy Nate would be the sweetest form
of revenge. After all, he blamed Nate for his lover's death.

"Call Mimi and tell her that you'll be spending the night,"
Nate said. "Then go pack a bag."

"Mimi's? You want me to stay with Mimi?" Cyn's gaze
questioned him. "I don't understand. I don't understand any
of this."

"Ryker knows where you live."

"But how—"

"How doesn't matter." If he told her about Carranza, she'd
think it was her fault and start feeling guilty. But she wasn't
guilty of anything except loving a man like him—a man who
had no right to let his emotions overrule his common sense.

"Dundee will stay with you at Mimi's until I talk to Romero and get a government man to protect you."

"No, please, Nate." She grabbed hold of his jacket lapels, tugging fiercely. "Don't leave me. Don't send me to Mimi's. Let me go home with you. You can protect me."

He held her face tightly, probing the depth of conviction that showed plainly in her rich brown eyes. He released her face and pulled away from her. "I can't protect you and fight Ryker at the same time. Try to understand that you're safer without me."

"Are you safer without me?" she asked.

He stood up, rammed his hands into his jeans pockets and strode across the room. "Yes."

She turned to face him, nodding her head in a gesture of understanding. "Why...why did he call you the Conquistador?"

Nate's face visibly paled. No one had used that damnable nickname in years. Hell, how had a label given to him by a friend turned into a curse? "It was my nickname. I acquired it in SEAL training at Coronado."

"Why—"

"Nick Romero dubbed me. Everybody called him Romeo because he was such a ladies' man. While we were in training I acquired a reputation. Because of my Hispanic looks and...undisputed abilities as a commando, Nick started calling me the Conquistador. The name stuck. In Nam, and for years after the war."

"I see."

"No, lady, you don't see." His voice was filled with all the pent-up rage he felt.

Nate cared for Cyn, more than he'd ever cared for another human being, but he hated himself for caring so damned much. He had allowed her to become far too important to him. He had put her life in danger by loving her. "You don't see a damned thing but some fairy tale legend about a couple of ancient lovers. Of all the men on earth, why did you pick me, huh? Why me?"

She gasped, new tears flooding her eyes as she huddled into a ball and hugged her legs up against her chest.

More than anything, Nate wanted to drop to his knees beside the sofa and put his arm around her trembling shoulders. But that sort of stupidity would solve nothing. This woman was one of his biggest problems. He had to get her out of his life—for both their sakes.

"You've made me weak." he stood with his back to her, fear and anger combining to strengthen the warrior within him. "I've never had a weakness before in my life, and it's the last thing I need right now. You are the last thing I need." When he heard her choked sobs, the anger inside him grew, building until he wanted to rage at the world, to appease that anger on Ryker. But Ryker wasn't here.

He turned on her then, facing her, afraid for her. "Ryker's going to try to use you against me. He's already using you. He knew when he called you that the first thing you'd do was get in touch with me, tell me what he said. It was his way of turning the screws, of prolonging my agony. He knows that, if you're with me, all I'll be able to think about is protecting you. I won't be thinking like a warrior, but like a lover. That kind of thinking could get us both killed."

"Are you saying that…that…"

"I don't want you with me. You're trouble, lady, more trouble than I can handle."

"Nate, please…" She reached out for him again, and felt as if he'd physically shoved her away when she saw the rejection in his eyes, the withdrawal in his stance. She was losing him, and she couldn't bear the loss. "If you loved me—"

"I don't!"

The pain was unbearable and yet she bore it. The tears that had only moments ago run so freely from her eyes lodged inside her, building the ache that threatened to choke the life from her. Nate had never told her that he loved her, but he had never said that he didn't. Until now. Did he honestly think that there was nothing more between them than the physical desire neither of them could deny?

"Call Mimi. I'll explain things once we get there." He could feel her pain, and it was almost his undoing. But he would not allow himself to comfort her. More than love and comfort, Cyn needed his strength. Only his strength could protect her.

"Should we…involve Mimi?" Cyn asked. "Won't my going there put her in danger?" An icy numbness had taken control of Cyn's emotions. She felt nothing, absolutely nothing. The pain of Nate's harsh rejection had spread through her so quickly that it had anesthetized her feelings.

"Dundee will make sure we aren't being followed. He'll stay with you and Mimi until an agent arrives." Hesitating for a brief moment, Nate looked at her. He hated himself for hurting her, but he hated himself even more for putting her life in danger. "Call Mimi. Change clothes. Pack a bag."

"Where will you go after you take me to Mimi's? Back to Sweet Haven?"

"No. I've already called Romero. I'll be meeting him."

Cyn walked on unsteady legs toward her bedroom. Pausing momentarily in the doorway, she turned slightly. "You're going after Ryker, aren't you? You're not going to wait for him to come to you."

"He's already come to me," Nate said, his voice deadly soft. "He knew exactly what he was doing when he called you. By threatening my woman, he issued me an invitation, one he knows I won't refuse."

The blessed numbness inside her began to dissolve, leaving her with the tiniest emotional sensation. He had called her his woman. "Is that what I am?" she asked. "Your woman?"

"The Conquistador's woman. That's what Ryker thinks you are," Nate said, and saw the spark of hope die in her eyes.

Chapter 12

Nate decided that Mimi Burnside was not only a sensible woman, but a human being with a heart of pure gold. He had liked the older woman the minute they met, but seeing her motherly concern for Cyn made him like her all the more.

"Don't worry about a thing," Mimi said as Nate laid Cyn's suitcase at the foot of her bed. "I'll call Brucie in the morning and tell him that I've come down with the flu or something and that Cyn is going to be playing nursemaid so neither one of us will be in to work."

Nate couldn't help but smile as he watched the big redhead, her graying hair rolled on soft pink curlers and her five-foot-ten-inch body wrapped in a blue chenille robe. Large-boned and buxom, Mimi Burnside looked more like an aging burlesque queen than a former factory worker turned housekeeper.

"You go ahead and put on your gown, honey child," Mimi told Cyn, then turned to Nate. "You come out in the living room with me while she changes."

Nate obeyed, following Mimi. Once outside the closed bedroom door, she leaned over and whispered, "I've got a gun. A

.25 automatic. I don't usually keep it loaded, but I've got the bullets for it.''

"Do you know how to use it?" he asked, not in the least surprised that she had a gun.

"Yeah. My first husband taught me how. Good thing, too, since I had to run off that no-good bum I married the second time. He tried to use me for a punching bag one time too many." Mimi pointed to the sofa covered with a bright flowered slipcover. "Sit."

"Are you sure you were never in the service? You sound a lot like my old boot camp drill instructor." Nate sat down, relaxing just a bit, certain that he had brought Cyn to the right place.

Mimi laughed, the sound hearty and unrestrained. "That Dundee fellow a friend of yours?" She nodded toward the front door.

"He works for me."

"A hired gun?"

"Something like that."

"When should I expect that government man?" Mimi asked.

"Possibly by morning. When I leave here, I'm meeting Nick Romero."

"You two going a-huntin'?" Mimi widened her slanted cat eyes.

"You just take care of Cyn and don't worry about me."

"We'll both worry about you," Cyn said as she opened the bedroom door.

Nate looked up. His heartbeat accelerated. She looked so small and fragile standing there in her aqua satin robe, her hair hanging loosely to her waist.

When she neared the sofa, he stood. He wanted to reassure her that everything would be all right. But he couldn't lie to her, and if he took her in his arms, he might never be able to let her go.

"This will all be over soon," he said. "Whatever happens—"

Her tormented cry ripped at his heart like the talons of a mighty bird. "Don't say that."

"Cynthia Porter has always been a strong woman, someone people could depend on. Be strong now." Silently he added, *"Be strong for me, Brown Eyes. I need your strength."*

"Go and do what you have to do." Silently she added, *"I'll be waiting for you…forever."*

Hastily, before his courage deserted him, Nate left. Mimi came up beside Cyn and placed a comforting arm around her shoulder. As Nate walked out into the hallway, Cyn noticed Dundee step out of the shadows. He came inside and closed the door.

"You ladies go on to bed whenever you like. I'll just sack out here on the couch."

Mimi squeezed Cyn's shoulder. "Come on, honey child."

"I don't think I can sleep," Cyn said, leaning her head against her friend's arm. "How can I rest not knowing what's happening with Nate, wondering if he's killing or being killed?"

Mimi led Cyn into her small bedroom. The light from an imitation Tiffany lamp spread a colorful glow over the unmade bed. "If you can't sleep, then we'll just have us a slumber party. We'll sit up the rest of the night and talk."

"It's not fair to involve you in this." Cyn turned to Mimi and was reassured by the smile on her face. "Nate seems to think we'll be safe with Dundee keeping guard over us."

Mimi gave Cyn a persuasive nudge, suggesting she sit. Cyn slumped down on the side of the bed. Mimi went around to the other side, got in, and propped several pillows behind her as she sat up against the headboard. "Nate knew what he was doing bringing you here. The only way that Ryker fellow could get to you would be through me."

Burying her hands in her face, Cyn cried silent, painful sobs. Mimi reached out and touched Cyn's back. "Go ahead and cry it all out. Better do it here with me than to let Nate see you like this. He's already worried enough about you."

After cleansing her heart with a torrent of uncontrolled cry-

ing, Cyn wiped her eyes with her hands, scooted up in the bed
to sit beside Mimi, and pulled a blanket up over her legs. "I
thought that losing Evan was the worst thing that could ever
happen to me, but I was wrong."

"You're not going to lose Nathan Hodges," Mimi said.

Cyn tried to smile at the firm conviction she heard in her
friend's voice. She wanted to believe. "I never knew you could
love someone the way I love Nate. It's…it's as if I've always
loved him."

"Since you were fifteen and dreamed about him for the first
time?" Mimi asked.

"It *was* Nate in my dreams. The same eyes. The same body.
The same strength." Cyn fumbled with the frayed edge of the
blanket with which she'd covered herself. "But the man in my
dreams was more than just Nate. He was…oh, Mimi, you'll
think I'm crazy if I tell you."

"So, tell me anyway. I'm probably crazy enough to believe
you."

"Do you know what Nate's nickname in the service was?"

"Does this have something to do with your dreams?"

"Yes." Cyn cleared her throat. "They called him the Conquistador."

Mimi sucked in her breath. "Who…but that's just a coin-
cidence, honey child."

"Maybe. Maybe not."

"You think the man in your dreams was the ancient warrior
whose soul is supposed to roam the beach at Sweet Haven with
his Indian bride?"

"Part the ancient warrior and part Nate, the modern warrior
who will set the lovers free to enter paradise."

"Well, I'm not sure I actually believe it." Mimi's nervous
smile could not disguise her doubts.

"I'm not sure I do, either, but…every time Nate touches
me, it's as if he's touched me a hundred times before. I've
known him for such a short time, and yet I feel as if I've known
him forever."

"I think you're tired and stressed out. In the last few weeks, your whole world has been turned upside down. If your belief that you and Nate are the lovers in the prophecy who will set a couple of ancient souls free helps you get through this ordeal, then who am I to think you're crazy?''

"He told me he didn't love me," Cyn said.

"When?"

"Tonight."

"Did you believe him?"

"I did when he told me," Cyn admitted.

"And do you still believe him?"

"No."

Cyn laid her head down on a large, soft pillow. Closing her eyes, she prayed for a few hours of sleep. Dreamless sleep.

Nate didn't spot Nick Romero's car when he pulled into the all-night diner's parking lot. No doubt Romero had used a government vehicle. Something a lot less conspicuous than the sporty 1968 silver Jag he drove.

When Nate entered the diner, the big plastic clock above the counter reminded him that it was after midnight. The aroma of strong coffee mingled with the fading smells of numerous meals and the ever-present odor of grease. The place was spotlessly clean, but the equipment and furniture had seen better days.

Nate glanced around the partially deserted eatery. A couple of guys sat at the counter drinking coffee, a middle-aged couple sat cuddled lovingly in a back booth, and an elderly man sat alone up front, reading a newspaper. Nick Romero sat in the second booth from the front door, and he wasn't alone. He was talking to a very attractive brunette.

Damn Romero, Nate thought. What the hell was he doing flirting with some dame? Nate knew that Romero liked women, and had spent over forty years living up to his nickname, but now wasn't the time for him to make a new conquest.

Nate approached the table, determined to control the urge to jerk Romero up by his collar and to send the brunette packing.

Romero looked up at Nate and smiled. "Sit down, old buddy, and let me introduce you to the lady."

Nate sat down on the opposite side of the booth and gave Romero a deadly look. "I haven't got time to meet any of your *friends*. This is business. Remember?"

Romero's smile widened. "Don't get bent out of shape. This lady is an agent. Donna Webb is going to be keeping an eye on Cyn until you finish things with Ryker."

Nate took a closer look at the woman sitting beside Romero. She appeared to be in her early thirties. Dressed in jeans, turtleneck pullover and a baggy plaid jacket, she could have passed for the average woman on the street.

Nate offered his hand. Donna took it. "I left Cyn at Mimi Burnside's. Dundee is with them."

"What did you think of Dundee?" Romero asked.

"I think he's capable," Nate said.

"Yeah, he's capable." Shaking his head, Romero laughed. "Sam Dundee was one of the meanest, toughest agents I ever worked with. He always reminded me a little bit of you."

"Then I'm glad he was available on such short notice," Nate said, then turned his attention to Donna Webb. "Cyn will probably feel more comfortable with a female agent. She hates the idea of having a bodyguard. I haven't told her yet that we're planning on sending her to her father's home in Savannah."

"You realize we can't force her to leave Jacksonville if she isn't willing to go," Donna said.

"She'll be willing to go," Nate said. "I can promise you that."

Nate spent the next thirty minutes drinking coffee, discussing the situation and making plans with Romero and Agent Webb. By the time the three of them left the diner, Nate felt reassured that Donna was as capable of protecting Cyn as any male agent.

Outside, the cool night air swirled around them. Overhead storm clouds obscured the pale moon and blackened the normally starry sky. Streetlights illuminated the parking lot, as did the huge neon Open 24 Hours sign flashing with bright, colorful light.

"Do you want to go with me to drop Donna off at Mrs. Burnside's?" Romero asked.

Nate shook his head. "No. I've already said my goodbyes."

"Okay. I'll meet you at your place in a couple of hours and we'll start tracking Ryker. If he can find you, then we should be able to find him."

Donna put her hand on Nate's arm. "Don't worry about Ms. Porter. I promise to take good care of her."

"Yeah, I know you will." Nate forced a fake smile, feeling nothing but loneliness and dread.

Romero and Donna headed straight for the brown sedan parked on the left side of the diner. Nate walked in the opposite direction toward his Jeep.

A speeding car flew down the street in front of the diner. No other traffic stirred at such a late hour. At first Nate heard the roar of the motor, then, out of the corner of his eye, he saw the vehicle swerve off the road, as if the driver had lost control.

Adrenaline pumped through his body like floodwater through a broken dam. Turning quickly, he caught a glimpse of a metal object sticking out of the car window, something held by the man sitting on the passenger's side. The moment his mind registered the object as a gun, Nate yelled out a warning as he dropped to the sidewalk, seeking cover behind the Camaro parked beside his Jeep.

The earsplitting sound of an Uzi firing repeatedly echoed in Nate's ears. Hunched on his bent knees, Nate made his way down the front of the Camaro as the Uzi's lethal clatter rang out a deadly toll. He saw Donna go down, her slender body crumpling, her arms flying about in midair as the force of the Uzi's bullets ripped through her. Then the attacker turned his attention to Romero, who had just pulled his automatic from his shoulder holster. His hand was in mid-aim, his gun pointed, when he took his first hit.

Nate opened his mouth on a silent scream of protest. Then suddenly, he felt a sharp pain lance his side.

As quickly as the car appeared, it disappeared. The silence

following the ungodly round of shots was morbid in its intensity.

Dammit all, he had never figured Ryker would try a sneak attack. He'd been so sure that he would want a face-to-face confrontation.

Running his fingers inside his jacket and alongside his rib cage, Nate felt the wet stickiness of his own blood. He knew he'd been hit.

As he struggled to stand, he noticed all the diner's customers coming to the door. But not one of them ventured outside. Nate saw that neither Donna nor Romero was moving. Blood covered both bodies. Nearby vehicles were dotted with splashes of red. Puddles of crimson formed on the sidewalk.

Nate checked Donna first. She was the closest to him. One of the bullets had taken off a chunk of her neck. She was dead.

Romero groaned when Nate leaned over him. "It's my leg," he said. "I'm bleeding like a stuck hog. I think he got the artery."

No matter how many times Nate had seen a comrade's body riddled with bullets or shattered by an explosion, the sight still sickened him. With trained instincts, Nate inspected the large hole in Romero's leg, then administered the correct amount of pressure to stop the flow of blood from the femoral artery which the Uzi's bullet had severed.

Turning his head toward the array of onlookers hiding inside the diner, Nate yelled, "Call an ambulance!"

The elderly man who had been quietly reading his newspaper stepped outside. "I done called 'em. Told 'em it was a shooting and to hurry." He hesitated in the open doorway. "Is she dead?"

"Yeah," Nate said. "She's dead."

"How about him?" the man asked, nodding toward Romero.

Nate looked down at his friend. "He's alive, and by God, he's going to stay that way."

* * *

By the time Dundee answered the insistent ringing of the doorbell, Mimi and Cyn were standing in the living room, belting their robes and yawning.

Cyn's heart beat overtime. She had never known such fear. Not knowing whether a killer or the bearer of bad news stood outside Mimi's apartment triggered a surge of adrenaline within Cyn's trembling body.

Holding his Magnum, Dundee motioned for Mimi and Cyn to step back inside the bedroom. With one quick move, he swung open the door and aimed his automatic.

"Put your gun away, *amigo,*" Emilio Rivera said.

"Who the hell are you?" Dundee asked.

Peering out into the living room, Cyn gasped when she saw Ramon Carranza's huge bodyguard. Mimi gave her a shove and they both took several tentative steps, stopping abruptly when Emilio glanced their way.

"What's wrong?" Cyn asked.

"Señora Porter." Emilio's dark eyes rested on her briefly, then looked over at Mimi. "Señora Burnside, you will help her dress. Please. Señor Carranza is waiting outside in the limousine."

Cyn moved forward, hesitating several feet away from Emilio. "What's happened? Why does Señor Carranza want to see me?" She grabbed the back of the sofa, clutching the flowery material in her hands.

"Señor Carranza will explain everything. But you must hurry, *señora,*" Emilio said.

"Now see here, one cotton-pickin' minute." Mimi put her hands on her ample hips, giving Emilio a warning glare. "You ain't taking this girl nowhere unless we get the word from Nate Hodges. Ain't that right, Dundee?"

"I'm afraid I must insist," Emilio said. "You can trust us, Señora Porter."

"Now that's where you're wrong, pal." Dundee, his automatic still pointed at Emilio, moved toward their uninvited visitor. "We know we can't trust you."

"*Señora,* surely after all Señor Carranza has done to help you, to finance your shelter, you can trust him." Emilio took a step toward Cyn.

Dundee moved quickly, placing his big body between Emilio and Cyn. "You go back downstairs and tell your boss that Ms. Porter isn't going anywhere with him."

"But he only wishes to take you to the hospital to see Nathan Hodges," Emilio said.

"What?" Cyn cried out. "What's happened to Nate?"

"Don't listen to him," Mimi said, grabbing Cyn by the arm. "It's some kind of trap."

Jerking out of Mimi's grasp, Cyn rushed toward the bedroom. Mimi caught her just as she swung open the door. "Don't be a fool, gal!"

Dundee edged closer to Emilio, who hadn't budged an inch. "What happened to Hodges?"

"He was shot in an ambush coming out of some seedy diner," Emilio said.

Cyn cried out. She clutched Mimi, feeling as if her own two legs weren't sturdy enough to hold her weight. If Nate was hurt, she had to go to him. Nothing and no one was going to keep her away from him. Not Ramon Carranza or Emilio Rivera. Not even Dundee. "I've got to go to the hospital."

"And so you will, honey child," Mimi assured her. "Mr. Dundee here will take you, won't you?"

Dundee never took his eyes off Emilio, but he nodded agreement as he stepped closer to his opponent. "You can go tell your boss that Ms. Porter doesn't need a ride to the hospital."

Emilio, as if reconciled to the fact that Cyn was not going to leave with him, turned toward the outside door. "I will relay your message."

"One more thing," Dundee said as Emilio opened the door. "Tell your boss that Ms. Porter won't be out of my sight for a minute. My job is to take care of her, and I always do my job, no matter what."

The minute the front door slammed shut, Cyn slumped into Mimi's arms. "What if...if Nate's dead."

"Honey child, we don't—"

"While you're getting dressed, I'll make a few phone calls," Sam Dundee said. "If I don't get some answers, we'll go straight to the hospital."

Pulling out of Mimi's comforting arms, Cyn rushed into the bedroom and began changing clothes. Mimi followed, closing the door behind her.

"Carranza was crazy if he thought you'd just go with him, and even crazier if he thought Dundee would let you go." Mimi flung open her closet, and, standing on tiptoe, reached up to the top shelf. Turning around, she held out a small hand-gun and a loaded clip. "I'll go with you if you insist on going, and I'll take along my little baby here."

Cyn stuffed her red blouse down into her navy slacks, pulled up the zipper and grabbed a sweater from out of her open suitcase lying on the bed. The minute Mimi laid the gun on the bed and began removing her housecoat, Cyn stared at the automatic. She had never held a gun. She hated them as much as she did knives. She despised any type of weapon.

"You aren't going with us, Mimi," Cyn said. "This isn't your problem."

When Mimi started to protest, Cyn held up a restraining hand. "I will not put your life in any more danger, but it seems I can't escape. I'm beginning to understand what Nate meant about having violence thrust upon you."

Cyn stared down at the gun lying on Mimi's bed. What if the only way to protect her life was to use that gun? What if the time came when Nate's life depended on her being able to defend him? Cyn, her hands wet with perspiration and trembling with uncertainty, picked up the automatic, inserted the clip and reached for her purse.

"I'll borrow this," Cyn said, placing the gun inside her leather bag.

"Be careful," Mimi said. "Let Dundee do his job. And call me when you find out something about Nate."

Several loud raps on the bedroom door interrupted any further conversation. "Are you ready, Ms. Porter?" Dundee asked. "I haven't been able to find out much over the phone. Hodges and Romero have both been admitted to the hospital."

Giving Mimi a quick hug and kiss, Cyn opened the door. She left the apartment with Dundee, pausing briefly in the hallway to wave a final farewell to Mimi.

As they walked down a flight of steps, Cyn asked her bodyguard. "Was Nate shot?"

"Gunned down."

"Oh, my God!"

"He and Romero and a female agent were riddled by an Uzi when they came out of a local diner about one-thirty this morning."

Cyn forced herself not to cry, not to faint. Walking briskly to keep up with Dundee, who held her securely by one arm, she followed him outside and into his car.

Cyn's worst fears had come true. Nate had been so sure that Ryker would confront him man-to-man. "Are they alive?"

"The woman is dead. My sources couldn't tell me anything about Romero or Hodges except that they were both still alive when the ambulance brought them in to the hospital."

Cyn leaned her head back against the seat. The thought of Nate hurt, maybe even dying, was almost more than she could bear.

The trip to the hospital seemed endless as the streets began to blur. The lights and the darkness merged. Cyn prayed. She couldn't lose Nate. If he died, they would be as doomed to an eternity without fulfillment as the ancient lovers were. If Nate died, she didn't want to live.

Chapter 13

Nate leaned against the wall just inside the first emergency room cubicle. He felt like hell. His side hurt despite the pain-killer the nurse had shot into his hip, over his stringent protests. And he had a headache the size of Texas. He picked up his jacket, belt and sheath off the nearby chair, placing the belt and sheath over his arm and covering them with his jacket. He ran his fingers over his bandaged side, grimacing from the pain that bending his arm caused. Looking down at his opened shirt, he thought about trying to button it, then decided it wouldn't be worth the effort.

J. P. Higdon, Nick Romero's boss, had just left. He had assured Nate that everything possible was being done to save Romero's life and that the agency was handling the situation with the local authorities.

For the last two hours, on the ride to the hospital and while the emergency room staff treated his gunshot wound, Nate had relived those few fatal moments outside the all-night diner. Had they been careless? How had Ryker known where they were meeting? Had Carranza had him under surveillance? Or maybe one of Ryker's associates in the Marquez syndicate? Nate felt guilty. He shouldn't have been so certain that Ryker wouldn't resort to an ambush. What hurt the most was knowing that he himself hadn't really been the gunman's target. Romero and Webb had been the intended victims. Webb was dead and Romero was hanging on by sheer willpower.

Ryker had issued a warning. Nate knew that, one by one, Ryker was going to attack the people closest to Nate. First John Mason. Now Nick Romero. There was only one person left... the most important person. And Ryker would try to kill her. Nate knew that as surely as he knew her death would destroy him.

Nate's big body shook, not from shock or pain, but from fear. Closing his eyes tightly, he sought to block out the fear, but instead the visions that flashed through his mind only heightened the terror. Dreams. The dreams of his brown-eyed lover that had once given him so much comfort. Dreams of Cyn lying dead in Ryker's arms.

Nate's eyes flashed open. He saw her. Her long golden hair hung in disarray over her shoulders, across her breasts, a vivid contrast to her bright red blouse. Her gaze moved in every direction, and he knew she was searching for him. God, it was good to see her. Not until this very minute had he realized how much he needed her.

She looked down the hallway. She stared at him, their eyes speaking a language only their hearts could understand.

She cried out and ran toward him. Dundee followed, rushing to keep up with her.

All the pain and fear and love that she felt came to the surface, full force, the moment she saw him. He was alive. Willing herself not to fling her arms around him proved to be the most difficult thing she'd ever done. She stopped, only inches separating them. With trembling fingers, she reached out and touched his face.

"Nate. Oh, Nate." Her voice was a fragile whimper.

She glanced down at his bandaged left side, wondering how serious his wound was and why he wasn't lying in bed instead of standing, partially dressed, just inside an empty cubicle. When he spread his right arm in a come-to-me gesture, Cyn lunged into his uninjured side. He pulled her up close against him, encompassing her within his strong embrace.

She eased one hand up and across his broad back and laid the other on his bare chest. Closing her eyes, she allowed her hands to explore the solid reality of his body. Tears fell in never-ending rivulets down her flushed cheeks, but she didn't care if her weeping was a sign of weakness. She had been strong all the way to the hospital, and she would be strong again in a few minutes, but right now she wanted nothing more than to rejoice in the knowledge that she had not lost the man she loved.

She could feel his warm breath against her ear, her neck, her cheek. She looked up into his dark green eyes. His gaze devoured her as his big arm tightened around her, almost painfully, and drew her closer. He nuzzled her face, seeking and finding her mouth. In one savagely possessive thrust, he captured her lips, and she accepted him with eager joy as the world around them faded into oblivion. Clinging to him, she felt her strength returning, as if she were absorbing his power.

He grasped her hip with his big hand, holding her quivering body against him while he continued ravaging her mouth. Finally, he released her, gazing at her with wild hunger in his eyes.

"How the hell did you find out what happened?" he asked, his voice harsh, but he still held her close against his side.

"Ramon Carranza," she said.

"Damn that man!" Nate didn't trust Carranza. The chances were pretty good that he and Ryker were connected in some way. But what bothered Nate the most was that Carranza was obviously keeping tabs on Cyn.

Noticing Dundee standing discreetly several feet away, Nate motioned him forward. "Carranza knew about the shooting? How did he contact Cyn?"

"He sent his bodyguard," Cyn answered before Dundee had a chance to reply.

"Carranza sent his goon to get Ms. Porter. He told her Carranza was waiting downstairs in his limo," Dundee said.

"Good thing you were there," Nate said. "Why the hell did you bring her here to the hospital? The point in having you around is to keep her protected and as far away from me as possible."

"The only way I could have kept her from coming here once she found out you'd been shot was to have knocked her unconscious, and I didn't think you'd want me to do that."

Cyn wanted to scream. These two big macho men were discussing her as if she weren't standing right there. She glared back and forth from Nate to Dundee. They were of equal height and about the same size. Sam Dundee's complexion was almost as dark as Nate's, but his short hair was flaxen blond and his eyes a cold, menacing blue.

"I want you to take her back to Mimi Burnside's," Nate said, then swayed slightly, bending his body in an effort to ease the pain shooting through his side.

Cyn held her fingers out over his bandaged side, longing to touch him, to soothe his pain, but she let her hand hover over his wound. "I won't leave you. You're hurt and..." She made an unsuccessful attempt to stop crying. "How...how...bad is it?"

Giving her another crushing hug, he tried to laugh. "Not so bad." He couldn't bear the agonized look on her face. "Hey, Brown Eyes, don't you know I'm too tough and mean to kill?"

"Oh, Nate, don't joke about this." She buried her face in his shoulder, sobbing quietly, relieved that he was truly all right and angry at the injustice of life.

"Don't fall apart on me now, Cynthia Ellen Porter. I'll be okay. All I need is for you to go back to Mimi's."

"Shouldn't you be in bed?" she asked, raising her head and brushing the tears from her eyes. She completely ignored his request for her to return to Mimi's.

"No. I'm fine. The bullet only grazed my side. I admit it made a nasty mess, but I've suffered far worse."

"I can't believe they've allowed you to get up." Pulling

away slightly, Cyn inspected him from head to toe, realizing, for the first time since she'd entered the emergency room, that Nate looked like a man ready to run. "You were trying to leave, weren't you?"

"I am leaving," he told her, then glanced over at Dundee. "I'm going back to Sweet Haven, and I want her to stay here in Jacksonville."

"Has the doctor said you could go? Have they released you?" Placing her hand on her hip, she glared at him.

"I told them I was going. I've got to check on Romero, then I'm getting a cab home." Nate took several staggering steps.

Cyn quickly placed a supportive arm around him. "What's wrong? Are you in pain? Mr. Dundee, find a nurse."

"Don't move, Dundee. I'm fine, dammit," Nate said, clenching his teeth. "They shot me full of painkiller. I told them I didn't need it, but they insisted."

Cyn smiled, a trembly, teary smile. Dear Lord, what was she going to do with this man, her big, brave warrior? "Mr. Dundee and I are taking you home if you refuse to stay here overnight."

"I don't want you anywhere near me." Since he held her against him with fierce protectiveness, his words were ineffectual, and totally contrary to his actions.

A petite silver-haired nurse entered the cubicle, and smiled when she saw Nate and Cyn. "I'm glad you have someone here to take you home, Mr. Hodges."

"Then it is all right for him to leave?" Cyn asked.

The nurse glanced over at Dundee. "We would prefer that he stay the night, but since Mr. Hodges has refused, he should have someone with him. We gave him a pretty high-powered injection. I'm surprised he's still on his feet."

"He won't be alone," Cyn said. "Is there anything special I need to do?"

The woman looked at Cyn. "Just keep his dressings changed, and see that he goes to the doctor for a checkup." The nurse turned to go, then glanced back at Nate. "Your friend is still in surgery. He's alive. Surgery could last several more hours.''

"What about his leg?" Nate asked.

"I don't know." The nurse shook her head sadly and left.

"What happened to Nick Romero?" Cyn asked.

"He got it in the leg. The bullet severed his femoral artery. There's a chance he'll lose that leg."

"Oh, Nate, I'm so sorry."

"Well, woman, don't you see?" Realizing he was still holding Cyn, Nate released her. "Ryker plays for keeps. As long as you're with me, your life is in danger."

"My life is in danger whether or not I'm with you." She nodded toward Dundee. "Otherwise, I wouldn't need a bodyguard."

Nate's knees weakened. The room began to spin slowly. He reached out, bracing himself against the wall.

Cyn willed herself not to rush to him. Maybe, just maybe, it would be better if he fell flat on his face, she thought. Then she and Mr. Dundee could just wheel him straight into a hospital bed. She watched him closely for several minutes, then realized that Nate Hodges was fighting the drug the nurse had given him, and, knowing Nate's strength and determination, he wasn't going to lose gracefully.

"Mr. Dundee, would you please call Mimi and let her know how Nate is. Tell her that we're taking him home." Cyn frowned at Nate, her hard glare daring him to protest. "Make the call as quickly as possible and bring back a wheelchair. I don't think Mr. Hodges is going to be able to stand up much longer."

Dundee nodded agreement, smiling at Cyn and then at Nate before exiting the cubicle.

"He thinks it's funny," Nate said.

"He thinks what's funny?"

"That you're bossing me around." Nate wasn't used to having anyone in his life care about him, and he certainly wasn't used to some take-charge female issuing him orders. "The last thing a man needs when he's…he's been shot is some loud-mouth feminist telling him what to do.''

"Oh, shut up, Nate." Cyn scooted a chair across the room, took Nate by the arm and eased him down. "Sit down and behave yourself. As soon as Mr. Dundee brings that wheel-chair, we're taking you home."

"Romero. Need to stay…see about…" Nate's words began to slur.

"There's nothing you can do for Nick. I'll keep in touch with the hospital, and you can come back as soon as you get some rest."

"And if I don't…won't…" Nate slumped in the chair, his eyelids heavy, his breathing deep.

"You're going home, and you're going to do just what I tell you to do. Understand? And I'm not leaving you. Have you got that straight?"

"Come here," he said, motioning for her to lean down close to his face.

"What?" she asked, staring directly at him as she lowered her head.

"You're a bossy wench, Brown Eyes."

Laughing and crying at the same time, Cyn kissed him on the nose. "You bet I am."

While the coffee brewed and the bacon fried, Cyn looked out the kitchen window at the slow, steady rainfall. It had been raining when she and Dundee brought Nate home a little after dawn this morning. That had been almost five hours ago, and Nate had slept the first four hours. When he had awakened, he'd refused to take any of the pain medication Cyn had found in his coat pocket, but she was determined that he would eat the hearty breakfast she was preparing in the makeshift kitchen. In her own kitchen she could have made biscuits, but since Nate's kitchen didn't have an oven, he would have to settle for toast.

She had found a wooden crate under the sink and had cleaned it to use as a tray. Laying a clean towel over the rough surface, Cyn set a plate filled with bacon, eggs and toast in the center and placed a mug of steaming black coffee to the side.

As she passed the den on her way to Nate's bedroom, she saw Sam Dundee admiring the varied array of knives that comprised Nate's extensive collection. A slight shudder passed through her at the thought of all those deadly weapons housed under one roof, indeed being proudly displayed by their owner. Perhaps she would never understand the warrior within Nate, the beast that lived within every man. She abhorred violence, but with her motherly nature, she could understand fighting to protect those she loved. She would fight to protect Nate, to keep him safe.

The door to Nate's bedroom stood open. Nate sat on the side of the bed wearing only his unsnapped jeans. For a brief moment, Cyn stared at him, at his hard lean body, at his long black hair. He was every inch a man. And that very maleness called to Cyn on some primitive level, telling her that she was his.

He glanced up, watching her as she came in and held out the crate-tray for him to take. Staring down at the tempting food, he grunted, then accepted her offering.

"Thanks, I'm starved." He gulped down the coffee, then attacked the stack of crisp bacon.

After picking up his rumpled coat and empty leather sheath, Cyn sat down in the chair beside the bed. She wondered what he'd done with his knife.

"It's still raining," she said. "Looks like it's set in for the day."

With his mouth half filled with egg, he mumbled, "Thanks for the weather report." He took another swig from the mug. "Where's Dundee?"

"Admiring your knife collection."

"Has Higdon called?" When he saw the puzzled look on her face, he said, "Nick Romero's boss. He's supposed to give me an update on Romero's condition, and...he's making arrangements to have you escorted to your father's place in Savannah."

"What?" Cyn jumped, throwing her body slightly forward. "I'm not leaving you, so you can just call this Higdon guy and tell him I won't need an escort anywhere."

"If Donna Webb hadn't been killed last night, the two of you would already be in Georgia."

"What are you talking about?"

"The woman who was with Romero last night was an agent unofficially assigned to take care of you until I finish things with Ryker. Plans were for her to drive you to your father's home and stay there with you."

Seeing the wounded look in Cyn's eyes made him hate himself for having to be so blunt with her. But dammit all, if he couldn't make her understand the real threat to her life, he'd never be able to make her leave him. "Your father has already been notified," Nate said. "He was told only what was necessary."

"Who called Daddy?" Cyn demanded, jumping up, balling her hands into fists and shaking them at Nate.

Setting the tray on the floor, Nate glanced up at Cyn. Well, she was mad as a wet cat and just as ready to spit and scratch. "If Higdon doesn't come up with some more unofficial protection for you, then I'm sending you off with Dundee."

"You're not sending me anywhere, Nate Hodges." Leaning over, she punched the center of his naked chest with the tip of her index finger. "I'm exactly where I want to be and exactly where I'm going to stay."

Nate reached out, closing his big hand around her stabbing fingers. Looking into her rich brown eyes, he saw fury and determination and…love. He couldn't remember a woman ever trying to help him, trying to take care of him. He hated to admit, even to himself, that he liked seeing her fuss and fume as she ordered him around.

Clasping her whole hand in his, he pulled her forward. Her forehead rested against his, his breath warm and coffee-scented against her mouth. "I've been shot," he reminded her. "When Ryker comes for me, I'll be at a slight disadvantage. If I have to worry about your safety, if I'm busy protecting you instead of myself, I'll be at an even bigger disadvantage.''

"Nate—" She couldn't think when she was so close to him, her lips hovering over his, her body straining for contact.

"Don't you understand, Brown Eyes, if you stay with me, you'll die with me?"

Their breaths mingled as her lips touched his with whispery softness. "Yes, I understand.''

She wanted to stay with him enough to die with him. The thought shot through him like a bolt of lightning. He knew she loved him, knew she didn't want to leave him and thought she understood the danger, but hearing her say that she was willing to die with him made him realize the extent of her feelings for him. This woman, his beautiful Brown Eyes, did nothing by half measures. She had a heart big enough to encompass every living creature, enough love and tenderness to soothe a thousand wrinkled brows, enough maternal instincts to try to mother the whole world. But she loved him, only him, as a woman loves a man.

Slipping his right arm around her, he pulled her to him as he pressed his lips against hers. She moaned into his mouth, opening for the potent thrust of his tongue. His kiss was frantic, wild with heady longing, ravaging with the need to possess.

Leaning into him, her slight weight toppled them over onto the bed. She fell against his uninjured side. He cradled her head on his shoulder, and buried his lips against her throat.

Dundee knocked on the open door, then cleared his throat. "Excuse me, but Higdon's here to see you.''

Nate released Cyn immediately. She sat up on the bed and straightened her slightly rumpled blouse. Looking down, she realized that, somehow, Nate had managed to undo the top two buttons. She stood up, turned sideways and hastily refastened her blouse.

Nate sat up, groaning silently at the soreness in his left side. "Tell him to come on back.''

"I'm staying," Cyn said, wanting Nate to know she had no

intention of letting him and some government agent make plans for her without her consent.

J. P. Higdon was several inches shorter than Nate, at least twenty pounds heavier and a dozen years older. He wore a three-piece suit, parted his thinning hair at an awkward angle in an effort to cover a bald spot, and had perpetual wrinkles in his forehead.

"How are you doing, Hodges?"

"I'm fine. How's Romero?" Nate asked.

Higdon glanced at Cyn and raised a questioning eyebrow. "This must be Mrs. Porter."

Cyn stiffened her spine, tilted her chin and smiled. "I'm Cynthia Porter." She offered her hand, which J. P. Higdon accepted in greeting. "I have no intention of leaving Nate so the two of you can have a private talk." Her smile widened. She placed her hand on Nate's arm. "So you might as well go ahead and say whatever you came here to say."

Higdon glared at Cyn, his round blue eyes wide with wonder. "I assure you, Mrs. Porter—"

"I'm not leaving," she said.

"She's not leaving," Nate told the other man. "How's Romero?"

Higdon ran his pudgy fingers beneath the tight collar that bound his neck, inadvertently loosening his tie. "Looks like Romero is as tough as you. The doctors say he'll live, but saving the leg is still iffy."

"Damn!" Nate wanted to strike out at something, at someone. He wanted five minutes alone with Ian Ryker.

Cyn felt the coiled fury inside Nate as she tightened her hold on his arm. His muscles hardened beneath her fingers.

"The bullet severed the femoral artery. If you hadn't known what to do and acted so quickly, he would have bled to death long before the ambulance arrived," Higdon said.

"When can I see him?" Nate asked.

"He's in the trauma unit. No visitors except family."

"He has no one except his grandmother, and she must be over eighty." Nate knew that Romero's childhood and youth had been little better than his own. Where Nate had suffered from neglect and abuse, Nick Romero had grown up in abject poverty.

"I'll arrange for you to see him, soon, but for now, I think you'll want to know that I've commandeered someone to take Mrs. Porter to Senator Wellington's." Higdon turned to Cyn. "Your father has been informed that you and Agent Bedford will be leaving Sweet Haven at approximately seven tonight."

Cyn started to speak, but kept silent when Nate took her hand in his and gave her a cautioning glance.

"She'll be ready," Nate said.

"I guess you know that this whole business with Ryker has become personal with us now that he's attacked two of our people." Higdon paused, but when Nate made no comment, he continued. "We're going to stick to you like glue until this thing is over."

"I don't think it'll be that easy." Nate squeezed Cyn's hand, not wanting to speak so frankly in front of her, but knowing she left him no choice. "When the showdown comes, Ryker will find a way to make sure I have no help. He'll want it to be the two of us."

"We'll see," Higdon said. "Agent Bedford will pick Mrs. Porter up here tonight at seven. And you can stop wasting your money on Dundee's services. We've already got our people in place."

"What do you mean?" Cyn asked, wondering if there was a combat squad surrounding the house.

"He means that there are men, strategically placed, who will be keeping an eye on me." Nate knew that Cyn must feel as if she had stepped into the middle of a badly written spy drama.

"Carranza's been making inquiries," Higdon said. "It seems he's very interested in the state of your health."

"Probably wants to give Ryker an update," Nate said.

"I can't figure out why that old Cuban involved himself in this mess with Ryker, even if he is in tight with the Marquez family." Huffing, Higdon shook his head.

Cyn felt Nate's whole body tense at the mention of the Marquez family. ''Who's the Marquez family?'' she asked.

''They're the top Colombian family working out of Miami. They sort of inherited part of the action from Carranza. He retired without giving them any trouble, so he's been able to maintain ties with them.'' Higdon glanced down at his watch. ''Good luck, Hodges. I'll keep you posted on Romero's condition.''

J. P. Higdon gave Cyn a courteous nod before leaving. Dundee appeared in the doorway moments afterward.

''I suppose you heard,'' Nate asked, knowing full well that Dundee had been standing outside in the hallway listening to the entire conversation.

''I'm as good as gone,'' Dundee said. ''I'll stop by the hospital and check on Romero before I leave town.''

''Thanks for your help.'' Nate offered his hand to the other man, who accepted it in a hearty handshake.

''Anything for a friend of Nick Romero's.''

Cyn waited until Dundee had walked away before tugging on Nate's hand as she looked up at him. ''Why should it matter that Ramon Carranza has connections to a crime family in Miami? That shouldn't come as any surprise considering his background. I don't understand what it has to do with anything.''

Nate took both of her hands in his and looked directly at her. ''Ryker is employed by the Marquez family.''

''Oh, my God!''

''Now do you understand?'' he asked. ''If Ryker has the Marquez family and Carranza behind him—''

''And I talked to Ramon Carranza about you, answered his questions. Told him things I shouldn't have. Oh, Nate.''

''When Agent Bedford comes tonight, you'll go with him. You'll stay at your father's until this is over.''

''I don't want to leave you.''

''Cyn—''

''Hush. I…I don't want to leave you, but I will. I don't want to make things more difficult for you. I don't want—''

Before she could finish her sentence, Nate swallowed her words, silencing her with the heated passion of his desperate kiss.

Chapter 14

The sun, only recently visible through the haze of gray rain clouds, lay against the western horizon like an overripe peach, fat and soft and brilliantly clothed in varying shades of yellow and red. The sky, coated with an eerie golden pink glow, seemed so close. Cyn shuddered, a sense of foreboding chilling her body.

A gentle after-shower breeze stirred her hair. She had pulled it back into a large bun at the nape of her neck, but fly-away tendrils had escaped and draped her face. She ran her gaze over Nate's unkempt garden. Knee-high weeds choked the grass and overwhelmed the spring flowers which were blooming in glorious profusion. Once, years ago, Miss Carstairs had attended this garden with the passion other women would have bestowed upon a lover. Even now, the remnants of her special care showed. It saddened Cyn to think how beautiful the grounds had been only a few short years ago.

She had left Nate in his knife-filled den. Ever since Dundee's departure over an hour ago, Nate had been on the telephone. First to the hospital, then to J. P. Higdon.

Cyn knew where she was going. She'd known the minute she had left Nate to come outside. The vine-covered rooms called to her. She felt powerless to resist; indeed, she had no desire to resist. There was darkness and death and mysteries long left unsolved lurking in the shadows, but there was more. There was love and commitment and hope. The Timucuan maiden and her conquistador had been married in the mission. They had made love in those rooms. And they had died there. Cyn didn't know how she knew; she just did.

The rooms had been a part of the old mission. They had not been the chapel itself, but the priest's living quarters. He had married them, that brave man of God, and had given them his bed in which to consummate their union.

Cyn's hand trembled as she reached out and pushed open the heavy wooden door. The air was oppressive, thick with mustiness, rich with the aroma of damp earth. Weak sunlight filtered through the boarded windows, casting the entire room into cold shadows.

Dear God, what was wrong with her? She felt hot and cold simultaneously. She was afraid, and yet realized she was safe. She knew things, felt things, wanted things that were alien to her.

It's why you came here, she told herself. *They are here. Waiting. Wanting. Needing.* With slow, almost trancelike movements, Cyn made her way across the cluttered room and toward a narrow wooden door in the center of the far wall. Behind that door lay the other storage room of the old mission.

Shivers of fear and excitement spread through her, stronger than the effects of any drug. Reaching out, she laid her hand against the cool wooden surface. Applying only slight pressure, she pushed. The door opened. Slowly. Ever so slowly.

She peered inside. The room was bathed in sunlight. Dark shadows had been forced into the four corners, leaving the center of the room filled with light...glorious, golden-pink light. Cyn sucked in her breath, awed by the almost sacred beauty of the room, her eyes seeing and yet not seeing that, except for the heavenly sunshine, there was scant difference between this room and the other.

She could feel the sun's warmth despite the chill in the ancient room. Her gaze traveled upward toward the source of the light. A huge section of the old ceiling was missing, leaving a jagged gap that permitted the outside world access within the coquina walls.

Although she had never been in this room before, it felt familiar. Memories flashed kaleidoscopically through her mind. Candlelight. Moonlight. The scent of fresh flowers. A soft blanket beneath her. A hard man above her. In her. Cyn shuddered.

They wanted something from her. Needed something so desperately. What? What do you want? she cried out silently. No one spoke the words and yet she heard them.

You and your warrior must be united as we could never be.

She didn't understand. How could she and Nate be united in a way the ancient lovers had never been? The maiden and the conquistador had consummated their marriage. They had been united. She and Nate had made love. They were already united.

Shaking her head, Cyn stepped backward toward the cool, shadowy wall. Her breath came in hard, shallow gulps. She trembled when she heard footsteps in the outside room. Who was out there?

Her mouth formed one word. Nate. Before she could voice his name, she saw the man standing in the doorway. He took a step forward.

She recognized him, and yet there was something different about him. He was Nate, her beloved Nate. And yet he was more. She was more.

In that one still moment when they stood staring at each other, Cyn knew. When he came to her, when they touched, when they loved, the fulfillment they found in each other's bodies would be shared by two ancient lovers. It had been that way before, every time she and Nate had made love, but only now did she realize the truth. A truth that should have frightened her, but didn't.

The love she and Nate shared had not begun a few weeks

ago when they'd first met. It hadn't even begun years ago when she'd first dreamed of him. It had been born centuries ago when an Indian maiden and a Spanish conquistador had fallen in love.

Nate felt suspended in time, as if, in entering this ancient room, he had stepped back into the past. His past, and yet not his past. Someone else's past.

And she was here. Waiting for him. For a few endless moments, all he could see were her eyes, those rich, warm, brown eyes that had haunted his dreams over the years. The eyes of the woman he loved, the woman he had loved forever.

He moved toward her, watching the way the sunlight turned her yellow hair to gold, the way her full lips parted in anticipation, the way her body hugged the wall.

He had wanted her before, more than he had ever wanted another woman. She had given him pleasure beyond his most erotic dreams, and yet he could never get enough of her. As soon as he felt sated, his heart and body fulfilled, he began wanting her all over again. He wanted her now. More than ever. His need was filled with desperation. Some unknown force within him urged him on, reminding him that life held no guarantees, that death was sure and often swift.

When he reached for her, she went into his arms, docile in her surrender. Gazing down at her beautiful face, he saw the adoration, the hunger, the love, and he was lost. Her expression mirrored his own inner feelings, passion riding him hard. Lowering his head, he sought and found her lips, taking them gently, nipping, licking, nipping again. He circled her moist lips with his tongue, then inserted the tip between her teeth. She sighed. He delved deeper. She took him inside, welcoming the marauding exploration, sharing the pleasure as her tongue raked the side of his.

With several brutal stabs, he conquered her mouth. Trembling with desire, he released her lips, burying his face in her neck, his teeth covering her delicate skin with love-bites. She clung to him, her hands searching his shoulders and back, glorying in the feel of his hard, masculine body. Reaching between their bodies, he ripped at her blouse, jerking it out of her slacks and off her shoulders. When he began working on the hook of her bra, she started unbuttoning his shirt. Two sets of eager fingers moved hastily over two hot, hungry bodies.

She wore nothing but a pair of red bikini panties, he only a pair of unzipped jeans.

"You don't know how bad I want to be inside you," he said, his chest rising and falling with the harshness of his breathing.

"I love you." She took his face in her hands, her palms covering him from cheekbones to chin.

"Come back to the house with me. I want you. Now."

"No. Here. It must be here."

He glanced around the dirty, musty room, a room stacked high with decaying boxes and littered with an assortment of furniture and old junk. "There's no place to—"

She covered his lips with her fingers. "You've been wounded. You mustn't overexert yourself."

"I've got to have you, woman. Damn my wound!"

Cyn knelt on her knees in front of him. The hard rock floor beneath her feet was damp from the rain, warm from the sun, and smooth from centuries of wear. Placing her thumbs beneath the waistband of his open jeans, she grasped the faded denim and pulled.

"What the hell are you doing?" He slapped his hands over hers where she held his jeans just below his hips. He could feel himself jutting forward, and was unable to control the fierce need eating at his insides.

"I want to make love to you." Her voice quivered with the intensity of her own arousal. "I've dreamed of this."

"Cyn..." She was offering him a precious gift, the fulfillment of a man's most carnal desire.

He allowed her to remove his jeans. He stood above her, big and strong and powerfully male, his body straining toward her, needing, begging, demanding.

Running her hands up his hips, over his lean belly and across his muscular chest, she caressed him, savoring the feel of sleek, hard smoothness. The very touch of him was intoxicating her, seducing her onward, toward a path she had never followed, into an unknown world of sensual power.

Hot, untamed sexual energy flowed through her, dominating her as surely as Nate's big body beckoned her to sample its delights. She ran her hand over him in wild abandon. Over every inch, from tiny male nipples to strong, supple calves.

When her mouth replaced her hands, he bucked forward, his manhood touching the side of her face. He looked down and saw himself caught in the web of her golden hair. He groaned, so great was his need.

Turning her head, she tasted him. He cried out, the sound a harsh, guttural shout within the ancient walls. All semblance of his control vanished as he reveled in her loving attention.

He was about to explode. He couldn't stand any more. He reached down, jerking her to her feet, swinging her up into his arms. Glancing frantically around the room, he sought and found the only suitable place he could use.

Setting her down atop a tall stack of dilapidated boxes, he spread her legs and stepped between them. If he didn't take her soon, he would die.

She surged closer, allowing her breasts to sweep across his chest as she grasped his tense shoulders. "Now," she said.

He slipped his hand between them, pinching her tight nipples until she begged him to stop. "No more."

Moving his hand downward, he palmed her. She keened, the sound thin and high and piercing. His fingers found her hot and tight and melting.

Uncontrollable in her need, she bit into the taut flesh of his upper arm. "Please, Nate, please. I'm hurting."

"So am I," he said and rammed into her like an animal intent on perpetuating his species.

The pleasure was so intense she thought she'd die. A lifetime of love consummated this mating. Cyn's love. Nate's love. The love of a Timucuan maiden and a Spanish conquistador.

Clutching her hips, he surged in and out, harder and faster, creating premonitions of ecstasy that prompted them to accept the knowledge that four hearts were beating as one.

She not only accepted the savagery of his lovemaking, but basked in his dominance, reeling with the promise each possessive thrust made, knowing that in the end, she would attain the supremacy...for it was within her body that their immortality could be created.

With a relentless, pulsating rhythm, he took her, and with equal fervor she took him. Quick and wild and hot, their bodies spiraled up, up, up into the heat of fulfillment. In one earth-shattering second, a scalding pleasure burned through them. He poured himself into her as she sheathed him, tightening her body's hold on his pulsing release.

Tremor after tremor shook her body, the untamed heat searing her. Her own flesh had become so sensitized that the mere brush of his lips against her throat was a pleasure-filled pain.

He lifted her into his arms and carried her out of the ancient rooms, through the secluded garden and into his bedroom. Laying her down atop his rumpled sheets, he stretched out beside her and pulled her damp body up against his.

Threading her fingers through his long black hair, she smiled. "I've dreamed of you since I was fifteen."

He looked down at her and saw the truth of her words in her eyes. "You dreamed—"

"I've dreamed of you for years. Oh, I didn't know it was you. Even after we met, I tried to pretend that you couldn't possibly be my dream lover."

"Your dream lover?" What was she saying? he wondered. Had she, too, been plagued by comforting dreams that ended with erotic lovemaking? "Tell me about your dreams."

He listened quietly, his heart hammering loud and strong as she told him about her dreams, when they had begun and why, and how, afterward, all she ever remembered were his mossy green eyes and the feel of his big body.

"Cyn." He kissed her tenderly. "I've dreamed of you, too. Since I was a kid. In Nam."

He felt her body tense, and ran a soothing hand over her back. "Did I bring you comfort?" she asked.

"Yes." He watched the play of emotions on her face and knew she was accepting the truth just as he must.

"And did I give you love?" she asked.

"Yes."

"And all you would remember afterward were my eyes and the feel of my body."

"Yes." He held her close, his lips against her throat.

"It wasn't just us," she said, arching into him. "It was them, too. They're a part of us. I can't explain it, but I know it's true."

"Yes, it's true." Nate realized that when a man lived as close to death as he had, he learned to believe in life.

She felt his erection pulsing against her and opened her legs to accept him. "We've loved each other forever."

He couldn't bear to think about what might lie ahead for them, the pain of separation, the agony of loss. If his most recent dreams came true, they would both die as surely as the ancient lovers had.

He thrust into her, glorying in her warmth, savoring the fact that they were both very much alive. At that precise moment, Nate knew that if only one thing survived this doomed earthly existence, it would be love.

The world outside the car blurred into one, long, endless streak of darkness punctuated by an occasional flash of light. The hum of the motor, the soft roar of the speeding automobile, the gentle whine of the night wind, all combined, lulling Cyn into a semirelaxed state. For the first hour out of Sweet Haven, she'd been tense and edgy, consumed with her need to stay with Nate, tormented by the fear that she would never see him again.

Agent Bedford had arrived precisely at seven. Nate had wasted no time in sending her away. She understood why. He loved her and wanted to keep her safe. Their goodbye, though brief, had been passionate. As long as she lived, she would never forget the feel of his arms around her, the taste of his mouth on hers, the look on his face when he pulled away from her.

Nate was probably at the hospital with Nick Romero. He'd been determined to try to see his old friend. She knew that Nate had only two real friends. John Mason, who had taken his family home to Alabama to keep them safe from Ryker. And Nick Romero, who had almost died from Ryker's ambush attack. What sort of monster was this Ian Ryker? she wondered. A man filled with hate, who lived only for revenge?

Cyn glanced over at Art Bedford, a muscular, dark-haired man with a thick mustache and wire-framed glasses. Nate hadn't known Bedford because he was a fairly new man. J. P. Higdon had assured Nate that he was fast becoming one of their best agents, and Cyn couldn't be in safer hands, not even with one of their most seasoned veterans.

They were only a few miles outside Jacksonville, on Interstate 17. Cyn had noticed the last road exit had been for Fernandina Beach. Although the Georgia line wasn't far, they still had the entire coastal expanse of Georgia to cover before reaching her father's home in Savannah. That meant a long trip lay ahead of them. She longed for rest, for sweet hours of sleep, but she was afraid to sleep, afraid of the dreams.

She closed her eyes and conjured up Nate Hodges. Sleek hard body, straight black hair, moss-green eyes, possessive words and loving touches. In a few short weeks, he had become the center of her universe, the reason for her existence. No, not in a few short weeks, she reminded herself. Love like theirs hadn't blossomed overnight, it had been growing silently in their hearts, waiting patiently in their souls for four centuries.

Even with her undeniably romantic nature, Cyn realized that if anyone had told her that she was destined to take part in the fulfillment of an ancient legend, she would have scoffed at the very notion. She would have found the idea irresistibly fascinating, but the strong, sensible part of Cynthia Ellen Wellington Porter never would have believed it possible.

But she believed now. And so did Nate. No matter what

happened with Ryker, even if somehow he managed to succeed in destroying Nate, the prophecy would be fulfilled.

The prophecy…the prophecy… She could hear Miss Carstairs's soft voice recounting the tale, the romantic myth that had fired the twelve-year-old Cyn's imagination. *A troubled warrior and the woman who could give him sanctuary would come to the beach, would abide within the walls of the old mission, and discover a passion known only by a precious few. And when their lives were joined as the maiden's and the conquistador's lives could never be, then the ancient lovers would be set free, their souls allowed to enter paradise.*

When Cyn felt the car slow down, she opened her eyes in time to see Art Bedford turning off onto an exit.

"Where are we going?" she asked, puzzled by the detour.

"I've got to check in, let them know we've crossed the state line. I'll find a pay phone. You stay in the car," he said, smiling at her. "I'll lock the door and keep an eye on you from the telephone booth."

Cyn shook her head in agreement. "Would you ask if there's been any update on Nick Romero's condition?"

"Sure thing. And if you want a cola or coffee or—"

"No, thank you. I'm fine." She closed her eyes again.

Bedford pulled into an all-night truck stop, parking the car close to the pay telephones. "I won't be long. And I'll be sure to ask about Romero."

Cyn glanced around the modern, brightly lit truck stop. Even with the windows up, she could hear the roar of engines, the beat of country-western music coming from somewhere inside and the loud laughter of two scruffy men in white T-shirts, faded jeans and ball caps with Budweiser embroidered across the front. One of the men lit a cigarette while the other bit off a big plug of chewing tobacco.

Looking back toward the telephone booth, she noticed Bedford was smiling at her while he talked. He seemed relaxed and self-assured, as if he didn't have a care in the world. He must be pretty sure of his abilities to protect me, she thought. If only she could be sure that someone was protecting Nate.

Her gaze searched the dark night sky, seeking and finding a bright star. With all the faith in her heart and soul, she prayed that a power far beyond any earthly force would keep Nate safe.

Cyn heard the back door directly behind her open. Jerking her head around she saw a man bending over, slipping inside. She opened her mouth to scream, but before she could emit one sound, the stranger tossed a large white envelope into the front seat, then pointed a gun in her face.

"I wouldn't cry out if I were you, Ms. Porter." His voice had a ring of familiarity. She looked at him, recognition dawning.

"Ah, yes, I see that you understand."

"You can't get away with this," Cyn told him, stealing a quick glance toward the phone booth. Bedford was standing outside, looking at her and smiling. What's wrong with him? she asked herself, can't he see the man in the back seat? Perhaps in the darkness, he couldn't. "There's a man with me. A government agent."

Bedford opened the door on the driver's side, bent over and peered inside. "You have my money?" he asked.

The man in the back nodded toward the front. "On the seat. Feel free to count it."

Suddenly Cyn felt disoriented, knowing and yet afraid to admit that she understood what was happening. She glared at Art Bedford. "You're handing me over to this man. You're betraying the agency for money."

"Smart, isn't she," Bedford said. "And pretty. You wouldn't care to share her with me before you confront Hodges, would you?"

Fear, searing and painful, choked her. The very thought that either of these men would touch her made her physically ill.

"Get in, Bedford," the stranger said. "You will drive us back to Sweet Haven, to Nate Hodges's home. And then you will leave. I suggest you disappear quickly. You can buy yourself a woman, a dozen women, with the money in that envelope."

Bedford obeyed, getting in, starting the car and pulling out onto the highway. "Oh, yeah, Ms. Porter, word is that Nick Romero has a visitor and that visitor has just received a message about you."

No, no, she wanted to scream. This was all a trap, a trap to capture Nate, and she was the bait. The man in the back seat lowered his gun, but continued holding it in his steady right hand.

"Don't think about doing anything foolish, Ms. Porter. I much prefer that you're still alive when Nate Hodges comes to me. You see, I have dreamed of the day I could take from him what he once took from me."

Cyn stared at the man, noting the sinister black patch over one eye. His other eye gleamed a silvery blue in the flash from an oncoming car's headlights. His left arm lay limp at his side. The sleeve of his expensive silk jacket, creased just above his wrist, hung loosely over the hidden stub of his hand.

"Turn around and relax, Ms. Porter. We have a long drive to Sweet Haven."

Cyn ordered herself not to tremble, not to cry, not to give this monster the satisfaction of seeing her fear. When he reached out and touched her shoulder, she cringed, but forced herself not to pull away.

"I'm sorry that I've been so rude. I just realized that we haven't been properly introduced, although I'm sure the Conquistador has spoken of me. I am Ian Ryker."

Chapter 15

Nate stepped outside the intensive care trauma unit. He hated hospitals, the smell of pain and death everywhere. Although he and Nick Romero had both suffered combat injuries in Nam, they'd both been damned lucky to be part of a highly trained unit where death had been the exception instead of the rule.

Romero looked awfully rough. He was so high on medication that his speech was slurred and his thinking confused. He'd been calling for a woman, the name familiar to Nate although he had no idea who she was. Once, years ago, Romero had mentioned her name when he'd been so drunk he couldn't stand. Nate had asked him about her later, and his old friend had laughed and said that she was the one blonde he'd never been able to forget. Nate wished he knew who she was and how to contact her. If ever Romero had needed someone to care about him, it was now.

In critical condition and the safety of his leg still in doubt, Romero was as tough as they came, and if anyone could live through something like this, he could.

Nate only hoped that he would be as lucky himself and be

the one still alive after his confrontation with Ryker. Life had never meant so much to him. He had always been reckless and unafraid. But that was before Cynthia Ellen Porter had entered his life in the form of a flesh-and-blood woman who loved him as he had never dreamed anyone could love him. He didn't want to die. He wanted to live.

Walking down the hall in a meditative daze, Nate accidentally bumped into someone. He looked up and saw J. P. Higdon. "Romero's still alive," Nate said. "And he's still got both legs."

"He'll make it," J.P. said. "You can't kill old battle-scarred warriors like you and Nick."

"I hope you're right." Nate noticed the strange concentrated stare Higdon gave him, the telltale nervousness as he shifted his feet repeatedly. "What's wrong?" Nate felt his heart in his throat, pounding loud and wild.

"We just received a message from Ryker."

Out of the corner of his eye, Nate saw Emilio Rivera standing several yards away near the elevators. "The message was for me?"

"Yeah, it was for you."

"Hell, man, quit beating around the bush and tell me."

"Ryker has Cynthia Porter."

Pain, intense and all-consuming, spread through Nate like high-voltage electricity. Anger more fierce than any he'd ever known claimed him. Grabbing Higdon by the lapels of his jacket, Nate shoved him up against the wall. "How the hell did this happen? You said Bedford was one of your best men."

Higdon, his eyes bright with fear, his upper lip coated with sweat, shook his head in a plea for understanding. "I have no idea what happened. Bedford could be dead for all I know. Does it really matter right now? Ryker has Ms. Porter at your place."

Nate knew immediately that Ryker had taken her to the storage rooms, to the old mission. In Nate's recent nightmares, Ryker had been in a dark, musty room when he had smiled triumphantly at Nate as he held Cyn's lifeless body.

"Ryker has threatened to kill her unless you come alone and we call off your protection," Higdon said, struggling to free himself from Nate's menacing hold.

"Then call them off." Nate loosened his grip. "And if Bedford isn't dead, he will be if I ever find him."

"You can't face Ryker alone. Your best chance of survival is to take some cover. Our boys can be discreet." When Nate released him, Higdon straightened his jacket, shirt and tie.

"Ryker is nobody's fool. I'm sure he isn't alone. He'll have lookouts just waiting for any sign of agents. He's probably got all the help he needs from the Marquez family." Nate glanced over at Emilio Rivera. "And from our friend Carranza."

"All the more reason for you to take backup," Higdon said.

"When I leave here, I don't want anybody following me. My survival isn't what's important to me. If I don't go alone, Ryker will kill Cyn." Nate knew his chances were slim, but that didn't really matter. The only thing that mattered was Cyn.

"How the hell do you think that you, one man alone, can rescue her?"

"I'm going to kill Ryker. Once he's dead, the Marquez family will have no reason to keep her, and they can do whatever they want with me once she's free."

Nate gave Higdon one last warning look before walking to the elevators. Punching the call button, he glanced over at Emilio Rivera. The big man nodded, but didn't say a word. The elevator doors opened. Nate stepped inside. Emilio stepped in beside him.

When the doors closed, Emilio spoke, his voice deep and quietly controlled. "Señor Carranza is waiting downstairs in the limo. He wants to speak to you."

"To hell with what Carranza wants!"

"You would be wise to speak with him, Nathan Hodges," Rivera warned.

Neither man spoke again as the elevator descended. The doors opened, and they stepped out onto the entry level of the hospital. Together they walked outside into the warm May night.

Nate hesitated momentarily when he saw Carranza sitting inside the back seat of the limo, the door wide open. When the old man caught a glimpse of Nate, he emerged from the black Cadillac.

Nate walked over to him, Emilio following. "I don't know what your stake in this is, Carranza, but I promise you that if Ryker harms Cyn Porter, your life won't be worth a damn."

Ramon Carranza's dark eyes clashed with Nate's unfriendly glare. "One of my former business associates is indebted to Ryker." He placed his dark, weathered hand on Nate's arm.

Instantly Nate retreated, jerking away, repulsed by the other man's touch. "What you're telling me isn't news. It's no secret that Ryker is part of the Marquez syndicate."

"You do not want to go up against these people alone."

Although the air was warm, almost balmy, Nate felt a shivering chill hit him. He hated Ramon Carranza and everything he stood for. The very thought that this man was deriving some sort of sick pleasure out of helping Ryker, by tormenting him, by threatening Cyn, made Nate want to rip out the man's heart. "Stay out of my way if you know what's good for you."

Gripping Nate's arm tightly, Carranza gave him a hard, penetrating stare. The two men looked at each other, eye-to-eye, man-to-man. "He plans to kill her regardless of what you do. He simply wants you there to witness her death."

The truth of Carranza's words ripped through Nate like one of his sharp, deadly daggers. "You've delivered Ryker's message, now you can take one back to him. Tell him that I'm on my way, and before I'm through with him, he'll be begging to die."

Releasing Nate's arm, Carranza slipped into the dark, private confines of his limo. Nate kicked the door closed with his foot. Every fiber of his being pulsated with a rage born of uncontrollable anger and a fear the likes of which he'd never known. If anything happened to Cyn...

Cyn could feel the rounded muzzle of Ryker's gun as he jabbed it into her back. Stumbling in the darkness, she steadied herself as they walked along the arched portico. Why, she wondered, had this crazy man taken her back to Sweet Haven, back to Nate's house? Where was Nate? Was he still at the hospital visiting Nick Romero? She had no idea what time it was, though she suspected it was near midnight.

When she slowed her steps, Ryker poked her in the back again. "Keep walking. We're almost there."

Cyn clutched her purse against her stomach and continued moving, praying for the opportunity to use Mimi's automatic that still lay nestled inside her leather bag. Violence had been thrust upon her, and her only chance for survival might well lie within herself. Did she have the strength and courage to fight back? Undoubtedly, Ryker hadn't even considered the possibility that she might be armed.

If she could manage to get hold of Mimi's gun, would she have the guts to use it? Was she capable of killing a man? Two men? she wondered, remembering that Bedford was still with them. Could she, to save herself, and perhaps Nate, go against her lifelong beliefs?

"Where are you taking me?" Cyn asked, but she already knew. There was anger and pain and fear inside the walls of the old mission as surely as there was passion and love and fulfillment.

"Just shut up and keep walking." Ryker's voice held a nervous edge.

With Bedford standing outside in the dark shadows, Ryker pushed open the storage room door with his shoulder and shoved Cyn inside. She turned on them, irrational fear controlling her actions. Like a madwoman, she flung herself at him. With one deadly backhanded slap, he knocked her to the floor.

Scrambling to find her purse where it had landed beside her, Cyn snapped the catch and rummaged around inside, unable to see in the darkness. Her fingers encountered the cold, deadly metal. Clutching the automatic in her hand, Cyn pointed it at Ryker. In that one heart-stopping moment, she knew that, if necessary, she would kill in order to survive.

With trained instincts, Ryker intercepted her attack. He raised his leg, expertly kicking the gun out of her hand. Cyn's fingers stung from the sharp blow as she listened to the sound of metal when the gun rattled across the stone floor.

Bedford's laughter rang out loud and clear. In the semidarkness, she could barely make out his stocky form as he entered the room, bent down and picked up her gun.

"She's a gutsy broad," the DEA agent said. "She almost got you."

Ryker growled, like a wounded animal. Cyn could see him, his one malevolent blue eye sparkling in the moonlight that poured in from the open doorway. Flinging his hand backward, he brought it down across the bottom of her face. Cyn jerked from the force of his blow. Blood filled her mouth. She spit it out, then ran her tongue over her split lip.

"Be a good girl, and I'll let you live to see your lover." Ryker motioned to Bedford and the two men turned and left the room.

Once the door slammed shut, Cyn scrambled to her feet and made her way across the room. Standing between the door and the partially boarded window, she listened to the muffled sound of male voices. She could make out another voice beside Ryker's and Bedford's. Who had joined them? she wondered. How many opponents would Nate have to face when he arrived? And she knew, without a doubt, that Ryker had contacted Nate, and that Nate would come for her.

When Cyn heard the door opening, she jumped, quickly moving toward the window. Ian Ryker came in carrying a gas lantern, which he set on top of some stacked boxes. Bedford followed, but no one else. Slowly, Cyn edged her way toward the corner of the south wall. She wanted to huddle into a ball and fall to her knees. But she didn't. She braced her back against the cool coquina wall and glared at Ryker, her eyes beginning to adjust to the new light.

He watched her with the intent curiosity of a cat studying a trapped mouse. She could almost hear him smacking his lips. As cold, deadly fear raced through her, she fought to maintain some semblance of composure. She would not let this animal get the best of her.

Hearing a noise, she glanced quickly over at Bedford, who busied himself pilfering through an assortment of old furniture. Suddenly she saw that a long, thick rope lay draped over his shoulder.

"Who were you talking to outside?" she asked, her voice steady despite her ravaged nerves.

"Curious little girl, aren't you?" Ryker smiled. His mouth was broad, his lips thick and his big teeth had a wide space between the front two. "I have powerful friends who are…assisting me. As soon as the Conquistador arrives, we will be taking a little helicopter ride to a safe place where I can kill you both, very slowly."

She knew that his powerful friends must be the Marquez family, men to whom killing was as commonplace as breathing. And perhaps Ramon Carranza was another friend. If rumors were true, the charming old Cuban could be as deadly as a poisonous snake. "Nate has powerful friends, too. He has the United States government behind him."

She hated the sickening smile on Ryker's face, as if he could taste her fear and was gaining strength from it. "Nathan Hodges will come alone. He knows that I will kill you if he does not. My friends are keeping watch, even now, for any sign of betrayal."

"Nate isn't stupid. He knows you'll kill me regardless of what he does." Why are you trying to reason with a madman? she asked herself. There was no answer.

"Ah, yes, but he will play the game by my rules because he thinks he can outsmart me and keep you alive."

Ryker moved toward her. Her body hugged the wall. Cyn stared at him, trying not to react to his nauseatingly sweet smile. Reaching out, he ran his index finger over her chin, down her throat and into her blouse, stopping between her breasts. When he popped open the top button of her blouse, Cyn glared at him, reaching deep inside herself for courage. Acting on the revolt she felt, Cyn spat in his face.

Wiping away the spit with a large white handkerchief he had slipped out of his pocket, Ryker laughed, then reached out and grabbed Cyn by the shoulders. He dragged her across the room and flung her into a rickety cane-bottomed chair that Bedford had set upright.

"Tie our little hellcat down," Ryker said. "Tie her hands behind her back and secure her feet to the chair legs."

Bedford obeyed, manhandling Cyn when she tried to resist. Within minutes, Cyn was bound. Fighting the overwhelming fear of helplessness, she opened her mouth on a terrified scream.

Ryker ripped his handkerchief in two pieces and tossed them to Bedford. "Here. Shut her up."

Bending down, Bedford stuck half the moist handkerchief inside Cyn's mouth. He laughed when she gagged on the cloth. After spreading the remaining material across her lips and knotting it behind her head, Bedford looked down at her, his eyes filled with such lust that Cyn shuddered. He covered her breasts with his fat hands, squeezing painfully with his thick, pudgy fingers. Cyn squirmed, emitting hoarse groans beneath her tight gag.

"It's time for you to leave," Ryker said, coming over to where Bedford still clutched at Cyn's breasts. "If you're horny, go buy yourself a woman. As a matter of fact, I've given you enough money to buy yourself a harem."

Bedford released Cyn and stood up, facing Ryker. "Want her all to yourself, huh?"

Ryker nodded toward the open doorway, then he and Bedford went outside, closing the door behind them. Alone and uncertain, Cyn prayed. She asked for the strength to endure whatever might happen and requested, with her whole heart, that she be allowed to help Nate survive his battle with Ryker.

Please, dear Lord, watch over Nate, and, if he has a guardian angel, please send him to us now.

Suddenly Ryker burst through the door, an Uzi strapped across his chest. Cyn watched, spellbound, as he neared her. Unable to do anything except groan at his touch, Cyn had to endure the humiliation as he ripped open her blouse, exposing her lace-covered breasts.

Terrified, she closed her eyes against his nearness, against the sight of his smile. But she could not escape the shrill, menacing sound of his laughter.

"You and I, my lovely, will wait for the Conquistador." He pulled a knife from a shoulder sheath and ran the sharp tip of the blade across Cyn's breasts, from nipple to nipple. "I regret, for your sake, that I cannot kill you quickly, but I will not deprive myself of the pleasure I will derive from watching Nathan Hodges's face. Your lover will suffer the agonies of hell as he watches what I'm going to do to you."

Crouched atop the roof, Nate secured the rope to a wide, sturdy beam. Overhead, the night sky closed in around him as he dropped the other end of the rope into the gaping hole in the back storage room ceiling. He checked the sheath on his belt and the hidden one in his boot, then hoisted the M16 to his shoulder. Grasping the rope, he slid downward with silent ease.

His feet landed soundlessly onto the stone floor. Moonlight poured through the roof opening, illuminating the cluttered room. With sleek, superior, trained movements, Nate made his way to the closed wooden door that connected the two storage areas. Like a jungle cat on a hunt for nourishment, he sought out the sound of Ryker's voice.

Nate grabbed the tarnished metal handle, gave the door a tiny push and waited for any hint of sound. Silence. He nudged the door again, a bit harder. With a minute squeak, it opened wider. Leaning back against the wall, Nate peered around the corner. A bright gas lantern lit the adjacent storage room. Ian Ryker stood, cowering over Cyn where she sat, tied to a wooden chair.

Nate knew he couldn't allow himself to think about how she looked, about what Ryker might have done to her. He had to keep a cool head if he were to have any chance of saving her.

Nate slipped his Fairbairn-Sykes dagger from its sheath, and pushed the door open, listening to the ominous creaking. Ryker jerked his head around, his one blue eye glaring at the doorway where Nate stood. Swinging his Uzi around, Ryker clutched the sinister weapon. Nate lifted his hand back, released the commando dagger, then jumped behind the safety of the thick coquina wall just as Ryker opened fire. Bullets riddled the wall.

Suddenly, with swift and deadly accuracy, Nate's dagger delved into Ryker's gut. Clutching his stomach with the stub of his left hand, he continued to spray the back wall with repeated shots. Finally, he slumped over, releasing the Uzi, and spreading his fingers into the blood dripping from his wound.

"Did you see her?" Ryker screamed as he fell to his knees in front of Cyn and grabbed her by the back of her head, twisting her hair around his hand. "You should come out and take a good look. She has blood on her face. Her pretty little mouth is all swollen and her soft knees are badly scraped."

Nate listened, his heart racing with outrage and torment. Wait. Wait, his instincts told him as he listened to Ryker's labored breathing.

Cyn wished that she could call out to Nate, to tell him that she was all right and not to let Ryker's taunts get to him. She glanced at the open doorway leading into the back storage room. How had Nate gotten in? she wondered, then remembered the roof. When she heard Ryker's harsh groans, she looked down at him just in time to see him jerk the long dagger from his stomach. Blood oozed out, turning his white shirt crimson. He held the knife up toward the heavens in a gesture Cyn knew he considered triumphant.

"I have your dagger, Conquistador." Ryker's voice held a hint of pain disguised beneath his victorious shout. "Come on out and see how I intend to use it on your beautiful lover."

Nate, his M16 on his shoulder, came through the doorway, putting himself in full view of the man sitting on the floor. Ryker held the dagger up to Cyn's chest, slicing through the sheer material of her bra. Red-hot fury seared Nate, branding every nerve within his body. Wild with the need to destroy the inhuman creature who was threatening his woman, Nate willed himself to stay in control.

Nate dragged his gaze away from Cyn's battered face, away from the look of sheer panic in her brown eyes. He studied Ryker, taking in every inch of the wounded man, noticing how profusely he was bleeding. At the rate he was losing blood, it was only a matter of time before he passed out. But Ian Ryker had the stamina of a battle-hardened soldier, and Nate knew he would fight to the bitter end. Given his strength of purpose, Ryker could well remain conscious long enough to kill Cyn.

"I'm going to take you and your woman with me," Ryker said, running the dagger's bloody blade up Cyn's throat, staining her satiny skin with the scarlet liquid. "I've got a chopper coming for us in a few minutes. They know you're here. They won't let me down."

"Who's helping you?" Nate asked, hoping to keep Ryker talking, postponing any desperate action on his part.

"I'm going to let you watch while I enjoy myself with her. When I think you've suffered enough, I'm going to kill you slowly, Conquistador, and let her watch you die." Ryker sucked in a deep breath, gasping for air, grunting with pain. "Oh, she won't be so beautiful when I've finished with her, but some of Marquez's boys will probably enjoy her for a while."

Nate stood perfectly still, never taking his eyes off Ryker. "You can't get away. Do you think a chopper can land on the beach without drawing attention?"

Ryker grinned. "You're too smart to have allowed any of Higdon's men to accompany you. You knew her life depended on your coming alone."

"Let her go, Ryker. This fight is between you and me."

"You didn't let Lian go. You and your bastard SEALs killed her."

"She got caught in the crossfire," Nate said, remembering that horrible day so long ago. "The bullet that struck her could just as easily have been fired by her own people."

"You killed my woman." Ryker rubbed the tip of the dagger

up and down, from Cyn's throat to her heart and back again. "I'm going to kill yours…but not quickly. Slowly, after many, many days. The last thing you'll see is your own dagger slicing away at her soft flesh."

Nate glanced at Cyn to gauge her reaction. He had never wanted anything more than to reassure her, comfort her, promise her that Ian Ryker would never live to carry through any of his diabolical threats. "I have no intention of dying. Not to give you any kind of satisfaction and certainly not to save *her* life." Nate nodded toward Cyn, and prayed that she understood what he was trying to do and why.

Ryker looked at Nate skeptically. "It won't work, my old enemy. You can't convince me that she means nothing to you."

"Oh, she means something to me." Nate took a quick look at her, his eyes pleading with her to forgive him. "She's the best lay I ever had, but that's all. When has a woman ever meant more to me than a night's pleasure?"

Ryker let the dagger slip down the front of Cyn's body, the blade skimming over her bare stomach. "I don't believe you, but even if it's true, your sense of honor will demand that you try to save her." He scooted closer to Cyn's chair, the nub on the end of his handless arm stroking his bleeding wound. Taking the dagger away from her soft, exposed flesh, he sliced through the ropes that bound her feet to the chair. "My friends will be coming soon." He pulled her hands up and over the back of the chair, then jerked her up, draping his arm around her and pressing the dagger against her side.

"I'm taking her outside," Ryker said. "The chopper should be landing on the beach soon. You can stay here, safe for the time being, or you can come with us, with me and your beautiful woman."

Ryker hunched over in pain. His movements slow and unsteady, he ushered Cyn outside and toward the road. Nate followed. Could he take a chance on his swiftness and accuracy? he wondered. If his life alone depended upon the outcome, he'd take the risk, but Cyn's life hung in the balance. Ryker's instincts could warn him if Nate tried to use the M16. But what about the boot knife? Nate asked himself. Could he remove it from his hiding place and strike Ryker in the back before the other man killed Cyn?

Once on the beach, Ryker fell to his knees, taking Cyn with him. Nate stopped a few yards away near the old cypress tree.

"You'll never make it," Nate shouted. "You're going to pass out."

"It won't matter." Ryker flung his handless arm around his wound. "My friends will take care of me, and they'll keep both of you safe and secure until I'm ready to dispose of you."

All three people on the beach heard the sound of the automobile as it pulled to a stop on the road in front of Nate's house. Three startled gazes watched while an enormous mountain of a man emerged from the driver's side.

Pulling Cyn tightly against him and placing the dagger's tip over her heart, Ryker shouted at Nate. "I told you to come alone."

"I did come alone. I swear."

"Then who's our company?" Ryker asked, nodding toward the two men who stood beside the limo.

What the hell was going on? Nate wondered. Having Carranza show up wasn't too surprising, but Ryker pretending he had no idea who the man was didn't make any sense.

"I don't know who the bloody hell you are, but you can stop right there or I'll kill her," Ryker said.

"I suggest that if you want to live you should release Señora Porter. There are three of us, you see, and if you harm her, one of us is bound to kill you," Ramon Carranza said, never slowing his stride as he neared the beach.

Ryker laughed, the sound shrilly hysterical as it carried on the night air. "There may be three of you, but I've got friends coming. A small army of friends who'll be carrying weapons. I suggest that you get back in that big limo of yours and leave, old man."

Carranza continued moving closer and closer to Ryker. Nate

wanted to reach out and grab him, but he was too far away. Carranza avoided getting anywhere near Nate.

"I'm warning you to stop." Ryker's hand trembled. Cyn could feel the knife pressing into her flesh.

"What are you doing here?" Nate, bewildered by Ryker and Carranza's conversation, knew he couldn't allow his own confusion to dull his senses or make him any less alert. This whole scene could be some elaborate hoax on Carranza's part. It was obvious the old man liked to play games. Just because Ryker didn't recognize him didn't mean they weren't on the same side in this battle.

Carranza spoke to Nate, but he never removed his gaze from Ian Ryker. "I had some important news for Señor Ryker. News that could not wait."

"What kind of crap is this?" Ryker asked. "Who are you? What sort of news have you got for me?"

"I am Ramon Rafael Carranza."

Ryker blanched, his face contorting into a frown. "What…what's the news you have for me?"

The sound in Nate's ears began as a loud buzzing, then quickly escalated into a thunderous roar. The old man had said his name was Ramon Rafael Carranza.

"My good friend, Carlos Marquez, regrets that he must sever his relationship with you," Carranza said. "He sends his apologies that he cannot assist you in this little kidnapping and murder scheme."

"You're lying. Marquez owes me. He's sending a chopper for me." Ryker's gaze searched the predawn sky as he cocked his head, listening to the silence.

Carranza took several steps forward. He was within a few feet of Ryker and Cyn. "Such a pity. In our business, a man cannot afford to put his trust in the wrong people. Marquez may, as you say, owe you, but his debt to me was far larger and much older."

Nate moved away from the trees. Good God, Carranza was going to try to jump Ryker. Was he a fool? Nate knew he had to intercede. If he didn't, Cyn would die. His nightmare would come true.

"Don't move, either of you." Ryker cursed Marquez, then dropped the dagger on the sand as he grabbed the Uzi and opened fire.

With trained instincts, Nate dropped to his belly as the shots rang out over his head. Suddenly, the Uzi's menacing roar quietened. Nate raised his head slightly and glanced around. Ramon Carranza lay on the sandy ground, blood pouring from his wounds. Ryker's lifeless body lay only a few feet away.

Nate jumped to his feet as Cyn struggled to hers, tears streaming down her face. Grabbing her, he jerked the gag out of her mouth.

"Oh, Nate."

He pulled her into his arms as he stroked her hair, kissed her face, and worked frantically to untie her bound wrists. Once Cyn was free, Nate looked down at Ryker. A small round bullet hole marred his smooth forehead. Nate could well imagine what the back of his head looked like. He didn't want Cyn to see it.

"Señor Carranza," Cyn said, her voice ragged and hoarse. "He's hurt." She tugged on Nate's arm, the gesture pleading.

Together they knelt down beside Carranza. Cyn took his head into her lap as she brushed back the strands of white hair that had fallen into his eyes. "You're going to be all right, Ramon," Cyn said. "We're not going to let you die."

Ramon Carranza looked up at Cyn as blood trickled from the corner of his mouth. "You will take care of him," he said as he gazed up at Nate.

Nate saw Emilio standing over them, the revolver that had killed Ian Ryker still in his hand.

"We must get him to a hospital," Emilio said, dropping the gun onto the sand, then reaching down to lift his employer up into his arms.

Nate helped Cyn to her feet and walked her toward the black limousine. Cyn got in first, then Nate helped Emilio place Ramon across the seat, his head resting in Cyn's lap.

Once Emilio started the engine and turned the big Cadillac around, Cyn looked over at Nate. "He saved our lives."

"I know," Nate said.

Chapter 16

Cyn sat beside Nate on the orange vinyl sofa. His head was thrown back, his eyes were closed, and his big arms were crossed over his chest. She wished he would allow her to comfort him as he had comforted her when they had first arrived at the hospital. While the emergency room staff had gone to work on Ramon, Nate had insisted that Cyn's scrapes and bruises needed immediate attention.

He had held her when the reality of what they'd lived through finally hit her. The nightmare was over. Ian Ryker was dead. Cyn and Nate were alive.

Cyn glanced around the surgery waiting room. A plump, middle-aged woman stood at the pay telephone, her voice hushed as she told the listener that her mother was still in surgery. In the corner chair, a teenaged boy flipped through the pages of a magazine with bored indifference. A young couple stood by the windows, his arm draped around her shoulders as he wiped her tears with a handkerchief and promised her that their little girl was going to be all right.

Two coffee machines sat on a metal table by the doorway.

One glass pot was empty, the other contained no more than a cup of liquid. The wastepaper basket beneath the table was littered with dozens of foam cups, plastic spoons and empty sugar and creamer packs.

Emilio Rivera stood outside in the hallway, his back braced against the wall. No one had given comfort to the big, quiet man, whose silent eyes and hard face gave away none of his emotions. Cyn wondered how long Emilio had worked for Ramon, how close their relationship was.

"I'm going to talk to Emilio," she told Nate. "I'll be right back."

Nate grunted an acknowledgment, but didn't open his eyes or move a muscle. Seeing Nate like this, so cold and withdrawn, broke Cyn's heart. It was as if he'd closed himself off from her, from the whole world, and refused to allow anyone near. Perhaps it was the only way he knew how to deal with everything that had happened, Cyn thought. Her kidnapping. Ryker's death. The knowledge that Ramon Carranza had risked his life to save them.

Emilio gave her a welcoming glance when she approached him. "How is Nathan?"

"I honestly don't know." Cyn touched Emilio's meaty forearm and looked up into his squinty black eyes. "Ever since they took Ramon up to surgery, he just sits there. He won't talk to me. He won't let me help him."

"*Si,* he is like his padre. A strong man who thinks he needs no one." Emilio patted her hand where it rested on his arm. "He needs you. He will accept your help, later."

As his words began to sink into her consciousness, Cyn wanted to deny her suspicions, but the facts could not be dismissed. Clutching Emilio's rock-solid arm, she asked him for the truth. "Is Ramon Carranza Nate's father?"

"*Si.*" A hint of a smile softened Emilio's battered face. "I have worked for Señor Carranza since before he met Nathan's mother. Since I was a boy of sixteen."

"You knew Nate's mother?"

"A most beautiful woman, Señorita Grace Hodges. As beautiful as you with her long blond hair and big green eyes. Señor Carranza loved her greatly.'' Emilio's eyes glazed over with memories.

"But Nate thought his father was dead.''

"*Si*, it was his mother's wish, and they agreed it would be best for the child. Under the circumstances.''

"You have to tell Nate, tell him everything. He has a right to know, and there is no one else who can tell him.'' She realized she was taking a chance that Nate would respond in a positive manner to the revelation that Ramon Carranza was his father. But regardless of how he would react to the news, he had to be told the truth.

"You think he wants to know?'' Emilio asked, giving Cyn a skeptical look. "He is a hard man. His heart may be closed to the truth.''

"There's no way to know unless we try.''

Emilio nodded, the tentative smile widening as Cyn took his hand, and together they entered the waiting room. Cyn sat down beside Nate. Emilio took a chair opposite the sofa. When she touched Nate's shoulder, he flinched, but still didn't open his eyes.

Cyn felt his big body tense beneath her touch. "Nate, Emilio wants to tell you—''

"That Ramon Rafael Carranza is my father.''

"You knew?''

"No, not until… Sitting here, I finally figured it out.''

"He was never your enemy.'' Cyn couldn't tell what Nate was thinking, but she could guess, knowing him as she did. "His interest in you was personal.''

"Yeah, I guess it was.'' Nate opened his eyes and stared up at the ceiling, then darted his gaze at Cyn. "But he was a little late in showing fatherly concern, don't you think?''

Nate closed his eyes again, and Cyn knew he was trying to blot out the truth—a truth he had yet to understand.

"Emilio can tell you about your parents,'' she said, longing to comfort him, to ease the pain she saw in his eyes, to remove the anger she knew was barely hidden beneath the surface of his falsely calm exterior.

Nate opened his eyes, uncrossed his arms and sat up straight. "What about them?" he asked, glaring at the huge man sitting across from him.

"You will listen, Nathan Hodges?" Emilio's dark eyes pleaded with Nate. "You will let me tell it all so that you will understand why you mustn't hate your father."

Cyn held her breath, praying for Nate's acquiescence. "Don't you think you owe it to yourself as well as your parents to know the truth?" she asked.

"So talk," Nate said, his voice brutally harsh. "I'm listening." Bending over slightly, he let his hands drop between his knees as he looked down at the shiny tile floor.

"Señor Carranza owned a casino in Havana. He was already rich and successful at thirty-five, and had very influential friends. The most prominent friend was his father-in-law, Luis Arnaz." Emilio hesitated briefly as he watched Nate for a sign of reaction. Seeing none, he continued. "Arnaz had arranged his daughter's marriage to Señor Carranza…a business arrangement ten years before…before your mother came to Havana."

"What was my mother doing in Havana?" Nate asked, finally glancing over at Emilio.

"She had just graduated from college and came down on a holiday with some of her friends. You must remember that Havana in 1949 was a playground for the rich and famous."

"She met him at his casino?" Nate couldn't imagine the sadly beautiful woman who had been his mother as a carefree young woman jaunting off to Cuba with her friends.

"I was there…that night." Emilio's voice cracked with emotion. "It was magic between them the moment they saw each other."

The words were like a tight fist squeezing at Nate's heart. Once, he would have thought the notion of love-at-first-sight ludicrous, but since meeting Cyn, he admitted that it was possible. Hadn't she trapped him in her spell the first night he'd seen her on the beach? Had it been that way for his father the first moment he'd seen the young and beautiful Grace Hodges?

"They were very much in love," Emilio said. "He wanted to marry her, was willing to give up everything to have her."

"Then why didn't he?" Nate asked, hating Ramon Carranza for allowing his sweet mother to have gone through the shame of giving birth to an illegitimate child.

"Luis Arnaz found out about your mother. He threatened her life." Emilio placed his hands on Nate's shoulders, his thick fingers tightening. "Arnaz demanded that your father break all ties with your mother. He swore that he would have her killed. Señor Carranza knew that his father-in-law was capable of carrying out the threat."

Jerking away from Emilio, Nate stood. He felt like running, hard and fast. But he knew he couldn't run away from the truth. Ramon Carranza was his father. He had loved Grace Hodges, and had deserted her in order to save her life. All the bitterness and hatred of a lifetime churned inside Nate, his anger nearing the boiling point. He needed something to hit, some faceless enemy to pulverize.

He balled his hands into tight fists, corded the muscles in his back and neck with such tension he could feel the strain in every nerve ending. And then she touched him. Gentle, soft, loving, her touch ignited the tinderbox of emotions within him. He turned on her, his eyes fierce with a slow burning heat that became white-hot.

Cyn gazed up into the eyes of the man she loved and saw such torment, such pent-up rage, that she couldn't bear to look at him. Mindless of anything except the need to comfort him, Cyn wrapped her arms around his tightly coiled body.

Swiftly, brutally, he encompassed her in his arms, hugging her to him with the savagery of a dying man holding on to his last hope for survival. "Cyn…Cyn…"

"I'm here. I'll always be here. I'll never leave you." She felt his body shaking as she held him, her hands caressing his broad back.

They heard a woman's commanding voice ask, "Is there someone here with the Carranza family?"

Nate and Cyn turned around. Emilio stood. All three of them moved toward the nurse who was waiting in the doorway.

"I'm Ramon Carranza's son," Nate said. "How is my father?"

"They've brought him down from surgery," the white-uniformed woman said. "You may go in to see him shortly, but Dr. Brittnell wants to talk to you first."

Ramon Carranza was dying. The doctors gave them no hope. It was only a matter of hours, perhaps even minutes. Emilio had sent for a priest.

For forty-two years, Nate had wondered about his unknown father, sometimes hating him, sometimes longing for him as only a child can long for a missing parent.

In the last few minutes he had remembered everything his mother had ever told him about his father. She had painted the man in glowing terms. Nate had never doubted that she loved his father, the mysterious man she had called Rafael. Grace Hodges had told her son that his father had been half Cuban and half Seminole Indian. That he had been a handsome man with a smile that could charm the birds from the trees.

When Nate had questioned her about why his father wasn't with them, Grace Hodges had told her son that his father was dead. As a child, he had not understood; as an adult he had accepted his mother's explanation as the truth.

"We can go in to see Ramon now," Cyn said, squeezing Nate's hand.

They entered the critical care unit together, hand in hand. Ramon looked very old and very tired as he lay on the pristine white sheets. But even surrounded by monitors and life-saving machinery, the big, dark-skinned Cuban dominated the room.

As he neared his father's bedside, Nate experienced a battle of emotions raging within him, creating uncertainty and dread. What could he say to this man? What would Ramon Carranza want from his only son?

The minute Nate and Cyn stopped by his bedside, Ramon opened his eyes. "Nathan." His deep voice was a whisper.

"I'm here." *Dammit all, I don't want to be here, Nate thought. I don't want to have to confront this man, to have to face all the ghosts from my childhood.*

Ramon tried to lift his hand, but was unable to do more than wiggle his fingers. Nate reached down and clasped the old man's hand in his.

"I promised her that…you would never be…a part of my sordid life." Each word seemed torn from Ramon, as if the utterance was painful. "I loved her so."

"It's all right," Nate said, squeezing his father's hand. "Don't try to talk."

"The day she died…" Ramon gasped for air, his lungs struggling for each breath.

"Hush, now," Cyn pleaded, her eyes filled with tears. This shouldn't be happening, she thought. Not now, when these two had just found each other.

"She called…she was so sick. I went to her." Ramon's limp hand tightened slightly around his son's tenacious grip. "I promised to leave you…with her brother…to never tell you…"

"It doesn't matter." Nate tried to reassure the dying man. "It was so long ago. Another lifetime."

"I wanted you…my son, but she did not want you growing up…in my world." Ramon's soft grip loosened, his hand falling limp within Nate's grasp.

"Father." Nate's voice trembled, his throat tortured with unshed tears.

"I love you. Always, I have loved you…my son." And with those tender words that said far more than the sentimental confessions of a dying man, Ramon Rafael Carranza accepted death.

"Father? Father!" Not yet. Not yet, his mind screamed. We haven't had enough time.

Emilio Rivera stepped forward from his watchful position by

the door. With her arms around Nate, Cyn turned in time to see the tears streaming down Emilio's battered old face.

Nate pulled out of her arms, staring at her with moist eyes, the look of a lost child on his face. "I need to be alone. Just for a while. Try to understand."

Cyn watched him walk away, stunned that he didn't want her with him, hurt that at the most traumatic time in his life, he didn't need her.

"So like his *padre*," Emilio said, placing his enormous arm protectively around Cyn's shoulder. "So much a man that he does not want his woman to see him cry."

"See him... Oh, Emilio, I didn't understand."

Emilio hugged Cyn to him, as together, Ramon Carranza's gargantuan bodyguard and Nate Hodges's woman cried for a father who had loved a son he could never claim, a mother with the courage to bear her married lover's child and a boy who had grown into a man without the love and protection his parents were powerless to give him.

Cyn slipped on her aqua robe, belting it tightly. Before leaving the bedroom, she gave Nate's sleeping body a loving glance. Quietly, she made her way to the kitchen, seeking out the coffeemaker. As she went about preparing morning coffee, she thought about the past two weeks since Ramon's funeral. It had not been an easy time—for Nate or for her.

Although Nate had spoken to her very little, preferring to keep his emotions bottled up inside him, Cyn had not left his side. Determined to carve out a future with the man she loved, Cynthia Ellen Wellington Porter was willing to wait it out, to give Nate all the time and space he needed to come to terms with his past.

She knew that Nate had already come to terms with Ryker's death, but not with her kidnapping. He still blamed himself for not being able to protect her. She realized that he probably always would. Even the fact that Art Bedford had been apprehended in flight to South America had not lessened Nate's self-imposed guilt.

Dealing with the knowledge that Ramon Carranza had been his father was difficult for a man like Nate, a man who'd spent twenty years dedicated to fighting for his country, to putting his life on the line for the principles of freedom and justice. His own father had been a part of the deadly cancer that had been eating away at the moral values of the United States for decades. And he was a part of that man, blood of his blood, flesh of his flesh. He could not deny the bitter legacy Ramon Carranza had left him any more than he could deny the vast fortune he had inherited.

Cyn's own attitudes had changed gradually since she'd fallen in love with Nate and had been thrust into the middle of his savage fight with Ian Ryker. Finally, she had come to terms with not only her own past, her husband's death and the murder of Darren Kilbrew, but she had come to terms with Nate's past. She did not condone violence, and yet she accepted the fact that violence had its place in mankind's never-ending struggle to survive. She realized that when violence is brought into your life, you inevitably have only two choices. The strong choose to fight back, to live, and hopefully restore peace. Nate was one of the strong ones, and now, she too, shared his strength.

More than anything, she wanted Nate to accept her comfort, to be receptive to the loving sanctuary she could give him. But all he had taken from her was the comfort of her body, the solace of hot, wild, frequent matings, as if making love to her could purge his soul of its torment.

Just as she poured herself a cup of freshly brewed coffee, Cyn heard the knock at the front door. Setting her mug on the table, she walked down the hall. Opening the door, she half expected to see Mimi, who had become a frequent visitor during the last two weeks. Instead of Mimi's smiling face, Cyn encountered Emilio's scowling expression.

"Good morning. May I come in, please?" Always polite and formal. That was Emilio.

Cyn stepped back and, with a gracious sweep of her hand, invited him inside. She noticed that he carried a small gray box under his arm. "Want some coffee?" she asked. "There's a fresh pot out in the kitchen."

"No, thank you. I am here to see Nathan." Emilio stood rigidly, though his expression softened when he looked at Cyn. "I have something for him. Something I found when we were packing away Señor Carranza's personal belongings."

"I see." Cyn glanced down at the small box, wondering about its contents. "I'm afraid Nate is still asleep, and I hate to wake him. He hasn't had a good night's sleep since Ramon died."

"I'm not asleep." Nate stood at the end of the hallway, his body bare except for unsnapped cutoff jeans, his long black hair disheveled, and two weeks' worth of beard covering his face. "Too much damned racket. What the hell are you doing here?" he asked, glaring at their guest.

Emilio lifted the box and held it out toward Nate. "These were your father's. They are something I know he would want you to have."

"I told you and I told his lawyers that I don't want a damned thing from him. Not one dime of his dirty, bloody money!" Nate said, his eyes burning with the conviction of his words.

Emilio handed the box to Cyn, who took it just in time to keep it from dropping to the floor. "These are letters Grace Hodges sent Señor Carranza. The dates indicate she wrote him regularly from the time of Nate's birth until shortly before she died."

Not waiting for a reply or a response of any kind, Emilio nodded to Cyn, then turned and let himself out. Cyn held the small box against her bosom, almost feeling the warmth and love contained within the wooden box.

Letters. Love letters. Cyn looked up at Nate who had grabbed her by the shoulders. He whipped her around to face him.

"Come back to bed," he said, running his hand along the side of her leg, raising her gown and robe up to her hip.

She stepped away and thrust the box out toward him. "I think you should read these."

Nate glared at her. "I don't want to read any damn letters my mother wrote to her lover."

"To your father," Cyn reminded him. "To the man she loved."

Clenching his jaw and narrowing his eyes, Nate reached out and took the wooden box. Dammit, he didn't want to know any more about his mother's love affair with Ramon Carranza. Wasn't it enough that he had to live with the knowledge that the man who had fathered him had been a criminal, and not just any criminal, but an underworld leader?

Two hours later, Nate found Cyn walking on the beach. He knew she'd been waiting for him to come to her, giving him the time alone he needed to decide his future—their future.

He walked along beside her for quite some time before he spoke. She accepted his silent presence, as she had accepted his anger and frustration and unforgivably selfish behavior during the last two weeks. Dear God, what had he ever done to deserve a woman like Cynthia Porter, a woman who loved him enough to stand by him, giving him her support and strength while she willingly submitted her body for his pleasure?

And he had almost lost her. His hideous nightmare had almost come true. Ryker had come very close to killing her. But he hadn't. Ramon Carranza had died to save both Cyn and Nate. No matter what sort of life the man had led, no matter how sordid and sinful his past, he had atoned for some of his transgressions in one final act of love.

"She loved him a great deal," Nate said. "She wrote him regularly from the time I was a week old until shortly before her death. She sent him pictures of me, told him about my first tooth, my first word..." Nate's voice trembled.

"It's sad that they couldn't be together." She could feel the warm May sun caressing her arms and face. She felt so alive, so beautifully, joyously alive.

"He came to see her the day she died." Nate reached down and took Cyn's hand, entwining their fingers.

"He wasn't all bad. There was a private side to him that had nothing to do with his business dealings." Cyn stopped walking, tugged on Nate's hand and raised it to her lips. "You inherited his good looks, his strength, his damn macho pride…but you are your own man and you have nothing to do with the dark side of his life."

"I have a dark side to my life, too, Cyn. Perhaps just as dark as his." Nate pulled her to him, trapping their clasped hands between his chest and her breasts. "Can you accept a man with such flaws? Can you spend your life with a battle-scarred warrior whose past sins put you in danger, put you at the mercy of a madman?"

"I've accepted the fact that terrible things happen in life. The strong survive by fighting back when they're given no other choice."

"I want us to be strong and survive together," Nate said.

"Are you asking me to marry you, Nate Hodges?" she asked, smiling at him, her heart swelling with the wonder of love.

Swinging her off her feet and up into his arms, Nate laughed. "Damn right, I'm asking you to marry me. I may not be the smartest man in the world, but I've got sense enough not to lose the best thing that ever happened to me."

Clutching him around the neck, Cyn laid her head on his shoulder. "I love you, Nate. You're all I'll ever want."

Holding her up against his chest, Nate began walking back toward the house. "I may be all you want, but would you be interested in my father's millions?"

"What?"

"I've decided that Ramon Carranza's money could do a lot of good in this old world. I'm going to accept my inheritance and let you help me choose what charities need it the most. Needless to say, Tomorrow House will never have to close its doors."

"Oh, Nate, that's wonderful."

When they reached the porch, he slid her body slowly down the length of his until her feet touched the warm stone floor.

Lowering his head, he brushed her lips with his in a tender, carefree kiss.

"I think Ramon would be pleased," she said.

Pressing his body against hers, letting her feel the throbbing strength of his arousal, he nipped at her earlobe. "Besides me and my father's money, I'd like to offer you something else."

Cyn laughed, swatting playfully at his chest. "You wicked man, offering me sex in broad daylight."

Rubbing his maleness into her femininity, he grinned. "The sex goes without saying, but that's not what I was talking about."

"Well, what else were you offering me?" Cyn asked.

"I think you and I would make awfully good foster parents, don't you?"

"Foster parents?"

"Bobby and Aleta. I think they need us. Bobby has no parents, and Aleta's mother has signed papers giving up any legal right to her in exchange for not bringing her up on abuse charges."

"I think," Cyn whispered into his chest, her tongue flicking over one distended male nipple, "that you will make a wonderful father."

Images of Cyn big with his child flashed through Nate's mind. The thought pleased him greatly. "Let's go inside and work on making you a natural mother."

Sunset in the western Florida sky, a mélange of colors, like the iridescent shades of a crimson-tinted rainbow. Evening of a hot summer day, the stirrings of a warm tropical breeze as purple shadows forecast the night. The ocean's heartbeat echoing along the shore as a sweet soprano voice sang, a cappella, the lyrics to "True Love."

Nathan Hodges dressed in a black tuxedo watched while the bridal procession made its way up the beach. At his side, Nick Romero, well on the road to recovery, sat in a wheelchair while John Mason and Bobby stood.

Laurel Drew Mason, wearing a tea-length dress of pale yellow satin, approached the groom, his best man and groomsmen. Aleta followed in a matching dress of a less mature design, and last but never least, Mimi Burnside, the matron of honor, strolled along the beach, unable to hide her wide smile.

The standing crowd of well-wishers held their breaths when Cyn, escorted by her father, passed by in her flowing gown of antique white satin, with Batenburg lace accenting the sweetheart neckline and butterfly sleeves. A Juliet cap covered with baby's breath sat on the back of her head and a short gathered veil covered her long golden hair, which was secured in a bun at the base of her neck. The bride carried an enormous bouquet of white orchids.

Hand in hand, Cynthia Ellen Wellington Porter and Nathan Rafael Hodges faced the minister and repeated their vows of love and lifetime commitment. Before God, their family and friends, they became one.

Nate kissed his bride so long and hard that his best man poked him in the ribs. And then the party began. Hours of food and champagne and music. Denton Wellington had spared no expense in giving his daughter the unorthodox wedding of her dreams on the Sweet Haven beach.

All the present residents and volunteer workers of Tomorrow House were in attendance as were Cyn's brother David, Bruce Tomlinson and Emilio Rivera.

While the crowd continued the revelry long after the sun had set and stars appeared in the black night sky, Nate swooped his bride up into his arms and carried her away…all the way across the street to his house.

Snuggling in her husband's arms, Cyn didn't even realize that Nate was carrying her straight to the storage rooms, to the old mission part of the house.

When he felt her tense, Nate hugged her to his chest. "All the bad memories, the pain, the ghosts of the past, will vanish tonight. From now on, these rooms will hold only happy memories."

The huge wooden door stood wide open. Cyn held her breath as Nate carried her across the threshold. The outer room was empty, swept clean, the windows unboarded and open. She clung to him, her heart beating wildly as he stepped inside the inner room. Cyn gasped at the sight.

Moonlight streamed down through the unrepaired opening in the roof and hundreds of candles glowed like flaming eyes all over the room. They flickered on the floor, in wall sconces, on a table filled with flowers, a table set with champagne and food, and they perched in the open windows like Titian-haired little guards illuminating the dark night. An old wooden bed, placed in the middle of the room, gained all of Cyn's attention. Cream satin sheets edged with delicate lace shimmered in the warm candlelight.

Nate set his bride on her feet, gazing at her with loving adoration as he drew her into his arms. "Do you have any idea how beautiful you are?"

"Am I as beautiful as you?" she asked teasingly, remembering how he'd sworn she'd never get him to wear a damned monkey suit.

"This is a once-in-a-lifetime deal, lady. You'll never see me in one of these blasted tuxedos again." He released her, pulled off his jacket and tossed it across a nearby chair.

Cyn began unbuttoning his pleated-front shirt. "You'll have to wear one when your daughter gets married."

"Aleta is only twelve, and since I'm not going to let her date until she's thirty, I won't worry about her wedding." Nate reached around and released the top button of Cyn's wedding gown.

Slowly, sensuously, with their gazes locked in the heat of a smoldering passion, Cyn and Nate undressed each other. With each garment removed, each new inch of flesh exposed, the desire within them increased until their hands trembled when they stood naked.

Nate picked her up, the feel of her bare skin exciting him, hardening his throbbing arousal. Lowering her tenderly upon the bed, he followed her down, covering her, his lips taking hers in a frenzy of wild abandon as his manhood pressed against her waiting femininity.

He had never known with any woman what he had found with Cyn, the passion, the uncontrollable thirst that could be quenched only with their heated mating, and a love that went beyond the here and now to stretch the boundaries of eternity.

She flung her arms around his neck, beckoning him to come to her. With his lips burning hotly against her neck, he buried himself deep within her. Cyn cried out from the pleasure of their joining.

With each touch, each kiss, each forceful thrust, Nate gave himself into her safekeeping, trusting her with his very soul.

"Ah, *querida, yo te amo.*" Nate spoke the words, but the sentiments belonged to an ancient conquistador as well as the modern warrior.

"And I love you," Cyn told him, her heart beating with the love of two women. "I'll love you forever."

Epilogue

As the last candle flame flickered into oblivion, dawn broke over the Atlantic Ocean. The first faint light of morning seeped through the windows of the old mission, covering the entwined bodies of two lovers lost in a passionate mating dance that united them for all eternity.

When fulfillment claimed them and their cries of pleasure shattered the tender silence, Nate planted within Cyn's receptive body the seeds of their immortality.

Outside, two spirits walked together along the isolated beach, their hearts rejoicing, their souls preparing for a final journey.

"It is time," she said.

"Yes, *querida*. They have set us free."

After four hundred years of waiting, the small Timucuan maiden and her big Spanish conquistador left the Florida beach where they had met and loved and died so long ago. On the day that Rafael Wellington Hodges was conceived, the souls of two ancient lovers entered paradise.

* * * * *

SILHOUETTE® SENSATION™

AVAILABLE FROM 20TH JUNE 2003

MD MOST WANTED Marie Ferrarella

The Bachelors of Blair Memorial

London Merriweather had turned Dr Reese Bendenetti's life upside down. But a crazed killer was stalking her—and before Reese could dream of a future with her, he had to make sure she lived to see tomorrow...

HER LORD PROTECTOR Eileen Wilks

Romancing the Crown

Lord Drew Harrington had to know if psychic Rose posed a threat to his royal family. She knew what he suspected—but how could she explain her gift...or tell him that *he* was her destiny?

CROSSING THE LINE Candace Irvin

Eve Paris and Rick Bishop went back to the jungle where their plane had crashed to learn what had really happened. And returning to enemy territory proved safer than revisiting the scene of their first heated kiss...

ALL A MAN CAN DO Virginia Kantra

Trouble in Eden

Getting up close and personal with the attractive new chief of police was part of reporter Tess DeLucca's job. But Jarek Denko knew that a relationship with the sister of a prime suspect could be his undoing...

THE DETECTIVE AND THE DA Leann Harris

District Attorney Kelly Whalen needed help from the last person she wanted in her life—her ex-husband Tony Ashcroft. The hot-shot detective still knew how to make her want him with a breathless hunger...

LOVE UNDER FIRE Frances Housden

In the two years since policeman Rowan McQuaid had saved her life, Jo Jellic had gone from beautiful to stunning. Now he found himself struggling to keep his passion from bursting into flames...

0603/18

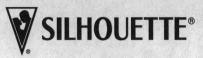

SILHOUETTE
HOT SUMMER NIGHTS
Make this summer the hottest ever!
Dallas Schulze
Maggie Shayne
Lindsay McKenna

FREE

4 BOOKS
AND A SURPRISE GIFT!

We would like to take this opportunity to thank you for reading this Silhouette® book by offering you the chance to take FOUR more specially selected titles from the Sensation™ series absolutely FREE! We're also making this offer to introduce you to the benefits of the Reader Service™—

★ FREE home delivery
★ FREE monthly Newsletter
★ FREE gifts and competitions
★ Exclusive Reader Service discount
★ Books available before they're in the shops

Accepting these FREE books and gift places you under no obligation to buy; you may cancel at any time, even after receiving your free shipment. Simply complete your details below and return the entire page to the address below. *You don't even need a stamp!*

YES! Please send me 4 free Sensation books and a surprise gift. I understand that unless you hear from me, I will receive 6 superb new titles every month for just £2.90 each, postage and packing free. I am under no obligation to purchase any books and may cancel my subscription at any time. The free books and gift will be mine to keep in any case.

S3ZED

Ms/Mrs/Miss/Mr ....Initials..........................
                                                                          BLOCK CAPITALS PLEASE

Surname..

Address...

....

....Postcode ....

Send this whole page to:
UK: FREEPOST CN81, Croydon, CR9 3WZ
EIRE: PO Box 4546, Kilcock, County Kildare (stamp required)